# MERELY PLAYERS

# MERELY PLAYERS

A DCI 'Percy' Peach Mystery

## J.M. Gregson

This first world edition published 2010
in Great Britain and in 2011 in the USA by
SEVERN HOUSE PUBLISHERS LTD of
9–15 High Street, Sutton, Surrey, England, SM1 1DF.
Trade paperback edition first published
in Great Britain and the USA 2011 by
SEVERN HOUSE PUBLISHERS LTD.

British Library Cataloguing in Publication Data

Gregson, J.M.
  Merely players. – (DCI Percy Peach mystery)
  1. Peach, Percy (Fictitious character)–Fiction. 2. Blake,
  Lucy (Fictitious character)–Fiction. 3. Police–
  England–Lancashire–Fiction. 4. Television actors and
  actresses–Fiction. 5. Detective and mystery stories.
  I. Title II. Series
  823.9'14-dc22

ISBN-13: 978-0-7278-6984-5  (cased)
ISBN-13: 978-1-84751-316-8  (trade paper)

*All Severn House titles are printed on acid-free paper.*

Severn House Publishers support The Forest Stewardship Council [FSC],
the leading international forest certification organisation. All our titles that
are printed on Greenpeace-approved FSC-certified paper carry the FSC logo.

MIX
Paper from
responsible sources
FSC
www.fsc.org  FSC® C018575

Typeset by Palimpsest Book Production Ltd.,
Falkirk, Stirlingshire, Scotland.
Printed and bound in Great Britain by
MPG Books Ltd., Bodmin, Cornwall.

*To David Browne, who read thirty-two of my books in eight weeks of a hard winter, and retained his habitual optimistic and good-humoured approach to life.*

'All the world's a stage,
And all the men and women merely players:
They have their exits and their entrances;
And one man in his time plays many parts.'

Shakespeare, *As You Like It*

# ONE

There was just enough light from the single street lamp outside for him to get his bearings. No need for the torch.

He stood perfectly still for five seconds, allowing his eyes to adjust to the dimness, registering in turn the panels on the closed doors, their brass handles, the frames of pictures on the walls. The stairs climbed steeply away from him into the dimness above. He knew the layout of the place, knew which of the invisible doors to open when he had climbed those stairs. As his vision improved and more landmarks of this familiar place dropped into their slots, confidence seeped back into him, coursing with the adrenalin through his veins.

The silence was profound. It was what he needed, of course, what he had expected and prayed for when he had planned this. Silence meant that the world around him was asleep, unaware of what he was about, of what he had come here to do and was about to achieve.

Yet just for a second he wanted noise, some neutral, indeterminate, masking noise, which might cover the next movements he had to make. Stupid and irrational: noise would have meant some other presence here, other ears, which might pick up the sound of his movements and forestall what he had come here to do. What he must do, unless he was prepared to spend the rest of his life within prison walls, with an eye perpetually on the watch for what other men in a place like that might do to him.

It was the thought of prison which freed his limbs from the fear of discovery which had for a moment immobilized him. He stole to the bottom of the stairs and began to climb them. His limbs moved in slow motion, with the exaggerated caution which in other circumstances would have been ridiculous. His battered trainers were set with elaborate care on the extreme left and right of each tread, so as to minimize the creaking that was surely inevitable in stairs of this age. His feet inside the shoes were like the paws of a cat, feeling each foothold carefully before committing the weight of his body to it.

It seemed to take him several minutes to climb to the landing, but he knew it was no more than fifty seconds. He had practised this over the years, knew to within a second or two exactly how long it took him to creep up a straight flight such as this. He paused for a moment when he reached the landing, casting his eyes to left and right as one did automatically on reaching a new floor, checking that everything he could see was silent and unthreatening, even though he knew that was how it would be.

Every door was closed. His eyes had now adjusted so completely to the dimness that he could make out some of the details on the pictures which were hung here. He could see high trees beside the glimmer of a lake in a painting, the white teeth and open mouth of a smiling child in a close-up photograph. Irrelevant. Too much information. Potential distraction. Cut out all emotion. Emotion was an enemy, when you operated in this trade.

He knew which door he wanted, knew also that it wouldn't be locked. The certainty about that was a tiny reassurance. The second door on the left as he turned at the top of the stairs and moved along the landing. He paused for a moment with his hand on the handle, nerving himself for the crisis, for the final, climactic seconds of the role he was playing in this. Not long now, but he had to be perfect in every move and every reaction. He took a deep, silent breath and depressed the handle with infinite care. The door opened soundlessly, as he had always known it would.

The curtains were thin at the single wide window, allowing the light from the lamp outside to show more than he would have expected of the room. He stood for a moment with his hands at his sides, checking that there was no one behind the door, that everything was as he had expected it to be. He knew that it had gone well so far. It must not be ruined now, in this last and simplest of its phases. Everything was as he expected: there were no chairs out of place, no stray shoes upon the floor which might trap him into a stumble and ruin everything.

He took in the glint of light upon the wardrobe, the whiteness of the door to the en suite, the clear definition of the slight figure beneath the blankets on the big bed. Then he moved across the room, stood for a moment beside the bed, and raised his arms to do what he had come here to do.

'Hold it right there, Phillips!'

The command was like a gunshot, unnaturally loud after the long silence which had preceded it. He whirled to the doorway of the en suite, face aflame with sudden fear, eyes flashing with the knowledge that he could never achieve what he had climbed the stairs to do. Framed in the doorway was the figure he had known he would see, with the pistol pointed steadily at his heart. 'What the hell—'

'CUT!'

The director's voice, the one they had all known must come at this point. The collective releasing of breath. The collective nervous laughter, loudest of all from that inert mass upon the bed which had played no part in the scene. The woman sat up, flinging aside the blankets, fully clothed, flicking her long hair back over her shoulders in the relief of the movement which was now allowed to her. 'I wanted to sneeze all the way through that! I thought I'd never last out!'

'What a trooper!' said the man who had burst out from the en suite to save her.

It wasn't clear whether he was sincere or ironic in that, but the director stepped forward on to the set and became for the moment the centre of interest. 'That was good, girls and boys! I'll need to run it through and check things out, but I think we have a take.'

'Can we fall out, then?' said the actor who'd sprung out to arrest the intruder in his murderous actions. He was clearly pre-eminent among the actors who were now emerging from various places around the set.

The director glanced at his watch, attempting to preserve the fiction that he and not their star controlled events here. 'I should think so, yes. It's too late to set anything else today. Good work, everyone! And I think you were right, Adam. That scene is more tense without any music at all. There's no need for us to gild the lily.'

'You don't think Jim took too long to enter the house and climb the stairs? I was beginning to think something had gone wrong by the time he actually arrived.'

'Always happy to build up an entrance for the star of our show,' said James Ellison, the actor who had played Phillips. This time there was no mistaking the sarcasm.

# TWO

The villain who almost committed murder in the television drama was not the star of the series. That was the man who sprung out of the en suite bathroom to interrupt his fell designs, a character named Alec Dawson. The actor who played this role was Adam Cassidy. He had a face which would have been immediately recognized by three-quarters of the people in Britain and a fair number in each of the hundred and eighty-four countries of the world in which the series was shown.

That is the power and the dubious influence of television on the diverse cultures of an ever smaller planet.

For many of the leading figures involved, television brings the easiest sort of fame. Men and women who half a century earlier would have been jobbing actors in repertory theatres, with a frenzied weekly workload and the perpetual fear of unemployment in an overcrowded profession, are now translated by television soaps into not only national but world stardom. Indeed, their dialogue is often dubbed into the tongues of people who have no experience whatever of the places in which these sagas are so assiduously set and documented. 'A mad world, my masters!' Nicholas Breton called our earth, and it is no less mad almost four centuries later.

It is a world in which vanity flourishes and has perforce to be indulged. It takes a remarkably detached and balanced man to withstand the pressures towards egotism, and Adam Cassidy was certainly not that man. His acting ability was not negligible, but it was limited. Like some of the stars of the great days of Hollywood before he was born, Adam had fallen by chance into a part and a persona which made the most of the attributes he had. The *Call Alec Dawson* series had brought him a success which meant that he could make millions of pounds without needing to step beyond his limited range.

Adam had always had the looks. Even when the greater talents around him at his drama college had confined him to carrying spears and speaking pathetically few lines, his looks had been noted. Others had dominated the stage in the modern and period pieces where Adam had secured his first small parts, but agents had noted his looks and his bearing. His voice was clear, but his projection was limited: his words did not carry to the back of the larger theatres. But he had an impressive profile, a charming smile, and a willingness to work. In due course he was taken on by an enthusiastic young agent.

He was given a small part in a television sitcom. Its story-line involved two established female stars sharing a flat. Adam was one of the many eligible bachelors who flitted through the strivings of the pair for permanent partners. A female reviewer in one of the tabloids noted him as the best of the beefcake in a modest series and the editor chose to set one of Adam's publicity pictures beside her column. There was an immediate response from readers. Moreover, this was in August, the traditionally slack time and 'silly season' for news. So the paper ran the beefcake debate for a full week. Some readers suggested alternative 'hunks' and others supported the original review in asserting Cassidy's physical charms. It was trivial stuff, cynically exploited, but for an obscure and not over-talented young actor, there is truly no such thing as bad publicity.

The industry which was to become Adam Cassidy had been launched.

The sitcom was a limited success and ran for only two six-programme series. But the writers noted that their previously unknown beefcake had now acquired that awful modern attribute, 'celebrity status'. He was given greater exposure and a few more lines in the second series. The two estab-lished female stars were made to swoon over him in private and compete for his attention in public. They were both more than ten years older than their quarry, so that writer and director saw fit to make their pursuit of their handsome hero increas-ingly desperate and a little ridiculous.

That didn't do the status of the young actor with the short speeches and the gorgeous profile any harm. When the sitcom's final episode was concluded, the general verdict was that although a tired format should be mercifully put out of its misery, a new television presence had been established.

There were enough offers of work to gladden the heart of

any agent. Adam now switched to one who was both shrewd and perceptive. Tony Valento was a failed actor himself. He told his clients that and very little else. Tony saw the limitations as well as the natural attributes of his young client. Television was Cassidy's natural metier, Valento assured him; privately, the agent congratulated himself that he need never canvas theatre producers on Adam's behalf again. Tony secured him a series of smallish parts in successful productions. He was an innocent young man among the highly experienced elderly cast in an episode of *Midsomer Murders*; he emerged as the innocent victim of a complex plot to frame him in the last scene. He was the idealistic young sergeant assisting a cynical superintendent in a forgettable one-off drama – he put his life on the line to save a young mother, and received a stern official police rebuke for his heroism, whilst the television audience applauded his actions.

When the BBC made their big-budget drama of the year, *Great Expectations*, it was Adam Cassidy who figured as that bright young man of the world, Herbert Pocket. The director severely pruned some of his scenes after seeing the rushes, and a couple of the older critics compared his performance unfavourably with that of Alec Guinness in David Lean's ancient film, but in the great television scheme of things, that scarcely mattered.

Adam Cassidy had his appearance in a classic. His agent duly added 'versatile' to his list of attributes. He was continually in work. He even managed to learn a little about his limitations, and became a more effective performer as a result.

Now, at forty-two, he was an undoubted television star and a national, even an international, name. The series specially written for him, in which he played Alec Dawson, a private detective who received a series of glamorous and perilous assignments, was now in its fourth series and more popular than ever. The plots were unlikely, even occasionally preposterous, but no one seemed to mind that. They weren't meant to be taken seriously, were they? And Adam Cassidy had the good sense to put exactly that idea forward in a succession of carefully timed chat show appearances. He announced that he didn't take either the series or himself too seriously. The British public liked that in their heroes.

As is quite usual in such situations, there was an increasing discrepancy between the way the public chose to perceive their star and the reality of the person himself. Very few people would turn their backs on stardom, but it is a difficult status to cope with. People stop telling you what they think and start telling you what you want to hear. That makes it difficult for you to be objective, and eventually you become unwilling to trust what people are saying to you. You can rely on very little of what you hear, and you begin to choose that little for your-self. In extreme cases, you begin to believe the greatest lies of all: your own publicity.

Your agent and most of those who work with you are riding on the back of your success. They note the signs of megalomania which are beginning to appear in you, but feel powerless to challenge them without jeopardizing their own fortunes. Only those closest to you can tell you the truths you do not wish to hear, and even they may do so at their peril. Adam Cassidy's first wife, Amy, warned him that he should not confine his contacts with his children to posing with them and their expensive toys for publicity photographs. 'I can't shut myself away in the house and play happy families, woman!' Adam had told her.

Amy didn't like that 'woman', didn't like the fact that he never wanted her to accompany him to film premieres, didn't like the fact that his being out and about meant visiting a succession of other beds.

The divorce settlement was expensive, but Adam could afford it. It became forbidden ground in interviews; the sooner the public forgot all about it, the better.

Two years later, Adam Cassidy remarried. The bride, Jane Webster, had been the damsel in distress in one of the most celebrated cases of Alec Dawson, television private detective and modern knight errant. There had been suggestions of their off-screen attachment in their enthusiastic screen clinches. For the millions of admirers of the series, it was a match made in TV heaven. A fair proportion of them chose to forget that their star had ever been married before.

In one sense, this second marriage proved the match Adam's fans wanted it to be. Jane Webster had looks and a presence which matched those of her new husband, even though her talent was limited. As the first fine bloom of her looks left her, the parts would certainly have declined. She declared that she was sacrificing her career to provide domestic security for her new husband, that wifedom and motherhood mattered more than stardom for her. She retreated demurely from the cameras as her pregnancy became more apparent.

Adam Cassidy was now a rich and successful man; the world was at his feet. That was the cliché with which chat show and other television interviewers often used to bring him on, possibly because it was the introduction suggested by his agent. Adam spoke earnestly of his love of the live theatre and the classics, of his desire to 'return to Shakespeare, the core of all our work'. He judged correctly that not many people would know that he had never played a significant Shakespearean role and that the few who did would not be foolish enough to display that knowledge.

The Alec Dawson adventures went from strength to strength, Adam explained, (his appearances were usually timed to publicize a new series). That made it difficult to find time for the serious roles he wanted to take on. He was grateful to television, of course, but she was a hard taskmaster. How wise the bard was when he said that all the world was a stage, and all the men and women on it merely players. Adam sighed, shook his head, and moved into the hilarious anecdotes about his co-stars that he had arranged to deliver at this point.

Each new series and each successful interview was another step in Adam Cassidy's progress towards becoming that distinctively British phenomenon, 'a national institution'.

On the evening after the scene which climaxed in his preventing murder by his timely intervention in the darkened bedroom, Adam drove himself home. He was using the big maroon Mercedes which was one of the three cars he now owned. He could have afforded his own driver, but he preferred to employ one only for special occasions like film premieres. He enjoyed driving; he could still remember the thrill of his first car, a battered Ford Fiesta with a dodgy gearbox. Each time he slid into the comfortable leather driving seat of whichever car he now drove, it was a reminder of those days and how far he had come since then.

It was well into autumn now, almost the end of October, and he felt the chill in the air, even at six thirty in the evening. There might be the first frost tonight, on the hills around his house and on the greater heights to the north. But German engineering was as efficient as ever; within three minutes, well before he reached the M62, the car was warm. By the time he struck due north up the M66, he was cocooned in that familiar, controlled warmth which made the weather outside irrelevant. The only real danger was of falling asleep at the wheel.

There wasn't much danger of that, with an active mind like his. He reviewed the events of the day and decided it had gone well. He had fluffed one line in the morning shooting, but the scene had needed to be re-shot in any case because of an oversight by one of the continuity girls about the levels of the drinks in the glasses. The director had severely rebuked her, whilst no one had said anything to him. That was how life was; the girl had better get used to it.

Cassidy got on well with his fellow-actors. They were mostly seasoned professionals and highly competent, but they knew facts of thespian life. They were delighted to have a part in a series which was highly successful, whatever the critics might say about it. Adam had been a little in awe of one of the theatrical *grandes dames* who was playing his eccentric aunt in this series. To find today that she was appearing in pantomime for the first time in thirty years gave him a lift and subtly altered the terms of their relationship. Adam congratulated Margaret on her bravery and energy, of course, but everyone knew that serious actors only accepted pantomime work when the other offers dried up.

He'd love to do panto himself, he said, when they broke for coffee; it must be great fun. But pressure of work meant that it was a pleasure Adam Cassidy must deny himself this year and for the foreseeable future.

He lived some forty miles from the studios in Manchester where he did most of his work. His house was just south of the Trough of Bowland, which the Queen had once said was her favourite place in the land. Adam revived that royal quote when he was given the opportunity in interviews, though he was careful to conceal the precise location of his residence. You needed privacy and seclusion once you became a television star. They helped you to preserve your balance, he said.

Once he left the motorway and struck off over the moors for home, the traffic became thinner. He listened to *The Archers* on Radio 2. He didn't hear it every day, but you picked up what was happening easily enough. It was pleasant and un-demanding. It added interest when you knew some of the actors, and it added satisfaction when you knew that some of these people who now seemed only modestly successful had been big names when he was struggling as an unknown. As the familiar jaunty signature tune marked the end of the episode, he switched to Radio 4 and heard the critic's review of the latest Pinter revival at the National Theatre. One of his contemporaries at RADA had a lead, and for a moment Adam was envious. But only for a moment; Adam Cassidy retained through all the adulation showered upon him a core of self-knowledge, which told him that he would never have made a lead at the National. It gave him a small, bitchy satisfaction to hear the critic saying that his friend's performance was flawed.

He sped north again on dual carriageway past the old towns of Whalley and Clitheroe, then turned west along lanes for the final part of his journey, where he scarcely saw a car. The house was modern and huge. He and Jane had originally planned to adapt the high Edwardian house in the centre of the spacious site, but eventually the architect had persuaded them to demolish it completely and build the house of their dreams. Or the house of the architect's dreams, Adam some-times thought wryly. But they had kept the old name for the house, Broad Oaks, and the original high walls at the boundary of the site.

He pressed his automatic garage door opener, watched the door rumble slowly upwards, and slid the Mercedes into the huge cave of garage beyond it. If the night was to be as cold as he expected, he didn't want his vehicle covered with white frost when he came to it in the morning. He'd rung Jane from his mobile an hour ago to say he was on his way. He watched her for a minute through the uncurtained windows of the kitchen when he got out of the car. She still had the blonde hair and large blue eyes which had secured her roles as a youngster. At thirty-seven and after two children, there was an inevitable thickening of the waist and the first signs of ageing in her face; the thought struck him that women with fair complexions aged more quickly or at least more visibly than brunettes. He was five years older than her, and no doubt showing signs of maturity himself. But a lot of men grew more attractive with age; everyone said that.

Jane had her apron on and was busy with pans when he went into the kitchen. He kissed her lightly on the forehead and stood behind her for a moment with his hands clasped around her waist, allowing the right one to slide down over the soft roundness of her stomach, caressing it for a moment with the fingers a million women would have loved to feel. 'Domesticity suits you!' he murmured softly into her ear.

'Domesticity will scald you, and me too, if you aren't careful,' she said with a grin. 'Why don't you go up and see the children? You might just have time to read them their story, if you go straight up.'

'I don't think I will. Not tonight, darling. I've had a very tiring day.' He sighed an elaborate fatigue, then added a happy afterthought. 'And Ingrid won't want me getting them excited and disturbing their routine.'

'Nannies are employees, not dictators, Adam. And I'm sure she'd be happy to see you reading to them. They don't see enough of you, you know.'

'One of the crosses of fame, dear. And they'll be tired themselves, after a full day at school. It wouldn't do to get them excited at the end of their day.'

'I know you're busy, but you'll regret it if they grow up without you. It's a precious time, this, you know.'

She was beginning to nag. Adam didn't like that and he wasn't used to it. No one nagged him about anything, now that his mother was dead. He sat in his leather chair in the dining room and read his mail until the dinner was ready. He told her a little about his day and his trials whilst they ate, and added some of the theatrical gossip which had passed around during the group whilst they drank coffee and waited for new sets to be mounted. 'And how was your day?' he said dutifully when they were on the cheesecake.

'Much as any other,' she said acidly. She didn't know whether he didn't notice her tone or simply chose to ignore it. This house and this life weren't proving as desirable as she had expected them to be, when she had been making her suggestions about the design of the kitchen and the various en suites and dressing rooms. She hadn't thought she would miss her fellow actors and the gossip of the theatre and the studios anything like as much as she now did. She had the children, of course, and she was delighted to watch the changes in them as they moved from infancy into childhood. But they limited her; they held back her own development; sometimes she thought she would scream her frustration, after another day of childish language and childish concerns.

Some of the other mothers she met at the village school said they felt the same: the favourite phrase was that they felt themselves 'becoming cabbages'. But most of them were country women, born and brought up round here, with families and friends about them. Jane Cassidy (she kept her professional name of Jane Webster in correspondence, but the school had insisted it was better for the children to register her married name there) was a city girl, who found herself at times desperately lonely in her magnificent, isolated home.

The women at the school gates were aware of her husband, of course; she was treated with a certain awe, and cultivated by those who sought to use her and the children to strike up some sort of friendship with the great man. But even that made her not a person in her own right but an appendage of her more celebrated partner. Fewer and fewer of her acquaintances seemed to remember her as Jane Webster, the actress.

She'd tried to talk about these things to Adam, but he listened for a few minutes and then switched to his own and greater concerns. It was the way of the actor, of course; egotism came with the profession and sometimes it seemed a necessary tool for success in it. Every theatre actor knew that if he collapsed with a heart attack they would be discussing the recasting of his role before the ambulance reached the hospital. But television stardom was something different: they couldn't stick a new face into a role overnight and hope for the same success. But Jane felt Adam should at least find the time to listen to her.

But Adam was Adam. She'd known that when she married him and she shouldn't expect something different. She lived in luxury on the back of his efforts, with a nanny now giving her the freedom she scarcely knew how to use. She couldn't expect sympathy or understanding from her husband for what seemed to him her petty problems. He would probably think she was a silly cow, or worse still an ungrateful cow. 'Jane Webster, you're pathetic!' she told herself sternly. She would need to find her own solutions.

When they went upstairs, Adam went into the two rooms at the end of the landing to look at his sleeping children. Jane, listening to the distant throb of the dishwasher beneath her as she undressed in the bedroom, wondered whether he had gone in there to please himself or to please her.

She might have been reassured if she had been able to see the change in Adam as he moved towards his children. The stillness of the scene in the first of the rooms, the slow, rhythmic breathing of the tiny figure in the big bed seemed to still also the thoughts and the pulse of the man who had fathered him. Damon was six now, a dynamo who seemed by day to have discovered the secret of perpetual motion. Yet, at this moment, you had to look hard to detect the tiny rise and fall of the blanket which meant that all was well with him. He had the blond curls that were so prominent in the pictures of his mother as a child, and skin 'as smooth as monumental alabaster'. Adam wondered where that phrase had come from, then realized that it was from *Othello*. Not really appropriate for the skin of a child, maybe, but it always pleased him when a phrase from the past came to him. He wasn't sure why.

He was beset with a sudden fear for the innocence he saw beneath him, for the damage which must surely be done to this tiny figure by the harsh world which awaited him. How could this sleeping cherub possibly become a grown man, with the weapons and the will to resist the hostility which must surely be turned upon him by that aggressive, dog-eat-dog world which awaited him beyond the walls of this luxurious citadel?

The room next door was identical, save for the pink walls which its imperious four-year-old mistress had demanded. Kate was not as deeply asleep as Damon had been. Her brow wrinkled for a moment as he watched her. The lips, small and delicate as the petals of a flower, mouthed words for a moment, but no sound came from them. Then a smile, tiny, mysterious, confident, settled on the small and perfect mouth. The sigh was as silent as the words had been. Then her breathing settled into a regular, quiet rhythm and you had to be close to her to detect any movement at all. He stooped and set his lips softly as the wings of a moth upon the infant forehead, then caressed with the back of his fingers the face which was so active and demanding when it was animated during the day.

Adam Cassidy stood for a moment at the door, looking

back at his sleeping child, relishing this moment of real life, which seemed at present to be increasingly elusive for him.

Jane was already in bed when he went into the master bedroom. She lay as still as the child he had just left, but with her eyes steadily upon him. He was suddenly self-conscious, for a reason he could not explain, and turned abruptly into the luxurious bathroom beyond the bed. He had intended to say things to Jane about the children, about the way she cared for them and the way he appreciated it, but the words would not come, even when he slid beneath the duvet beside her five minutes later. He put out the light and stared for a moment at the invisible ceiling. Then he said, 'I love you, Jane.' It emerged not as he wanted it, but as if it were somehow a statement which surprised him. He said after another few seconds, 'But you know that, don't you?'

'It doesn't do any harm for you to say it occasionally, does it? Or for me to hear it, for that matter.' She turned on her side and slid her arms round him, feeling the muscles on his back, moving her hands down from the shoulder blades she knew so well to the bottom of his back and the top of the cleft there.

Both of them knew that they were going to make love, but there was no need to hurry things on. He held her tightly for a moment, then leaned her back and stroked her breasts, in the foreplay they both knew she enjoyed. Then passion took over and he rejoiced in the sudden urgency of her movements, of her nails digging into his shoulders as he brought her to a climax and she urged him on with the familiar blunt commands.

Then they relaxed, unclasping their limbs as unhurriedly as they had begun, and lay on their backs with hands entwined as a prelude to sleep. It was good to have the experience, to know what would excite a woman and give her sexual pleasure. That was his last, consoling thought before he turned on to his side and lost consciousness in the big warm bed.

Actors are more self-centred than ordinary men. It did not occur to Adam Cassidy that the pleasure they had just enjoyed might also owe something to Jane Webster's experience in other places.

# THREE

Eight hours later and twenty miles south of Adam and Jane Cassidy, in a house which would have fitted comfortably into the four-car garage at Broad Oaks, a very different couple were preparing themselves for the challenge of a new day.

Detective Chief Inspector 'Percy' Peach surveyed his breakfast table and Mrs Peach with a satisfaction that his enemies might have called smug. He wasn't short of enemies among the criminal fraternity of North Lancashire, and he even counted one or two among the police service on the other side of the great divide. He set his hands on the shoulders of his wife's dressing gown and said with conviction, 'I've decided I like being married.'

'I'm not sure I do,' said Lucy Peach 'Not at work, anyway. I'm getting tired of all the stale jokes about having sex on tap.'

'But you know how to turn the tap on full flow,' he said with a smile, allowing his right hand to run for a moment through her luxuriant chestnut hair.

'Speaking of taps, it was bloody cold in that bathroom of yours this morning!'

'Language, our Lucy!'

'Our Lucy's language will get a lot worse, if you don't do something about the heating in there before the winter sets in.'

'You were warm enough last night,' said Percy dreamily. 'If I could have plugged in to that, I could have heated the house for a week.'

'If you're going to comment on my bedroom performance every morning, I shall become inhibited. You'll be giving marks out of ten next.'

'Nine point five for technique, ten for artistic impression,' said Percy promptly. He looked sadly at the bowl of muesli in front of his new wife, then slid a slice of white bread provocatively on to the pan in which his bacon and egg was frying.

Lucy tried to convey the correct distaste when he banged

the cholesterol-laden plate down opposite her two minutes later, but feared that she had managed only envy. 'This is how sausages should be, nearly black all round but not burnt,' said Percy. The sausage disappeared down the chief inspectorial throat with a rapidity that was matched only by the consumer's relish. 'Nothing wrong with a bit of cereal, lass, but you need a fry-up to follow before you meet the rigours of the day.' He dipped a piece of his fried bread in the yoke of his egg and downed it with a predictable sigh of satisfaction.

'If I breakfasted like that, my bottom would look big even in a kaftan,' Lucy informed him.

'Tha's got a gradely backside, lass. If tha'd been a cricketer, tha'd have needed a gradely backside. One of the requisites for a fast bowler, John Arlott always said.'

'And who was John Arlott?' said his wife innocently. She was ten years younger than Peach's thirty-nine, and she liked to remind him of that occasionally.

'Wash thi mouth out this instant, lass!' Percy shook his head sadly. 'If tha doesn't behave thisen, I shall have to tell thi mother that tha didn't know who John Arlott was. And then tha'll get thi arse tanned. Delectable though it undoubt-edly is,' he reassured her, dropping his Lancashire dialect for the purpose. Unlike most newly married men, Percy found his recently acquired mother-in-law a pearl amongst women.

Lucy thought it wisest to divert his thoughts to the subject of work. 'I've got to go into the Muslim community again today. We're still following up the associates of this terrorist suspect they arrested in London last week.'

Lucy had been Percy's detective sergeant until their marriage, learning much from his maverick style and his aggressive interviewing techniques. But police practice demands that couples with a close relationship do not work closely together. Only the fact that the head of CID, Chief Superintendent Tucker, was completely out of touch with the staff whom he nominally controlled had permitted them to work together for so long. Everyone else in the station except the man in control of CID had known for the last three years that Percy Peach and Lucy Blake were an item. But even Tucker could not miss marriage. DS Lucy Blake was now employed in different detective teams and on cases which were not the concern of her new husband.

Percy missed her presence at his side more than he cared to admit, even to himself. She had counterbalanced his direct, confrontational style, often gaining cooperation from witnesses he would have challenged head-on, bringing a different sort of insight from his own to complex cases. 'Have you found anything significant about this Akmal bloke?'

'He was militant Muslim all right. And he was planning some sort of attack. But we knew that when we started. We need to find out who his associates were and how far the cell extended. They've got to be plotting more mischief. Probably suicide bombings, which we all know are such a sod to detect and prevent. I need to know more of the Muslim culture – more about how they think and feel. Most of the Asians we speak to are only too anxious to help us – they realize that the reputation of their whole community is in danger of being wrecked by this lunatic fringe.'

'Then what's the problem?'

'They don't really trust us, because we're police. We need more Asian officers. We've got just three in Brunton, and two of them are new constables still wet behind the ears. None of them are women, of course. The only one with any service is a DS who's working beside me. We're supposed to be getting a couple of Asian DCs on temporary assignment from Manchester, but there's a national shortage of Asian officers. The people I interview tell me just as much as they want to. I'm not able to sense if they're holding anything back. I felt I could do that when I was working with you and dealing with people of a similar background to myself.'

Percy had downed his fry-up and two slices of toast with amazing speed and was already washing the dishes. Lucy decided she must have been talking too much. She realized that she didn't want to hear that he was getting on famously without her. Nevertheless, she downed her mug of tea and said dutifully, 'How's it going with you?'

'Very dull, at the moment. All shop robberies and petty violence. We could do with a good juicy murder.'

Adam Cassidy wasn't required in the studio until two o'clock. They were filming some of the small takes with extras during the morning and the director had taken care to inform him of that. He didn't want a star kicking his heels around the place; idle stars tended to make trouble, and no one wished to risk a confrontation.

Adam allowed himself the luxury of a lie-in. He couldn't sleep late, of course. The excited noises of young children preparing for a school day ensured that. But he lay contentedly, listening to the high-pitched tones of Damon and Kate and the responses of mother and nanny. He couldn't catch a word of what anyone said beyond the close-fitting door of the bedroom, so he amused himself by imagining the tussles being conducted between adults and children. Five minutes of this was enough; it was like trying to follow a play without the dialogue. He switched on the radio and listened to John Humphrys making his latest political victim squirm in the ten past eight interview. It was like a brisk stage exchange, he thought, with Humphrys scarcely allowing the minister to complete a sentence before he refuted a statistic or provided a less favourable one of his own.

He didn't know why the politicians put up with it. But probably both Humphrys and his victim had agreed the main lines the interview was going to take before it started. Bit like improvised drama really, where they gave you a situation and invited you to improvise the dialogue. He'd never liked that very much; others had always been quicker thinking and more inventive than he was. But he couldn't see the point of it. Written dialogue, with all the time for thought and revisions, was always going to be better, wasn't it?

His reflections were interrupted by the sudden shrill of the phone beside his bed. He waited for someone else in the house to answer it. When no one did, he switched off the radio, snatched up the receiver and rapped out his number.

'Adam? Is that you?'

He sighed, already irritated. His elder brother, by three years. The dutiful plodder of the family, whose rectitude felt to Adam like a constant rebuke to his own lifestyle. 'Of course it's me, Luke. You should know my voice, after forty-two years.'

'I'm at Dad's house, Adam. He's not well. You should come and see him.'

'I will, as soon as I can make the time.'

'You said that last time. That was now five weeks ago.'

'It can't be.'

'Five weeks yesterday, mate.' An attempt at the old intimacy which had long since deserted them.

'Trust you to be counting. You don't seem to realize how busy my schedule—'

'He's ill, Adam, and he's been waiting for you to come. He doesn't complain, but you can see when he's disappointed. Or you could if you were ever around.'

'Look, if all you want to do is to—'

'I think he's had another heart attack. Only a small one, if indeed it is one at all. I'm waiting for the doctor to come now.'

'All right. Give me a few minutes and I'll see what I can do.' He put the phone down before Luke could speak again. He had a free morning and he knew what he was going to do, but there was no reason to let his brother think it was easy. Luke might do the bulk of the caring, but he must realize that Adam had a lifestyle which didn't allow the domestic complications that the less eminent had to cope with.

He gave it seven minutes, heard in the sports news that another Premiership football manager had been sacked, then sat up and picked up the phone. 'I've managed to reschedule this morning's appointments. I hope you're not exaggerating, because it wasn't easy.'

'I think you'll be glad you did it, when you see Dad.'

Luke's voice had restraint and dignity, and for a fleeting moment Adam envied those qualities. 'I'll be there by about half past ten. You can tell the old bugger I'm coming.'

He levered himself out of bed, made for the bathroom and the power shower, then changed his mind. He slipped on his dressing gown, making sure that the cord was securely tied; you had to be more careful about your dress, now that there was a nanny permanently in the house. He went downstairs and found the children where he had calculated they would be, with coats on at the front door.

'Give Dad a hug before you go!' he called from the stairs. They turned and ran to him, flinging arms wide as they reached him. He swung each of them around him in turn, clasping them to his chest, feeling the smallness of the torsos beneath the clothes, envying them the spontaneity which would drop away from them for ever as they left their childhood.

Jane Webster thrust aside the thought that he could have

arrived earlier, rather than turning up belatedly for the rituals rather than the substance of love. She waved to him, then clutched a small hand in each of hers. She could have got nanny to take the children to school, but she enjoyed this morning walk, when her small charges confessed their fears and hopes for the day.

Adam was finishing his breakfast when she returned home. She had planned a discussion about the children and their progress with him, but he said whilst she was still taking her coat off in the hall, 'I've got to go and see Dad this morning. Luke thinks he's taken a turn for the worse. He's probably exaggerating, as usual, but I said I'd go.'

You poor bloody martyr, thought Jane. Aloud, she said as she came into the kitchen, 'Of course you must go.'

The actress who had been the slight shape beneath the bedclothes in the scene shot on the previous day was Michelle Davies.

In earlier scenes, she had caught the flavour of the series excellently, showing a capacity for comedy as well as romantic melodrama. The unwritten subtext beneath the unlikely plots in the Alec Dawson series was that it didn't take itself too seriously, and Michelle had immediately struck the right notes. She had the looks and the talent to do well on stage and television. So far she had not enjoyed the third and most important thing you needed in an overcrowded profession: luck. Over the eight years since she had left RADA, she had managed to hone her craft by securing regular parts in the theatre. She had been almost continually employed, but it was precarious and not very well paid work.

Playing opposite Adam Cassidy was her first big break. Anyone who did that was certain to be noticed. With the worldwide appeal of the Alec Dawson series, it was almost like becoming a James Bond girl in an earlier generation. One episode didn't mean a lot, of course, but the plan now was that she would become Dawson's regular girlfriend in the next series. Once she had a regular role like that, her fame and her fees would rocket in harness and the offers of stage and film work would pour in. Her agent said so. And whilst Michelle Davies knew that agents always promised jam tomorrow and never gave guarantees, in this case his optimism made good sense.

The director professed himself pleased with her work; he had assured Michelle that she was part of the producer's plans for the next series. This morning she had a meeting with that producer and she hoped that he was going to tie things up. Directors lived in the present and dealt with problems day by day, but the producers who provided the human and other resources to set up series had to plan well ahead.

She hadn't spoken to James Walton in the four months since he had taken her on to play the part of the damsel in distress in the episode they were currently filming. He was an erect, distinguished man of sixty, which in the ephemeral world of television was very old. He was also one of the few men in the Manchester television centre who wore a suit and tie. Michelle Davies felt a little like a sixth former summoned to an interview with the headmistress as she took a deep breath and knocked at his door.

Walton had silver hair, keen grey eyes, and a confidence which emanated from age and experience. He stood and asked her to sit down when she came into his office. He would have offered the same courtesy to any woman, whether she was a theatrical dame or the newest recruit being accorded her first small part. He saw Michelle into her chair, then went back to the other side of the desk, sat down, and asked her whether she had been enjoying her work in the one episode under-taken so far.

It was good to be treated like a lady, in a profession where most people were careless of such things, Michelle told herself. Yet she found Walton's politeness inhibiting; she would have preferred a quick and informal confirmation of the offer she hoped desperately was coming to her. She said carefully, 'Everyone's been very friendly to me – they've made me feel as if I'd been one of the team from the start.'

'That's good. Sometimes it's not easy coming into a team where everyone seems to know each other and know the form for the production. You don't need me to tell you that acting is a very insecure profession; most people in it seem to have their fears and their hang-ups, so they can be suspicious of newcomers.'

'There's been nothing like that. They've made me feel one of the team from the start.' It was broadly true, but she would have delivered the thought even if it hadn't been. Producers didn't want new people coming in who would rock the boat. She didn't want anything raised against her at this stage; there were dozens of women with attributes similar to hers who would bite this man's hand off for the offer he was going to make. Once she became a regular on the series, with a well-known television face, she would be much more difficult to dispense with. Until then, she must play her cards with care.

'I'm glad you feel like that. We like to think we have a happy ensemble on the *Call Alec Dawson* series.' Walton turned a sheet over on the desk in front of him, though she had the feeling that he knew exactly what he was going to say and was using the paper as a prop to add weight to his words. 'Well, as you know, Ms Davies, it is my job to plan ahead and make sure that everything is ready to go when we begin the filming of the next series.' He smiled a broad, genuine smile at her; things were always easier when you had good news to offer.

'I understand that. And it's Michelle, by the way.' She answered his smile, feeling strangely coquettish, in a Jane Austen sort of way. She was sure this man had never employed the casting couch which she had been warned about all these years ago at RADA.

'Well, Michelle, I have what I hope will be good news for you. Our director is eminently satisfied with your work in the episode currently being shot in the studio and on location. The rest of the cast are also happy, but you know as well as I do that it is the opinion of the director which counts most. Now: the details of storylines are not yet finalized, but we have already decided that Alec Dawson should have a perman-ent girlfriend in the next series, and, if that goes well, for the series which follows that. I cannot make you a formal offer this morning, but I wish to know whether you would be interested in undertaking this role.'

What a splendid, old-fashioned, roundabout way of putting it, Michelle Davies thought. She wanted to fling herself across the executive desk and embrace the man. She did nothing of the sort, of course. She found it a test of her acting talents to keep the excitement out of her voice as she said, 'I should certainly be interested. I'd be a fool not to be, wouldn't I?'

He smiled at her. For once he was at a loss for the polite phrase, now that she had stepped out of her part and become

spontaneous. 'It will mean a considerable rise in your remuneration, of course. Perhaps you would prefer that I discuss
this in due course with your agent.'

'Yes, I would. Make him earn his fees, eh?' she gave a
strangely brittle laugh, which told her how nervous she had
been.

'Is there anything you would like to ask me at this stage,
Michelle?'

She thought for a moment, feeling a vague wish to prolong
this moment of triumph. 'Am I allowed to let the rest of the
cast know about this?'

He steepled his fingers and frowned briefly, enjoying the
moment in his muted, courteous way. 'I can't see any reason
why you shouldn't do that. They will no doubt find you a
most welcome addition to the regular team. Have a word with
your director first. If Joe Hartley has no objection, I certainly
haven't.'

Walton stood up, signifying that their exchange was at an
end, and came round his desk towards her. Michelle thought
he was going to shake her hand, but he merely ushered her
towards the door; perhaps the handshake was reserved for the
formal contract. She was almost through the doorway when
he said. 'Our star has an ultimate veto over casting – that is
the television way of things, I'm afraid. But I'm sure there
won't be any difficulties there.'

# FOUR

The narrow street rose with increasing steepness towards the pewter sky. The terraced houses shut out the light, so that the eye was drawn naturally towards that rectangle of pale grey light and that invisible world beyond the grimy bricks of the frontages. When these tight little houses had been built in the nineteenth century, clogs had clattered through the noisy winter darkness to the mills at the bottoms of streets like this. The mills had been the focus of life for the folk who lived here. These cheap houses had often been rented from the mill-owners themselves, who wanted their workforce close to the looms which dominated their lives. The town of Brunton had been a jewel in the empire of King Cotton.

The cobbles had gone and the street was tarmacked now: the tight houses had neither gardens nor garages. At weekends and overnight, there were unbroken lines of cars down the street, making it seem even narrower. At half past ten in the morning, there was ample room to park. Adam Cassidy locked the Mercedes carefully; it was by far the newest and most expensive car in the street. But he didn't fear damage to it, as he would have done in a similar area in Manchester. This was still what its older residents deemed a 'respectable' area. That familiar word might be difficult to define, but everyone in old industrial towns like Brunton knew what it meant.

Adam Cassidy stood motionless for a moment, looking up and down the deserted street, glancing up at the low clouds above, hating the place and what it meant to him. The scene should have reminded him of how far he had risen in the world, of how he had climbed to success from an unpromising environment like this, of everything he had achieved in his life. Instead, it depressed him. He wasn't ashamed of his roots. Indeed, when he gave 'in depth' interviews for papers or magazines, he stressed his humble beginnings and how they encouraged him to keep his feet upon the ground and treat those twin impostors triumph and disaster just the same. But whenever he came back here he felt dejected, not uplifted.

The door of the house opened straight on to the street. Some of the older women had still sand-stoned their doorsteps every week when Adam had been small, but no one did that any more. The brown paint on the panels of the door was flaking and needed attention, but it was opened before Adam could knock.

Luke Cassidy looked more than three years older than his brother. At forty-five, his hair was receding a little but still plentiful; it was, however, already streaked with grey. His face was deeply lined. He looked past Adam for a moment to the gleaming Mercedes. Then he smiled at his brother and said, 'It's good that you could come. It will give Dad a lift; you're still his favourite, you know.'

'I doubt that. The old lad's not daft. He knows how much you do for him.'

But families weren't like that; Luke knew it, if Adam didn't. Feelings weren't formed on the basis of logic, particularly those of parents towards children. Their dead mother had probably always marginally favoured her first-born son, though scrupulously fair in any material measure of things. Their father had always loved Adam most, had always indulged him as a child, had even tolerated his demand for drama training where he would certainly have refused anything so esoteric for his elder son.

Harry Cassidy believed in education, in its power to lift his children beyond the skilled manual labour which had been the limit of his own development in the years after Hitler's war. But he had been happy to see Luke get a degree and become a teacher. It was almost as if this conventional success had been a prerequisite for the more exciting and experimental development of his younger son. People from Alma Street in Brunton didn't become actors; that was a ridiculous idea. When Adam Cassidy had defied the odds and done it, his father had been delighted, had revelled in telling his wife that he'd been right after all, hadn't he?

Harry struggled hard to get out of his chair when Adam came into the living room with his wide, infectious smile. Then he fell back and beat the arms briefly in frustration. Adam watched the giant of his childhood and felt a sharp stab of pain in the present frailty of the old man. He said with breezy cheerfulness, 'Good to see you, Dad! Sorry it's been so long, but you know how it is.'

He proffered his hand. Harry, who didn't know at all how

it was in the world of his younger son, took it after a moment's surprise and held it in both of his. 'And it's good to see you, son. Good of you to make the time for your old Dad.'

Adam glanced at Luke. He knew it had been the wrong gesture to shake hands with his father. It was far too formal for father and son. It showed that it had been a long time since he had been here and it showed that he felt awkward in the family home. He turned back to the thin grey face with the welcoming smile and said, 'How are you today, Dad? I believe you've not been too good.'

'Better for seeing you, Adam! And I'm not that bad, really. The old pins aren't what they were, but you have to expect that when you're nearly eighty.'

Luke Cassidy, who had brought a meal in each day for the last fortnight, thought wryly that the old man was behaving as he did with the doctor, minimizing the pain and the restrictions which his advancing arthritis visited upon him. That left it to others to make out his case for him, to try to get the help in the house which he now warranted and direly needed. He had lately acquired the old person's urge to boast about his age. Harry was barely seventy-eight, but that had now become 'nearly eighty' whenever the opportunity arose. You noticed these things in those you loved, when you were with them for most of the time.

But Luke was a generous man, and a loving as well as a dutiful son. It gave him pleasure to see the old man's face light up with Adam's presence in the house for the first time in many weeks. 'Sit down and talk to Dad, Adam. Bring him up to date on the latest happenings in the world of show business. I've got to get off to work, but I'll make you two a quick pot of tea first.'

Harry watched his elder son disappear into the kitchen, then said conspiratorially to Adam, 'He fusses about as much as ever, you know. Brings me in a meal Hazel makes for me most days, when I could easily manage for myself. He's nipped down here in a free period at his school so that he could be here when you came. But he's a good lad really.'

Adam felt guilty that his elder brother's necessary ministrations should be minimized in this way. He said rather feebly, 'He's more than a good lad, Dad. He really cares about you and he does his best to get you help when you need it.' And he takes the weight off me and allows me to neglect you for weeks on end; it was better not to voice that thought.

'Tell me what you've been doing, lad.' Harry leant forward eagerly in his chair.

'Oh, we've been very busy filming the new *Call Alec Dawson* series. Each episode takes only an hour on the screen, but it takes weeks to make, you know.'

'Oh, it must do.' The old man knew nothing at all about it, but if his son said it was so, then he wanted it to be so. 'It must really take it out of all the cast – and particularly you.'

Adam was about to enlarge on the hardships when Luke came back with a pot of tea, two china mugs, and a plate of shortbread on a tray. 'Hazel made you the shortbread, Dad. I've put the rest of it away in the tin.'

It wasn't meant as a rebuke, but it seemed like one to Adam. He should have thought to bring something from home, or at least picked up something on the way here. He was left smiling awkwardly at Luke. 'How is Hazel? And how are the kids? Still doing well at school, I expect.' The last bit sounded resentful, when he hadn't meant it to be so.

'Young Harry's holding his own at the comprehensive. Rather more than that, I think. Ruth should join him there next year.'

'Good. That's very good, isn't it, Dad? But they have an advantage with you, Luke. I expect you can give them a helping hand whenever it's needed. I wish I had the time to do the same with mine. Or the ability, for that matter. You were always the bright one of the family.'

And much good it's done me, thought Luke. Living in a nineteen sixties semi half a mile away from where I was born and teaching at the local comprehensive. With a reputation as a good teacher, in a calling which Adam despises and most people think of as dull. With a routine marriage and two kids who are quite bright and are about to visit upon me all the joys of their adolescence. Looking after a homophobic and racist old father whose prejudices I understand but can't share. Watching him move a little further away from me each year as age takes him over. Yet needing more of my time and my care – and yes, even my love – as each year passes. Luke watched Adam's perfect teeth bite into the shortbread and said, 'You were bright enough, kiddo, and you always knew exactly where you wanted to go.'

Adam grinned at the old appendage. He couldn't remember

Luke using it for years. Not since the days when the world had been smaller and simpler, and the frail figure who now sat with a blanket over his legs in the armchair had ruled this house with a rod of iron. A tiny part of him whispered insistently that he had been happier then, in that world he had understood and controlled. But it could not possibly be so. The feeling must be mere nostalgia for youth, for the cosiness of family, for the dead mother who had sat every evening in the chair where he was sitting at this moment.

He went with Luke to the door and said quietly, 'He seems worse since I last saw him. Is he getting everything he needs?'

'He's getting every help I can get and every help he will accept. He's growing old fast, Adam. He's better than usual today, because he perked up as soon as he knew that you were coming. Stay here as long as you can and talk to him. Tell him when you go that I'll pop in on my way home from school as usual.'

'I'll pay, you know. If you get someone in to give this place a face-lift, I can pay. If you want someone to come in every day, I'll—'

'He won't take it. You know that. It's us he needs. If you can just make the time to come in more often, that would be the greatest help. You can see what a lift it gives him. If you'd seen him yesterday, you'd know what I mean.'

'All right. Don't go on about it. I do what I can. We don't all live on the doorstep. We don't all have the kind of life which lets us pop in whenever we feel like it. I'll make sure I get here more often. It should be easier in the next few months.' But each of them knew in that moment that he wouldn't come, that Luke would have to be on the phone to him before he drove here again.

He went back into the room which he knew so well and yet knew now not at all. The old man and he made a few stabs at conversation, searching desperately for topics, where once they would not have needed to search. 'You won't be able to get to see the Rovers now,' said Adam.

'Haven't been for two years. Luke took me with the boys. We had seats in the stand. It's all seats now, you know. Not like when you were a lad and I used to take you.'

Adam had been very keen, until he'd left the town and never gone back. He still played up his Brunton Rovers allegiance in interviews, when he was being his man of the people. But he didn't know many of the players, so that the father and son's discussion of the latest struggle to stay in the Premier League soon foundered. He tried to tell his dad about the making of the Alec Dawson series, and the old man seemed interested for a moment or two. Then he said suddenly, 'You go careful when you're on location, our Adam. They tell me there's puffs and fairies round every corner in your business.'

'There's a few. But gay people really aren't a problem, Dad. They don't bother you, when they see you're not interested. They're quite easy to work with, most of them. Well, as easy as anyone else in our business!'

He meant it as a joke, but the old man told him not to turn his back on them and not to trust them. He reverted to a familiar theme. 'Our lads would never have won the war if they'd had shirtlifters around.'

Only when Adam talked about his new family did Harry Cassidy show any interest. Adam found a small snap of the kids taken a year earlier in his wallet and watched the wizened fingers take it with immense care. He promised to bring a bigger and more up-to-date selection when he came again. Harry seemed to have got the children from his son's previous marriage mixed up with the present ones. Not surprising, really, since he hadn't seen either pair for at least a year.

It made Adam feel guilty once again when he realized that. But he didn't want to bring Damon and Kate here, even though Jane told him they'd like to see where he'd grown up. There was nothing for them in this dim terraced house with its fusty old carpets and his fusty old Dad. That sounded harsh, but it was a fact of life, wasn't it? He said, 'You must come and see us, Dad. You'd like our new house. It's almost in the Trough of Bowland, where you used to walk as a lad.'

'Ay. I'd like that. Happen Luke'll bring me, and let his bairns see their cousins.'

'That's a good idea! I'll arrange it, as soon as this series is in the can and we have a bit more time to ourselves. You'll be surprised to see how they're growing, Dad.'

'Ay, that I will. It's been a while.'

'It has, hasn't it? Life's so hectic, nowadays. Speaking of which, Dad, I've got to be on my way, I'm afraid. Can't leave a lot of actors waiting for their leading man, can I?'

Harry Cassidy levered himself from his chair with an immense effort and used his stick to hobble to the door with his younger son. There he put his hand suddenly upon Adam's forearm, panting hard with the effort he had expended to move those few yards. 'Those lasses they surround you with in these things. You keep your hands off them, lad.'

'Oh, you get used to pretty women, Dad. It's a fact of life in the business. Don't you worry, you get so that it's water off a duck's back.'

The father looked up into his son's face with a grim little smile. 'Not for thee it's not, lad. You've never been able to resist a nice bit of skirt, especially if you got the chance to put your hand up it. Just think on, you've got that nice lass Jane and a family to look to. Don't go pissing in thee own nest lad.'

The old man had never spoken to him so crudely before. It must be something to do with his advancing age. Adam put the warning out of his mind as he eased the big maroon Mercedes away from the grimy kerb, but it would return to his mind several times in the days to come.

Later that day, Detective Chief Inspector Percy Peach climbed the stairs towards the top storey of the impressive new Brunton police station with a sinking heart. It wasn't the weather that caused his depression. The clouds of the morning had lifted and this was a pleasant late-October afternoon. The view over the old cotton town to the autumn colours of the trees and hills beyond it became more extensive with each passing floor.

It was people rather than the world outside which made Peach gloomy. And one person in particular: the one who occupied the penthouse office whence he was bound. He paused for a moment before the familiar bold lettering on the door which informed him that behind it there dwelt the head of CID. Then he took a deep breath, pressed the button on the right of the door, and watched the light which lit up the ENTER slot with a sinking heart.

Chief Superintendent Thomas Bulstrode Tucker sat behind the biggest desk in the station, in the same model of round-backed leather chair as that afforded to the Chief Constable. He was better fitted for the trappings of power than the exercise of it, in Peach's view. But even Percy would have had to admit that he was hardly an unbiased witness. Tucker now glared at his junior over the rimless glasses he had recently adopted and said, 'What is it now, Peach? I'm very busy.'

It was a Pavlovian reaction to his arrival, thought Percy, sourly surveying the vast yardage of empty desk surface. Tommy Bloody Tucker was always very busy. A cynic would have said that his busyness had accelerated alongside his inefficiency over the years, as he had become ever more remote from the crime-face. But Peach wasn't a cynic: 'realist' he would have accepted, but not cynic. He said with immense patience, 'It wasn't my idea to come up here, sir. You sent for me.'

'Did I? Ah, yes, Percy. Things to discuss, you see. I like to keep my right-hand man fully in the picture, don't I?'

Percy took this as a rhetorical question and afforded it a guarded smile. He didn't like it when Tucker used his fore-name; it usually meant some particularly tedious or tricky assignment was coming his way. 'Trouble in the offing, is there, sir?'

'Trouble? Why no, not at all. On the contrary, I'm always glad when we reach this date in the year. You should try to present a more cheerful face to the world yourself, Percy. Gives the public confidence in the service we offer them, a cheerful face does.'

'Yes, sir. What is the significance of the date, then?'

Tucker leaned forward confidentially. 'Well, Percy, it marks another landmark in my service. I now have less than two years to go to retirement.'

'I'm very pleased for you, sir.'

'I don't mind admitting to you that it will be a happy day when it comes.'

'I'm sure everyone in the CID section will rejoice with you,' said Peach inscrutably.

Tucker looked at him keenly for a moment, then belatedly remembered why he had called him to enter the rarefied air of this sanctum. 'Meanwhile, we have things to do, Percy.'

'Indeed we have, sir. Crime never sleeps, as your perpetual vigilance reminds us.'

'That is so. You and I, though, have to take a wider view of things, as senior men. We must never be sanguine, but I think it is fair to say that at the moment we have no really serious cases on our patch.'

'But we know not the time or the place, sir,' Peach reminded him gnomically.

'And in the absence of complicated investigations—'

'We are involved in a complex search for the roots of terrorism. The Home Secretary thinks that is about as serious as it can get,' said Percy desperately. He sensed from long experience that Tommy Bloody Tucker was lining up some tricky assignment for him.

'And are you personally involved in this search?' The question showed an unusual perspicacity; it thus took Peach by surprise.

'Well, no, sir. Not directly. A specialist unit has been set up to investigate the militant Muslim element in our Asian population. I have a tenuous connection, in that DS Peach has been drafted into that unit.'

'DS Peach?'

'My wife, sir. The former DS Lucy Blake, whom you assigned to me as my detective sergeant some years ago.'

'Ah, yes. I trust the married state is everything you expected it to be?'

'Everything and more, sir.' Percy cast his eyes ecstatically to the ceiling for a moment, hoping thus to suggest the bedroom bliss which was surely denied to his chief with the formidable partner Percy had christened Brunhilde Barbara. 'I miss her at my side during the daily grind, but we can of course no longer work together.'

Tucker had allocated a female sergeant to this most masculine of men as a punishment. The move had gone spectacularly amiss. He said tetchily, 'This is all very well, but I'm afraid I haven't time for gossip. It is time to think of the community and our part in it. The modern police force does not exist in a vacuum.'

It was one of his favourite phrases over the last year, and one of his most meaningless. Peach could see now where this was going. He said heavily, 'You're good at public relations work, sir. It's one of your strengths. It was never one of mine.'

'Then you must make it so, Percy. You must address your weaknesses.'

Still his forename. There was a shitty job coming up, for sure. 'I pride myself on collaring criminals, sir. Whereas – well, you're good at public relations.'

'We have been asked to speak to our Asian community –
to build on our already good relationship with them. I want
you at my side on the platform. I shall deal with the general
questions, you will provide practical examples of how good
policing is helping these people, even though I find some of
them are suspicious and uncooperative. This will be valuable
experience for you.'

In other words, you'll deliver the general, meaningless
platitudes, but if we collect any tricky questions about discrim-
ination, they'll be passed to me. 'This isn't one of my
strengths, sir.'

'Then it damn well ought to be! I'm acting on the chief
constable's instructions here, Peach. If necessary, this will
become an order.'

At least 'Percy' had disappeared, now that the cards were
on the table. He said heavily, 'In that case, I shall put my
limited talents at your disposal, sir.'

It was a view of the great northern city that would not have
been possible thirty years ago, when the rows of tightly terraced
houses which had given *Coronation Street* its setting were
still being demolished.

From the fourteenth floor of this new block, Adam Cassidy
now looked out over the new Manchester. The spectacular stainless steel and glass of the Lowry Art Gallery glinted in the soft
autumn sunlight, with the water of the ship canal setting it off
on two sides. On the other side of the slim arc of the lifting
footbridge, the newly completed Imperial War Museum North
rose impressively, moving the eye on to that arena of more
peaceful contests, the football ground at Old Trafford. The
Theatre of Dreams, the publicity boys had labelled it. Well,
Adam Cassidy was here today to further his dreams.

The man who stood behind his shoulder as he looked out
at all this did not hurry him. Accommodation in this spectacular high-rise building had been expensive to acquire and
he now paid plenty in council tax for an office suite with this
impressive view. So let it do its work and impress his visitor.
He hadn't met Adam Cassidy before; two brief phone conver-
sations had been the extent of their previous communication.
The actor was a little older and a little shorter than he had
expected, but that was usual when you met men who had acquired

a degree of glamour. He waited until Cassidy turned away from the big window, then gestured towards the armchair and took the one opposite it for himself.

Mark Gilbey wore an expensive lightweight suit and a silk tie. His features were tanned so deeply that he might have been from the Middle East. He had small, neat features, of which the most remarkable were his deep-set, dark-brown eyes, which gave the impression of continually seeing more than the actual scene in front of him. He wore a small gold earring, which was easily removable for those of his clients who preferred a more conservative appearance. His visitor had refused tea but accepted a dry sherry, in which Mark had joined him. He sipped from his glass and waited for his visitor to take the initiative; most show business people liked to feel that they were controlling things. He would keep his eye on Cassidy's sherry during this exchange, replenishing it if necessary. It was always good to know from the outset if a client was a drinker.

Adam sat back and appeared at ease. An actor could always simulate relaxation, even if he did not feel it. He said, 'I must make it clear from the beginning that anything we say to each other this afternoon must be completely confidential.'

Gilbey offered his most knowing smile, the one that said that already they had an understanding, that they appreciated each other and their respective needs. 'That goes without saying. It is my normal practice. Anything disclosed to the media will normally be on my client's initiative, not mine.'

'You should understand that I am under contract to another agent at the moment.'

'Most people who come to us currently have other agents. That is because we do not need to take on people who are not already successful.' An easy, confident smile. Let the prospective customer know that you do not need to grovel for trade. Tell Cassidy that whilst you might welcome his custom, it will not be the end of the world for you if he doesn't sign up.

'I would need to be convinced that you can offer me wider prospects, that you can secure the kind of work I envisage for myself in the next few years.'

'I look forward to convincing you, Mr Cassidy.'

'I want film work.'

The usual story. Get yourself a television success and move on to Hollywood and world glory. It was understandable enough, considering the obscene sums still volunteered to stars by film moguls. And this man had possibilities. Others before him had moved on from television leads in adventure hokum to James Bond; if Roger Moore could do it, there was certainly hope for Adam Cassidy. The kind of popular success he was enjoying in television was surprisingly easy to sell to Hollywood, now that such series were sold around the world. Mark Gilbey noted down a few details of Cassidy's career to date. He already had most of this on the profile his PA had prepared for him, but it was always interesting to hear how actors saw themselves.

Gilbey pursed his lips, then delivered his prepared speech. 'You're seeking to move into a very competitive world, as you no doubt appreciate. But in your case I consider it is a realistic aspiration; you've done the spadework with your Alec Dawson series. We have good contacts both here and in America. I suggest I conduct some exploratory work on your behalf and then come back to you. You will need to sever your ties with your present agent to facilitate this process.'

'That seems a sensible approach.'

'There will be no fee at this stage. If we eventually secure you an acceptable offer, I would expect you to sign up with the agency at that point.'

'That is eminently acceptable.' Adam found himself trying to use phrases Gilbey might have used to him. It was always a temptation for an actor; sometimes the last person you wanted to present was yourself.

'This preliminary procedure will probably take a week to ten days. May I ring you then at the number you gave me?'

'Yes. And only at that number, please. It is my home number. But I would prefer that you spoke only to me about this.'

'Good. That is understood.' Gilbey made a final note and stood up. 'I look forward to doing business with you, Mr Cassidy. And I hope ours will be a long association.'

Adam tried to control his elation as the lift bore him back to earth. He had at that moment no knowledge of how long this new association would last.

# FIVE

Adam Cassidy had secured his first small role after leaving drama school in 1990 in a revival of *An Inspector Calls*. The lead part had been played by Dean Morley.

Dean was only five years older than Adam and he had taken the raw young actor under his wing. He had helped him with the delivery of his lines. At Adam's request, he had taken him through his one major speech in private, showing him how he could make a greater impact if he could make himself take it more slowly. You could give greater impact to ordinary phrases if you delivered them after a pause, could make dialogue seem better than it was if you made it important to yourself. They must have talked about such things at drama school, though Adam couldn't remember it. In any case, this was the first practical application of it for him. He had learned the lesson eagerly at the time, and found it still useful with the occasionally stilted dialogue of the *Call Alec Dawson* series.

Dean had continued to help Adam in his first few years in the business, putting in a mention for him with casting directors, recommending him to the agent who secured him a tiny part in a low-budget British film, and, most important of all, using a contact to get the eager young man his first small speaking roles in television. It was not entirely altruistic, of course: few things are in a cut-throat and overcrowded profession. Morley realized that a young man with Cassidy's looks and common sense might make progress, and eventually be able to reciprocate these favours.

More immediately, the twenty-two-year-old Adam Cassidy was a young Adonis and Dean Morley was homosexual. He was not one of the prancing queers more common in fiction than in fact. He was never aggressive and always discreet. Nor was he stupid; he saw Adam giving attention to the young women who were always at hand in green rooms and could not ignore it. But there was always a chance that he might be bisexual; there were many precedents for that, in a business which seemed to redistribute hormones copiously and ambiguously. Dean Morley was an optimist.

He was also well used to refusals. When Adam decisively rejected his advances, he shrugged his shoulders and got on with the acting life. There were always other possibilities and Dean exploited them cheerfully. Life wasn't to be taken too seriously, he told everyone. He maintained a boisterous exterior and trusted that no one would see the quiet desperation which besets the lives of all men.

In any case, his early kindnesses to Adam Cassidy were certainly not wasted. As the younger man's television successes rapidly surpassed those of Morley, he remembered those early days. Dean found that a succession of supporting roles came his way as a result of the rising star's recommendations. He was forty-seven now, and he found he was increasingly playing villains and character parts, but that did not matter. Dean had seen too much of the business to worry about the roles which came his way; the important thing was to keep working, which he generally did. A well-known television face could always secure theatre work.

Now the fourth series of the Alec Dawson adventures was almost complete and the casting was already proceeding for a fifth. There was a plan to give Alec Dawson a regular opponent, who would be repeatedly frustrated by the latest Dawson swash and buckle. A modern version of Moriarty, the Napoleon of crime, who had set his mighty talents and intellectual acumen against the even mightier ones of Sherlock Holmes. Dean Morley saw himself as a natural for this part. He had a wide experience of playing villains by now; he knew how to be smooth and sinister at the same time, which he saw as the vital combination for this super-villain. And he knew how to play off the personality and acting idiosyncrasies of his friend Adam Cassidy, didn't he? He could make Alec Dawson into an even bigger star by forming an intriguing duo with him.

Acting is the worst profession of all for fostering illusions.

Dean Morley had settled down now. After his years of cheerful promiscuity, he had acquired a regular partner and bought a flat. They had even talked of a civil ceremony next year, when he had secured the regular villain's role in the *Call Alec Dawson* saga and with it financial security for life. The repeats around the world already brought in a steady income,

and he would be able to pick and choose his theatrical roles
once he became the regular foil for Alec Dawson. Even Iago
might not be out of the question, once the public had him
classed as a villain; after all, he was the right age for it now.

The illusion was getting a firmer hold.

Three days after Adam Cassidy had visited Mark Gilbey,
he was relaxing with a mug of coffee with Dean Morley and
other members of the Alec Dawson cast. The short scene they
had been shooting had gone well, but they were awaiting the
director's verdict after his viewing of the shoot. Adam liked
these interludes, where he could be just one of the cast like
the others, yet find his opinions treated with a little more
respect than anyone else's. It was the sort of respect accorded
to the head of the gang's pronouncements in his school days,
subtle and unspoken, but quite definite. It was power, of course.
The leading actor in a series always acquired power, whether
he wanted it or not. Most people did want it, and Mark was
no exception to the rule.

Even though technically it was the casting director who did
the hiring and firing, the opinions of the star were always
heeded. The bigger the star, the greater the heed. At the back
of every decision was the unspoken thought that if the star
withdrew his presence, the whole project would collapse; it
was very unusual for a leading role in an established series
to be recast. The public were comfortable with the lead who
had established himself; many of them did not clearly distin-
guish the actor from his role, so that they did not take kindly
to a new face usurping that persona.

When the latest theatre gossip was exhausted, the bit players
went off to check whether their services would be needed
again that day, leaving Dean Morley together with his old
friend and one-time protégé. Adam watched the blue smoke
curling slowly upwards from Dean's cigarette and said with
the righteousness of the ex-smoker, 'Be the death of you, those
tubes, if you keep on using them.'

Dean nodded, stubbing out a fag which still had a few draws
left in it. 'I'm not sure it's allowed here any more. No one's
objected, so far.' Green room practice tended to avoid the
rules, in a situation where stress and anxiety were constant
facts of life. 'I still use them to relax at work. I've given them
up altogether at home.'

'How is Keith?' Adam was pleased with himself for remembering the name of Morley's partner.

'He's doing fine. He sold a painting last week. That always cheers him up. But this week he's painting the lounge, so I expect him to be in a foul mood when I get back. I think I'd better pick up a bottle of gin on the way home.'

Adam was grateful for the clues. He remembered now; Keith had a part-time job as an art gallery curator, but aspirations to be a full-time professional artist. He said conventionally, 'It can't be easy, trying to sell serious art when you're not a big name.'

'It isn't. But we get by. And we're happy with each other.' Dean wanted to tell people about that, but no one ever asked you, the way they asked heterosexuals about their liaisons. He wanted to tell everyone that at forty-seven he had discovered the most important love of his life, but no one gave you the chance to do that. There was a pause before he said, 'You're doing well. New series lined up, and more to come after that if you want it. You've come a long way from that lad playing a motorcycle courier with two lines.'

He hadn't intended to mention that, but the temptation to harp back to the help he had offered in Cassidy's early days had been irresistible. Adam gave a little frown before he smiled his recognition of those far-off times. Dean glanced towards the door, wondering how long this privacy would last. It wasn't easy to get Adam on his own, these days. He didn't want to ring him up. He needed to drop his question into a more casual situation: a situation like this, in fact. 'I'm looking forward to being your regular foil in the next series. Be like old times, eh?'

'Regular foil?' Adam knew what Dean meant, but he wanted time to think. It was part of that power which leading actors had, making people spell out the things they didn't want to.

Dean took a deep breath and strove to keep it light. 'The criminal mastermind who's worthy of Alec Dawson's mettle. The villain whose machinations seem to have every chance of success, until they meet the energy and intellect of Alec.' He was trying to treat the role upon which his whole future rested as if it were a curious trifle.

Adam frowned again, for a little longer this time. 'It seems to have been accepted that that's the way we'll go. But as I understand it, the role hasn't been cast yet.'

'But it's as a result of my performance in this series that a permanent opponent for you is envisaged. There is surely an understanding that the part should be mine. I think both the producer and the director envisage that.'

'Really? Well, in that case, you've nothing to worry about, have you?' He gave his old comrade a bland smile, then glanced at his Rolex.

It was that gesture which filled Dean Morley with a sudden horror. He knew that he should leave it now. Pleading with stars was like pleading with departing lovers; it emerged only as a sign of weakness. But he couldn't help himself. 'It's important to us, this, Adam. Keith doesn't earn a lot. This part could mean security for us.'

A moderately successful actor, begging him to secure the future of a couple of puffs. Adam Cassidy enjoyed the feeling of power in that dismissive phrase, though he knew that in an hour or two he would despise himself for it. 'Then I hope it all works out for you, of course.'

'You can put in a word for me, Adam. You know the way it works. If the star's happy with a support player, his opinion counts. And you're a big star now. Perhaps even bigger than you realize.' Dean despised himself for the shameless flattery of the phrases, even as he delivered them. But he must make the man see how crucial this part was for him, for Keith, for the rest of their lives.

'Oh, I'm just a jobbing actor who's been lucky, Dean. You should know that better than most.' Adam smiled his modest television smile; this was almost a rehearsal for his next interview. 'I'll do my best, of course, but I don't think you should count any chickens until they're very fully hatched.'

'Who'd you say it was?'

'Granada Television, sir.'

'Put them through.'

'Superintendent Tucker?'

'It's Chief Superintendent Tucker, actually.'

'Sorry. Granada TV here. I'm Pat Dolan. Your name was passed to me by Janet Jackson from our newsroom staff. I think she's met you when you've held media conferences about serious crimes.'

Tucker was immediately wary: his last TV encounter hadn't

gone well. 'I remember Janet, yes. But I'm happy to say we have no high-profile murders for you at the moment.'

A sudden cackle of laughter made him move the receiver two inches away from his ear. 'Oh, it's nothing like that, Chief Superintendent. This is a very different request. I'm wondering if you'd like to appear on Gerry Clancy's afternoon programme. We usually have either two or three interviews, with people from very different backgrounds. The emphasis is on entertainment. You'd counterbalance show-business personalities for us.'

'I wouldn't wish to endure a hostile cross-examination about police work.'

Another, less strident, laugh; more of a chuckle, this time. 'Have you seen Gerry Clancy's programme, Chief Superintendent Tucker?'

'Not often, no. Scarcely at all, in fact. Pressure of work doesn't allow me to—'

'Gerry doesn't go in for hostile cross-examinations. We leave those to *Panorama* and *Newsnight*. Mr Clancy is no Paxman. This is a light-hearted afternoon programme.'

'I see. May I ask who else would be taking part?'

'Well, that isn't finalized yet. I'd like you to treat this as confidential at the moment, but we're hoping to secure Adam Cassidy for the big interview on that afternoon.'

'I see.' Thomas Bulstrode Tucker strove to control an excitement he felt was quite unsuitable in one of his rank.

'He's the star of the Alec Dawson series.'

'Yes, I'm well aware who Adam Cassidy is.' Barbara refused to miss an episode. She considered Cassidy a tremendous 'hunk'. She would be mightily impressed to see him sharing a sofa with the star.

'Sorry! In that case, you will appreciate that it would be quite a coup for us if we get him. With the advance publicity involved, you'd have quite a big audience for whatever you chose to say about police work. If we get someone as big as Adam Cassidy to appear, we'll probably only have two guests on that programme – you and he.'

'I see. Well, I shall certainly consider your offer. The police service gets a lot of bad publicity, most of which is quite unjustified. If I can do anything to put that right, I would feel obliged to consider it.'

'There'd be a fee.'

Tucker fought back the impulse to ask how much. 'That is not a consideration. I shall have to clear this with my chief constable. If he has no objections, I would see it as my duty to appear.'

Pat Dolan wanted to tell him to loosen up, that this was a bit of fun in the afternoon, that his function was merely to be the PC Plod foil for a series of stories and bon mots from Cassidy. But she had sensed despite his formal tone that he was hooked; the big showbiz name had its magic, even for a staid chief superintendent who should know better. 'I shall take that as a qualified yes, Mr Tucker. I'll be in touch again as soon as I have further details for you.'

A sharp, cold, November Saturday. The market in Brunton has been a covered one for many years now, but the market hall is chilly today. The men and women serving fish and vegetables wear mitts and flap their arms across their chests between serving their early customers. The nation moved its clocks an hour back and returned to Greenwich Mean Time a fortnight ago; the town has its first ropes of coloured lights and the shops their first posters announcing that Father Christmas will be in attendance from the beginning of December.

Lucy Peach is shopping, secretly enjoying the novelty of being a housewife. She is meeting her mother for lunch at twelve; she has resigned herself to being quizzed about married life and her views on producing grandchildren at an early date. Percy Peach is playing in the monthly medal at the North Lancs Golf Club, seeking to reduce his already respectable handicap of eight. He sniffs the cool, clear air and looks to the north, to the heights of Ingleborough and Pen-y-Ghent: the mountains which look surprisingly close as the sun climbs a little higher. Not many better places to be on a day like this, he remarks to his companion; it is always easier to feel like this after landing a 5-iron on to the green at a par three. Percy has always preferred the cool sun of winter to the more torrid temperatures of June and July.

Ten miles north of Peach, on the moors which rise beyond Clitheroe and Waddington, Adam Cassidy is also relishing the day and its sport. There is a carpet of frost up here this morning,

but the whiteness is disappearing now, except in the shadow
of the dry stone walls. There is the first dusting of snow on
the top of the great mound of Pendle Hill to the east. A great
morning to be alive and on the moors, he and his companions assure themselves repeatedly.

Adam had never thought when he was a boy that he would
join those shooting grouse on the moors: only toffs whose
lifestyle was totally outside his experience did that. Yet that
seemed to him a very good reason why he should be here
now. He held his shotgun in the crook of his arm and chatted
happily to the landowner who had invited him to shoot with
his party. Adam wasn't an expert shot, but he didn't need to
be. There were others here who were as bad as him – and in
one case plainly worse. Shooting was expensive, and the invitation to participate was used to cultivate acquaintance or to
return favours. In his case, it was one of the more acceptable
rewards of celebrity. People, even people who had standing
and influence, wanted to be seen with you, wanted to feel that
they were in touch with the glamorous world of show business and television. So why not take advantage of that, when
it could bring pleasure to others as well as yourself?

It was his third shoot in all, but his first of this autumn.
One of his first television appearances as a young actor had
been as a servant in a play about Edward VII and Lillie
Langtry. His function had been to hand the portly monarch a
loaded gun and then say 'Good shot, Your Royal Highness!'
whilst the corpse of a bird plummeted in the background. He
remembered it vividly and with affection, not least because
the well-known actress playing the Jersey Lily had taken him
into her bed for a brief fling. That had been a memorable
experience in itself. More importantly, it had raised the
standing of the unknown young bit-part player on the gossip
grapevine which flourished amongst actors and directors.
Being noticed was very important at the outset of a career,
and young Cassidy had taken full advantage of the opportunities which resulted.

He brought down a couple of grouse early on, which
established his credentials and made the rest of the day more
enjoyable. He enjoyed the trappings of the day more than the
shooting itself. In a relatively small party, he was able to relax,
almost in fact to be himself. He was so much on show

nowadays that he had almost forgotten exactly who that self was. But there were no cameras here, no journalists looking for a juicy quote and waiting all day for a moment of indiscretion. His companions enjoyed the fact that he was in the party, that they would be able to drop casually to others in the coming week that they had been 'shooting with Adam Cassidy at the weekend', but they weren't seeking to trip him up.

He enjoyed the moment when they opened the hampers and brought out the home-made pies and sandwiches and the booze. He enjoyed sitting with his host on a rock in the heather and looking at Pendle Hill on the one side and the fells which ran away towards lower ground and eventually the Ribble estuary and the sea on the other. He had expected to be among the 'county set', but the party was much more mixed than that. There were only two women, one of them the wife of the owner and the other one a twenty-five-year-old niece of his, who made a point of seeking out the man who played Alec Dawson, She was thoroughly star-struck. That pleased Adam, though he wouldn't take it any further. He didn't want to risk antagonizing his host, and there were ample opportunities for him elsewhere.

There was also a young farmer, who was one of the few who didn't cultivate Adam's acquaintance. He had the healthy open-air countenance you would expect and a pronounced Lancashire accent which in this company you wouldn't. Adam thought he'd seen him somewhere before, but he couldn't be certain where – he met so many people, he said with a smile to the man of whom he made his enquiry. Paul Barnes was the farmer's name. He farmed in the valley over there, said his informant, gesturing with a wide sweep of his arm towards the Trough of Bowland. 'Round my neck of the woods, then,' said Adam.

He remembered then where he had seen Barnes. It was on one of his rare excursions to the school gates with his children. Must be months ago now. Paul Barnes had been there and he must surely remember him. Adam wondered why he did not come across and speak to him, then spoke again to the owner's pretty niece and forgot the matter entirely.

# SIX

The meeting with the Muslim community which involved Chief Superintendent Tucker and Detective Chief Inspector Peach took place on the sixteenth of November. It proved far more successful than Percy had dared to hope.

The theme of the meeting was law and order in the town, and the senior policemen shared a platform with three prominent local councillors, one of whom was himself an Asian. The questions and the answers were for the most part constructive. The audience listened politely, though it was sometimes difficult to be certain how many of them agreed with the arguments being put. Under pressure, Percy would have had to admit that as a partnership, he and Tommy Bloody Tucker had on this occasion made an effective team. The older man had briefed himself well on the general lines of police policy and avoided any gaffes, whilst Peach was able to illustrate the generalities with particular instances from cases the CID had handled in the last couple of years.

Although the session was conducted in a hall adjoining the largest mosque in the Asian quarter of Brunton, it had been billed as an open meeting. Predictably, a dozen or so National Front party members made a noisy entry into the hall two minutes before the meeting was due to begin. There was a strong presence of uniformed police around the doors, but at Peach's insistence the Front group were allowed to remain, on condition that they conducted themselves in an orderly manner.

Most of these men – there were no women in the group – were known to Peach from previous confrontations; some of them had convictions for affray in the constant frictions between white and Asian youths in the town. They were no more pleased to see DCI Peach on the platform than he was to see them filling a group of seats at the side of the hall and conferring with each other about how they could best make mischief.

For twenty minutes, things went smoothly. Tucker gave a surprisingly succinct summary of the policing of this predominantly Muslim area of the town and outlined some of the problems. Many of these arose when male police officers had to deal with female Muslims, particularly when the wearing of the Burka made communication difficult and led to suspicion on both sides. There were career opportunities for Asian police officers, who were desperately needed not only in Brunton but in most urban areas of the country.

The National Front youths had grown increasingly impatient during these exchanges. A young man with a union jack on his tee shirt and tattoos on his forearms now called out, 'These buggers are too busy collecting welfare benefits to work for a living in the police!'

A woman town councillor had the figures ready to refute a charge she had obviously met many times before. She quoted figures to show that among Asian males of working age there was less unemployment than among other ethnic categories and that relatively few Asians were receiving council tax support.

It was when the young man's neighbour was frustrated by this calm statistical refutation that he shouted, 'They're all on the fucking fiddle!' Counter-shouts arose and chaos threatened.

Peach rose to his feet and waited for the relative silence which eventually fell. He looked with undisguised disgust at the group who had come to disrupt this meeting. 'Some of you still purport to be Christians. They at least should recall their leader's direction that it should be those without sin who cast the first stones. I recognize in your group at least three faces who have been prosecuted for falsely claiming benefits.'

The group looked at each other in confusion. There were mutterings about 'bloody Peach' and worse. Then the youngest of the group, a pimply youth not long out of school, glared at the rest of the hall and said, 'These bloody people make no fucking attempt to integrate!'

A hand went up at the other side of the room. A small, elderly white woman whom neither Peach nor Tucker had noticed before rose to her feet. Percy noticed her now, not least because his new wife was sitting beside her, looking up with consternation at her mother. Agnes Blake was seventy, but no more afraid of speaking her mind than she had ever been. 'One of the very first Pakistani visitors to this town was certainly prepared to mix. His name was Fazal Mahmood.'

There was bafflement among the mass of her audience, though a few of the bearded Muslim elders around the room nodded their recognition of the name. Mrs Blake hastened to explain. 'Fazal Mahmood was one of the leading cricketers of the world – perhaps the greatest seam bowler of his day. He won Pakistan their first Test victory in England at the Oval. But he knew how to mix. He was a very popular man when he was a professional at East Lancs, and he enjoyed his time in the town. My late husband played against him and knew him.'

The youth whom she had answered was baffled by this unexpected intrusion. He shouted across the hall as belligerently as he could, 'You're talking about before I was bloody born, lady!'

Peach spoke decisively from the platform. 'Before I was born too, laddie. But the lady has a point. One of the first Muslims the town had seen was welcomed here and was happy to mix with the natives. Nowadays, we've lost that. No one pretends mixing's easy with the numbers involved, but it's the only thing which will work in the long term.'

He was interrupted by a voice from the National Front group. 'It's not us as won't bloody mix, Peach! We had to pass under that damn great arch over the road to get here tonight. Told us we were entering the Paki ghetto, that did!'

'There are religious reasons for that arch!' a Muslim voice from his left on the platform reminded him.

Peach held up his hands as the shouting around the hall threatened to get out of hand. 'I know there are, but there are political reasons as well. I agree with our young friend on that arch. It's the wrong sort of symbol. It's crystallizing the very divisions we are saying tonight that we want to abolish. The children of Brunton are being educated together, going out from school into a common world. We should be working to break down barriers, not erecting new ones.'

He was surprised at how hard he was breathing. A voice from his left whispered, 'Easy, Peach!' and for once he was glad of Tucker's intervention.

The National Front leader was on his feet now, full of righteous indignation. 'These bastards are trying to blast everything we stand for to kingdom come! And you're asking us to lie back and take it!'

The man's violent words reminded Peach of a poem from his past, proclaiming that in dangerous times,

'The best lack all conviction, while the worst
Are full of passionate intensity.'

Yeats, he thought. And what an appropriate and prophetic summary of the thirties and the rise of fascism. But that didn't matter now. He felt the charged atmosphere in the hall and forced himself to be calm, to speak quietly, to avoid reducing himself to a yeller of meaningless slogans. 'This is an important time for all of us, for Christians and for Muslims, for atheists and for agnostics. I, along with everyone on this platform tonight, am appealing for calm and for reason. With all their faults, this country, and this town within it, are places which are worth preserving: places where we want to live in peace alongside each other. The National Front voice we have just heard is determined on a violent reaction to the changes we see around us. There is also a tiny minority of Muslim people who are interested in furthering an ideology by violent means. There may even be some such people in this hall tonight. If anyone knows of cells of terrorism, I urge them to declare their knowledge to the police. We need the cooperation of the Muslims in our community to eliminate this murderous violence. I cannot urge too strongly that all people with moderate views should help the rest of their communities by declaring any knowledge of planned murder and mayhem at the earliest possible moment!'

Peach had surprised himself by the rising volume and passion of his speech. He had intended when he came here to listen and scarcely speak at all, but the combination of the National Front faction and the startling presence and brave words from Lucy's mother had roused him. The cynical, worldly-wise policeman was his preferred stance, but the words from a sturdy woman who could scarcely have spoken in public before had brought a compulsion in him to support her. Remarkably, his words seemed to have worked. There was sporadic applause from his largely Asian audience. Some of it was no more than politeness, but there were pockets of genuine enthusiasm, much of it among the older sections.

A bearded man in the front row rose to his feet and turned to face the mass of people. He was obviously known to most of them; they fell instantly silent. 'What the officer says is right. If we want to be a part of the community, an integrated part, we have to denounce terrorism and the fanatics who use it. There may be people in this hall tonight who are aware of plots against the state. If any of you know anything about these cells of murderous violence, you must tell the authorities. That is not only fair to them but fair to us, the ordinary Muslim people who want to practise our religion and live at peace in this country. Every act of terrorism sets back our cause.'

There was general applause for this. Everyone seemed to be clapping save the National Front group. The chairman on the platform had the good sense to wrap things up quickly, sensing the mood of the meeting and divining correctly that this was as far as they could go tonight. He made a brief reference to the ways of voicing local grievances, then reiterated the general need for cooperation and the benefits this would bring to all.

Peach had for ten years been accustomed to going home alone and making his own assessments of the work of the day. As he left the hall and his pulse returned to its normal rate, he found the presence of a wife a most pleasing change.

'Did you know your mum was going to speak, Lucy?'

'I most emphatically did not! I'd have held her down if I'd even thought she might.'

'Good thing you didn't. She had a great effect.'

'Except that hardly anyone knew the man she was talking about.'

'Fazal Mahmood? I knew about him. People still talk about him at East Lancs. And some of the older people in the audience were nodding their heads tonight. They like their cricket, you know, Pakistanis. And Agnes picked on one of their great heroes. She struck a positive note when those yobbos were trying to disrupt the meeting.'

As they moved into Percy's shabby house, which she was slowly improving, Lucy thought how fortunate she was that the two people she loved most in the world were so fond of each other. 'I think she only insisted on attending the meeting because she knows I'm involved in trying to unearth the militant faction.'

'She's a good woman to have on your side.'

'And yours. I don't think she'd have gone there tonight if you hadn't been on the platform. She said she never gets the chance to see you at work. And you rose to the occasion.'

'Perhaps I shouldn't have spoken like that. It was to support her, I think. I realized how much it must have taken for her to get up at all.'

Lucy stifled a sudden yawn. 'It's been a long day.'

Percy's face cracked into a delighted grin. 'I never heard a more blatant effort to get a man into bed. But I'm putty in your practised hands, as usual.' He leapt gallantly to his feet. 'Lead the way up the stairs, my shameless darling!'

Paul Barnes was one of the fortunate ones among British farmers early in the twenty-first century. He had inherited not only his own farm but a sizeable sum of money six months later. In the rich pastures of the Ribble Valley, Barnes ran one of the few mixed farms remaining in the county, including a valuable dairy herd. He had the money to tide him over hard times, to develop the potential of his land, and to employ skilled and trustworthy assistance.

It was reliable help on the farm which had allowed him leisure time to join the shooting party where Adam Cassidy had enjoyed himself on the previous Saturday. Five days later, Paul was able to leave the milking in capable hands whilst he took his single child to school. The boy had a mass of fair hair and the fresh complexion of his father. He raced into school without a backward look, greeting his friends as he went. The father watched him go, standing a little to one side of the school gates beside his Land Rover, whilst the overwhelmingly female group on the other side of the gates chattered eagerly. There were glances cast towards this tall, personable man, but if he was conscious of the attention he disregarded it, staring fixedly towards the village school and the shrill-voiced children disappearing into it.

Barnes climbed into his vehicle but did not drive away. It was only after the crowd of mothers had dispersed that the single one who remained moved slowly towards the Land Rover. He did not look up from the document he was studying, though he was acutely aware of her presence. The passenger window of the vehicle was already down when she arrived beside it. 'Can I give you a lift home?' Paul said with a smile.

'It's scarcely worth it. I haven't far to go,' the woman said. Nevertheless, she reached up to open the door and climbed into the Land Rover, whilst Barnes started the engine.

'What news?' he said tersely, staring not at her but at the road ahead of him.

She glanced at the last two of the mothers, who were still in animated conversation forty yards away. 'I'll tell you when we're somewhere more private,' said Jane Cassidy with a smile.

Jane's husband had left the house two hours earlier. He had a full day's location filming scheduled, on the bleak slopes of the Pennines near the Snake Pass. It was important to use the limited daylight to shoot as much as possible on this sunny day of settled weather. Very soon now, the full rigours of winter would overtake this high, remote place.

The site wasn't far from the burial places of the children killed in the horrifying 'Moors Murders' of Ian Brady and Myra Hindley half a century earlier. The body of one of them, a twelve-year-old boy, had never been discovered; it lay somewhere beneath the peaty earth around here. Adam shuddered at the thought as he drove on to the site, where the film crew were already assembled at eight thirty in the morning. Despite his sheepskin coat, he was glad of the hot coffee handed to him as he entered the caravan where he would change.

The two continuity girls were busy. Television drama scenes are not shot in chronological order. Location shooting dominates the planning, because it is more difficult and infinitely more expensive than studio work. They had already shot the end of this episode, when Alec Dawson intervened as the villain was about to strangle the sleeping heroine. It was important that both the length of hair and hair styles remained the same here as in other scenes. Adam had his hair cut in the same style each month and he was already in the trousers and sweater he had worn for previous outdoor scenes. He needed only minimal make-up for open air shooting.

'Such a professional!' one of the star-struck continuity girls sighed, as they moved on to the next caravan.

'And way out of your league, girl!' said her older companion with some satisfaction.

Michelle Davies, the actress playing the damsel who landed herself in distress, had a leading role alongside Adam in this scene. They were fleeing together across the moor from the villainous gang who were pursuing her. Just when they appeared to have eluded their pursuers, a helicopter was to appear above them and cause renewed consternation. Very John Buchan, except that a helicopter had replaced the monoplane. 'Just like *The Thirty-nine Steps*,' said Michelle. 'One brave man and a girl who fascinates him against an evil world!'

'Very Alfred Hitchcock, more like!' said Adam, who had read Buchan avidly as a boy and didn't remember many women.

It was bitterly cold up here, but the scene was supposedly taking place in the summer, so that they could not be warmly clothed. Director, camera crew, everyone save the actors, wore bobble hats, scarves, gloves and thick coats or anoraks, but Adam and Michelle were hatless and coatless. They moved as quickly as they could along a predetermined route over the small stony path. As they were supposed to be fleeing for their lives, the haste which kept them marginally above hypothermia was quite appropriate.

Adam wondered if this speed would prevent them synchronizing with the arrival of the helicopter above them. The plot called upon them to look at each other in horror at the first faint noise of the helicopter, then fling themselves between rocks and coarse grass to utilize the minimal cover available. But the pilot did not let them down. As they neared the prearranged spot, the characteristic whirlybird note of the machine could be heard behind them.

The cold and their haste meant that they were panting appropriately as they whirled to identify this latest enemy. The helicopter was not visible at first, but its note grew steadily louder as they looked at each other fearfully. Michelle made herself wait for a second or two, glancing from her saviour towards this new source of danger. Then she delivered her line. 'It's them! I know it's them. What the hell do we do now?'

She timed it exactly right. A second later, the helicopter rounded the hill behind them and came into full, terrifying view. The noise of its blades redoubled. Adam took one look upwards, another sideways, and said 'Quick! In here!'

He flung her face down ahead of him between the mossy

rocks, then threw himself alongside her with his arm protectively around her. They had a considerable off-camera pause now, whilst a different camera specially set up for the moment tracked the helicopter circling above them and coming lower, winding up the melodrama as the audience wondered whether the villains would spot the fugitive pair beneath their minimal cover.

Michelle turned her face sideways and grinned at him. 'Not great dialogue, is it?'

He smiled back, still breathing hard from his efforts and the tension of performance. 'Effective enough, though. I don't expect people say very much when they're in fear for their lives! More to the point, it's bloody cold and wet here. What happened to that rug they were going to leave for us?'

'Joe decided it might show up in the aerial shots, so it had to go.'

'They could have bloody told me! Joe Hartley's not the one who has to lie still on this freezing ground.' He shivered a little, holding her body tight against him, feeling the warmth of her through their summer garments. Then, impulsively, he kissed her, letting his tongue enter her mouth softly, feeling her teeth before her tongue, firm and exploratory, answered his.

She pulled away after a few seconds, so that her deep brown eyes could study his face through her dark hair, which had fallen over her face. 'That was nice! Nicer still for being un-expected.'

'All part of the service, madam! It will help the chemistry we're supposed to display for the rest of the day. Speaking of which, we'd better be ready for our cue.'

'Do you think Joe will allow me a brandy if I tell him I've wet my knickers in the cause? From the outside, I hasten to add. It's fucking cold in here!'

She had the actress's determination to swear as hard as any man in the company. At that moment Adam found it quite exciting. He waited for his cue, which was the disappearance of the helicopter noise and the infernal machine with it. He had a sudden, farcical fear that he would stand up with an erection when the cameras were on him. He daren't let Michelle in on the thought, or they'd have been corpsing together when that moment came.

He waited until the noise grew very faint, then cautiously raised his head and watched the helicopter move round the curve of the hill to the east and disappear. He stood up, eyes searching the clear blue sky. 'Looks like we got away with it, for the moment. But we've got to move fast. They could be back at any time.' He took her hand and broke into a trot along the path, hoping that the cold did not show in the stiffness of his movements.

After a few more lines of terse dialogue between them, the call came to cut. In the finished version, there would be a scene slotted in here involving the thwarted enemy heavies, discussing among themselves their frustration and what they would do next. The filming plan for today was that Adam and Michelle would resume after lunch with the conclusion of their flight across the moorland. They trooped back hand in hand to the location site centre. Michelle complained to their director about her freezing wet belly and was duly accorded her brandy.

'I'm pretty sure it didn't show on camera in that last shot,' Joe Hartley reassured her. 'Fortunately, you had your backs to the camera in that, except for the facial shots.'

'Typical bloody director,' grumbled Adam. 'You can catch sodding pneumonia so long as he gets his shot and can pretend it's high summer!'

A few minutes later, after much-needed visits to the Portaloos, they took their hot soup into Adam's caravan and tried to thaw out. 'It's much more luxurious in here than where we have to slum it,' said Michelle, reviewing the place before she sat down. She made a mock curtsey. 'But I suppose we have to keep the star happy!'

She had rearranged her lustrous dark hair into its usual style. Her brown eyes looked bigger in the limited space and light of the caravan; as the colour heightened in her cheeks and the warmth flowed back into her limbs, she looked very pretty. Adam said with a smile, 'The star is very happy at present!' He stepped forward and kissed her, then held her slim body tight against him as he felt her respond. He ran his hands over her shoulder blades, then down her back and, for a delicious moment, over the curve of her bottom. He felt a tiny shiver run through her frame. He was not quite sure whether it was the last of the cold or a shudder of desire. But it was certainly not resistance; she held him tightly, and made no further move until he pulled away a little and held her at arm's length.

He studied her for a moment, relishing the nose that should have been a little too long for perfection yet in her was just right. Then he smiled, deliberately breaking up whatever there was between them for the moment. 'That was nice! We mustn't go any further yet, or I won't be able to carry you in this afternoon's scene!'

Michelle noticed that 'yet' and was pleased by it. She too wanted time to think. The fact that he was a married man wasn't very important for her. Lots of actors, male and female, enjoyed a sexual fling with each other when the occasion offered it – usually on location shooting, when they were far from home. She was sure now that she would enjoy such a fling with this man. He had the looks, plus the power which is always an aphrodisiac – he didn't seem to take himself too seriously, but both of them knew that the star of a series always has power. It would be nice to consolidate her bigger role in the next series.

The afternoon's scene Adam had mentioned involved their transfer to a different section of the Pennines. She was supposed to sprain her ankle as the speed of their flight across the moors told on her. Adam was to help her along with her arm round his shoulders as she grew increasingly exhausted. Then, as they sighted the welcome lights of a farmhouse through the near-darkness, she would faint and he would carry her the last seventy or eighty yards, making light of his own fatigue as he rose to the demands of heroism upon his stamina.

It was supposed to be almost ten o'clock on a summer evening; this was the climax of twelve miles of fear, tension and the physical effort needed to outwit their pursuers. Here the early winter darkness was a help again. There were no trees and little vegetation at this height, which was one reason why the Pennines had been chosen. By four twenty, Adam was panting gallantly beneath his delightful burden and hammering on the door of the farmhouse, whilst casting a final anxious glance at the darkening landscape behind him.

Darkness meant they could do no more today, but everyone waited anxiously to know whether they would need to come up here again tomorrow to undertake repeat shootings. By five twenty, Joe Hartley was assuring them that he was delighted with his early viewing of the afternoon's shoot in the director's caravan and that they were shutting down the generator for the day. Everyone, from the leading players to the assistant carpenter, breathed a sigh of relief and prepared to abandon ship. The temperature had dropped sharply with the disappearance of the sun and a bitter wind was sweeping over the Pennine slopes, making departure more welcome than ever.

The actors voiced their relief in noisy congratulations to one another, to the cameramen, to anyone who had been involved in the day's work, very much in the manner of the nervous relief which follows the first night of a play. Michelle Davies was now wrapped in a padded brown coat with the collar turned up high around her chin. Her woollen bobble hat meant that only a fraction of her face showed as people hurried to their cars. She glanced quickly over her shoulder to check that Adam Cassidy was behind her, making sure that her invitation would extend only to him. 'Irish coffee available at my place if you fancy it,' she said cheerfully.

Both of them knew that it was more than that she was offering, but she said it as lightly as she could, so that a rejection would be less humiliating if it came. Cassidy took a moment to answer, watching his footing in the darkness on the uneven ground. Then he said, 'That would be nice. It would let the traffic get away before I venture north. I'll follow your car. I don't know exactly where you're based, so don't do a Jenson Button on me!'

The traffic thickened on the M62 as they approached Manchester, but he had no difficulty in following her red Mazda sports car as she turned off at junction 17 and headed north towards her eventual destination of Darcy Lever, an exotic name for a village on the outskirts of Bolton. She waited for him whilst he parked the Mercedes, then led the way into the ground floor flat nearest to the outer door in a newly erected block. Neither of them turned down their collars until they were inside the flat. It was one of the prices of television fame that you were likely to be stopped by strangers at inopportune moments.

'This is nice!' he said conventionally, as he eased himself out of the sheepskin and looked around the place. And it was.

The rooms were much more spacious than in most modern developments; the fittings in the kitchen he could see to his left were of excellent quality.

She smiled at him, grateful for the fact that even the man who played the suave Alec Dawson seemed as uncertain as she was over the next move. 'I'll put the kettle on and get the whisky out.'

As she turned her back to move towards the sink, he slid his arms round her waist and put his face against the back of her head. Her long dark hair was still damp from the hills and the winter darkness; he fancied he could smell the wildness and freedom of the Pennines still upon her in this civilized, comfortable place. He breathed the single word 'Later!' softly into her ear and felt the face he could not see breaking into a smile.

The heating was on in the bedroom and he pulled the thick curtains swiftly shut. He slid beneath the silk sheets on the big double bed with scarcely a shiver and took her naked into his arms. Her love-making was urgent and direct. He had no need for foreplay or any skilled technique. She led the way, urging him on as much with her movements as with her brief and scarcely intelligible cries. His contribution was but to synchronize his excitement with hers, ensuring that they came together, then held each other afterwards for a long, delicious moment of climax and satisfaction.

A few minutes later they lay contentedly upon their backs and stared at the ceiling. 'You needed that,' he said with a smile.

She did not respond, so that for a moment he thought she had been offended by the comment. Then she said softly, 'It's been a while.' She gripped his hand beneath the sheets for a moment, then slid away from him. 'I shan't be long. Don't go away.'

He heard the cistern flush in the bathroom, then muffled movements in the kitchen they had left so peremptorily. It was ten minutes before she was back, carrying two china beakers upon a small silver tray, her face filled with the concentration of a schoolgirl bringing her latest triumph before admiring adults. 'Irish coffee! You really meant it!' he said with delight.

'I never default on a promise,' she told him earnestly. 'The skill is to get the whisky beneath the cream, so that you can drink it through it. It's not the Irish brand, as it really should be, but I defy you to tell the difference.'

She watched him as he took his first exploratory sip, knowing well what was required of him. The hot, sweet coffee with its generous lacing of whisky and its subtle touch of cream passed deliciously down his throat, warming his chest an instant later. He took another sip, expanding the joyous, silly tension of the moment as she waited for his verdict. 'Best I've ever had!' he said. He took a third sip before he set the beaker carefully on the bedside cabinet and reached out to enfold her in his arms and tumble her back into the bed.

She still had her dressing robe on and they dissolved into laughter at the confusion of its removal. 'You actors know how to please a girl!' she said mockingly. 'But we never know whether to believe what you say, do we?'

'Oh, it's true all right. Best I've ever had.' Then a moment later, 'The Irish coffee, I mean, of course!'

She punched him playfully on the chest and they chatted contentedly about the director and the people they worked with in the ten minutes it took them to finish the coffee. Then, as both of them had known they would do, they made love again, slowly and less frenetically this time, as confident as if they had done this many times before rather than a breath-less once.

They were looking at the ceiling again when she said, 'Shouldn't you be looking at your watch about now?'

'My watch?' He had in fact been wondering what the time was, but he was too experienced to make the mistake of searching for it.

'Isn't this the moment which reminds the mistress of her place? The moment when the married man takes over from the randy lover and she realizes she's just the bit on the side?'

He didn't want her to consider herself his mistress. Even his bit on the side was running a little too far for the moment. He said, 'It was all spontaneous today, you know. It wasn't planned.' Even as he said that, he wondered if it was exactly true.

'Was it, Adam? I don't think I can really claim that. I hadn't planned anything, but I suppose I was wondering what it was like all through this episode of the series.'

'Yes, it's been good. Pity it's the last one.'

'There's another series planned though, isn't there?'

'Oh yes. Already commissioned. Many of the storylines are already in place. I haven't had time to look at them yet. I believe in giving all my attention to the work in hand.'

'Yes. I noticed that tonight!' She giggled a little, feeling her thighs and her side tight against his. 'Still, we should be able to work together more regularly in the next series, when I'm your regular girlfriend.'

There was a pause which was a little longer than she had hoped it would be. Then he said in a carefully neutral voice, 'Been cast, has it?'

'I believe so, yes.' Suddenly she was trying to keep it light, to keep any anxiety out of her voice. 'James Walton seemed to think it was a done deal.'

'Did he, indeed? Well, what the producer says goes, as we are all aware. Speaking of which, as you so tactfully reminded me, I must be on my way.'

He was abruptly distant and cold when she wanted him to be intimate. He dressed quickly, held her for a few seconds in an embrace, kissed her forehead, and was gone. He had smiled at her before he went, had said something conventional about doing this again.

But he had said nothing more about working together. Half an hour later Adam Cassidy was nearing his house and his wife and his sleeping children. And Michelle Davies was still trying to thrust from her mind the producer's final reminder to her that the star still had the final veto over casting.

# SEVEN

C hief Superintendent Tucker would never have admitted it, but he was not immune to the celebrity culture which seemed to have captured British society in the second decade of the twenty-first century.

He was as anxious to catch his first glimpse of the actor who played Alec Dawson as any of the eager audience for the afternoon chat show. He had accepted his wife's injunction to have his hair cut specially for the occasion. He decided he was pleased with the effect, as he surveyed himself in the mirror after the make-up girl's rather perfunctory attention to his solid fifty-four-year-old features. His hair was thinning a little, but still plentiful enough when brushed skilfully; the silvering at the temples would give just the correct degree of gravitas to the considered opinions of a senior policeman.

He realized by the polite applause which greeted his introduction that he was to be merely the warm-up act for the eagerly awaited appearance of Adam Cassidy, but he didn't mind that. It would take the pressure off him in a television world where policemen were sometimes not the most popular presence. And he had confirmed that he was to stay on set even when Cassidy appeared. Barbara would be delighted to see him accorded equal status with the great man, sitting beside him in the studio armchairs and exchanging friendly conversation.

The host of the programme was Gerry Clancy, a bright Northern Irish man who had for ten years risen at four each morning to present the early morning show on Channel Four. It was his liveliness there which had earned him the right to this more relaxed and leisurely afternoon ITV assignment. The vehicle was ideal for him; he had a quick wit and an ability to mine the richest veins of ore among a wide variety of guests. Clancy knew the importance of preparation; one of the paradoxes of television chat was that to appear spontaneous you had to put in a modicum of research and the proper degree of forethought. Gerry had noted that Chief Superintendent Thomas Bulstrode Tucker was a senior policeman who was a little nervous and a little pompous. He was even more aware than his guest that policemen were not the most popular of public servants.

He said as much to Tucker as soon as he had greeted him and set him politely in the chair opposite his.

His interviewee had resolved to picture a doting wife rather than the sprightly and hostile Percy Peach as his audience. He smiled patronizingly at this man who was fifteen years his junior and plainly in need of enlightenment. 'The public needs us and we need them, Mr Clancy. Our job is more difficult than it has ever been, and we do not always receive the cooperation we deserve from the public.' He shook his head sadly.

'Deserve, Superintendent? Surely trust has to be earned? If suspicion of the police is greater now than it has ever been, there must be good reasons for that.'

Tucker allowed his eyebrows to lift a fraction, indicating surprise and disappointment. His demeanour conveyed that he wasn't going to be worried by this modern tendency towards aggression in his interviewer. He was never at a loss for a platitude. 'There is an unfortunate tendency in modern society to resent any form of authority, Gerry. Police officers suffer from that, as do teachers and anyone who has to enforce the rules. But I assure you, there would be chaos without us.'

'I think everyone accepts that, Mr Tucker. Otherwise we shouldn't be paying millions of pounds each year for your services. But some of us have begun to wonder whether that money is being well spent. We have more police officers each year. If we take account of the huge amount of what was formerly police work but which is now being done by civilians, we have almost twice the number of officers we had ten years ago. And yet the clear-up rates for so many crimes seem to get not better but steadily worse.'

Behind his professionally calm exterior, T.B. Tucker was trying hard not to panic. They should have warned him that the man intended to say things like this. But he could hardly say that now. 'Oh, I'm sure that if you compare like with like and examine the real figures—'

'What would you say is the crime which besets and worries most people in their daily lives, Mr Tucker?'

'Well, I'm sure that you'd get a variety of—'

'Burglary, Mr Tucker. The criminal most likely to affect

most people's lives is the burglar. I should have thought you might have known that.'

A titter among the audience, alerting Tucker to the fact that things were moving against him, that in this bear-pit he was the amateur and Clancy the professional. He cleared his throat. 'In the modern climate, where terrorism and all sorts of other violence threaten our society, burglary has necessarily assumed a lower profile than in former years.'

'Indeed it has, Mr Tucker. It is an increasingly attractive proposition for our youth, many of them hooked on the illegal drugs you also seem unable to control. If I were a young man with no morals and in need of quick money for drugs, I should consider burglary a very easy option. Especially in view of the fact that well over eighty per cent of burglaries go undetected.'

Laughter and applause, this time. Gerry Clancy let it run for a moment, then held up his hand, signifying to his audience that he wanted the chief superintendent to have a fair opportunity to refute this view. Tucker smiled a superior smile. 'Statistics can be very deceptive, Gerry.'

'And in what respect is this particular one deceptive, Chief Superintendent?'

Tucker sighed, then offered the patient smile which was meant to convey that mere amateurs couldn't expect to understand these things. 'One has to allocate resources economically. Burglary is one of the pettier crimes, you know. It cannot always be accorded a high priority.'

This time there were murmurs of discontent in the audience, many of whom had suffered from this crime. Clancy nodded thoughtfully. 'So the public just has to accept that even a much enlarged police service is incapable of dealing with petty crime.'

Tucker's smile was now covering an increasing desperation. 'I did not say we were incapable.'

'No, you didn't admit to that. Then are we to presume that you *choose* to neglect burglaries, Mr Tucker?'

'We have to allocate resources, Mr Clancy. It is part of every senior police officer's duty to decide on priorities.'

Gerry Clancy turned directly towards his audience. 'And it seems that this particular senior officer chooses not to prioritize the very crime which every survey shows the citizens of Britain find most disturbing. Food for thought there, certainly.'

He shook his head solemnly, then let his face light up. 'But now to happier things. It is time for us to meet the actor who was last year voted Britain's favourite television star. Ladies and gentlemen, Adam Cassidy!'

Adam gave it a full two seconds, whilst the clapping swelled in volume. Then he walked briskly on to the set and smiled with modest thanks at the studio audience. It might be some time since he had appeared on a stage, but he hadn't forgotten how to milk applause. He sat down carefully between his host and Tucker, making sure that the adulation lasted for a few seconds more, plucking at the trouser creases of his superb light-grey suit, smiling first briefly at Tucker and then more warmly at his host.

Clancy radiated good humour and welcome; this was a good star to hitch your wagon to. 'We've all seen what Alec Dawson's been up to. Haven't we?' He flung the question at his audience, who roared an enthusiastic affirmative, and then turned back to Adam. 'How does it feel to be a national institution?'

'Oh, I don't know about that. I might prove to be just a passing fancy!' Adam smiled at the women in the audience, who loudly refuted any such heresy. 'Theatrical institutions are people like Jean Simmons, who built up a body of work.'

Clancy knew his cue. 'You worked with our late lamented Jean, didn't you?'

'I did indeed. In one of my first television assignments, back in 1990, Jean was Miss Havisham in *Great Expectations*. She was a great actress who was also tremendous fun. I learnt an enormous amount from her.'

'You played Herbert Pocket, if I remember right. And how was the great Jean to work with?'

'Oh, entirely approachable. A great pro. She was very kind to me when I was an inexperienced young actor. People thought of her as a grande dame of theatre and cinema, which she was. But as I say, she had a wicked sense of humour!'

He launched into a well-rehearsed, mildly bawdy, anecdote about the great lady. He had learned early in his career that it was always safest to attach your stories to a dead thespian, who could no longer challenge the verity or the detail. He struck the right humorous, slightly daring, note. The audience gasped in surprise, then roared with delighted laughter, which culminated in a round of applause that Gerry Clancy dutifully encouraged. Laughter was infectious; if the studio audience was relaxed and amused, the television viewers would be happy in front of their sets with their afternoon cups of tea.

They moved on to Alec Dawson, so that Adam could feed in the excellent viewing figures for the present series and the announcement that a new series was already commissioned for next year. Clancy spoke about the appeal of the series. Was it not strange that this type of multi-action adventure, usually favoured by men, should have such a high female quota among its audience? What was the reason for that?

Adam said he'd never thought about that. He couldn't think of any reason. Surely, his host said, the appeal must stem from the looks and personality of its star? The prolonged round of applause pleased both host and guest. Then Clancy leant forward a little on his chair, always an indication that something a little more serious was to be introduced.

'Hand on heart, Adam, how seriously should we take Alec Dawson and his adventures?'

Adam leaned forward in turn. He spoke confidentially, as if imparting a confidence which should go no further. 'Between you and me, Gerry, it shouldn't be taken very seriously at all.' A collective gasp, then delighted enthusiasm from the audience for his candour. It was as if they had been the first people who had been privy to this revelation: Adam Cassidy, the man who played the dashing Alec Dawson, did not take himself too seriously. Adam beamed at the rows of laughing people, as if the revelation had been a relief to him. Then he said without warning, 'What we put together is what my old English teacher used to call interesting yarns. We make them as entertaining as we can, but we don't take ourselves too seriously and we don't expect our viewers to think of them as real life. Real crime is a different and more serious thing altogether, as this gentleman is well aware.'

He turned unexpectedly towards Thomas Bulstrode Tucker, who had been relaxing in the thought that his torment was over and with luck would be forgotten in the shadow of this bright torch of celebrity. He managed a weak smile of acknowledgement. 'I can certainly confirm that. Real crime is nasty.'

'And also dangerous. I was listening with interest before I came on, Chief Superintendent. As you may know, I was born and brought up in Brunton.'

Tucker did not know. He gave a weak smile and managed a 'Really?'

'My father and the rest of my family still live there, indeed. I was disturbed to hear how little control you seem to have over crime in the area. My poor old dad did his bit for Queen and country, but he's an invalid now. He won't be pleased to hear how likely he is to be burgled. Still less to hear that the thugs will more than likely get away with it. I only hope he doesn't try to take things into his own hands.'

Murmurs of approval and a few 'Hear hear!'s from an audience now hanging on his every word. Tucker's smile was a mistake this time; it signified complacency to his listeners. 'He shouldn't do that, Adam. We always advise the public against—'

'Frustration makes ordinary people desperate, Chief Superintendent. Tough old codgers like my dad believe in looking after themselves, not leaving things to the nanny state. When they see yobbos getting away with things, they do not always behave rationally. Wouldn't you agree?' He turned directly to his audience in a blatant piece of demagoguery. They burst into massive applause, as if they had been waiting for exactly this cue.

Tucker said, 'Policing is more difficult now than it has ever been. We have more officers than we have ever had, but more crime as well.'

'More officers, yes. But how often do we see the copper on his beat nowadays?' More shouts of approval. Adam had an actor's sense of when the audience was with him and he knew how to harness the conditioned reaction. 'I think most people believe that a visible police presence would itself prevent of lot of petty crime. And prevention is always better than cure, is it not? But who am I to say that? You're the man with the expert knowledge, Chief Superintendent.'

'Yes. Well, in fairness to my officers in Brunton, I must point out that we have more serious crimes on our patch than burglary.'

'Indeed you have. We live in dangerous times, do we not? The terrorist threat is ever present, and cells of militants have recently been unearthed on your patch. I'm sure the people here and those watching this afternoon would be interested to hear about your progress in this area.'

'We have a large Muslim population. The overwhelming majority of them are law-abiding citizens, who are peaceably disposed towards their neighbours.'

'And as you imply in saying that, there is also a tiny and highly dangerous minority, who are anxious to take innocent British lives. Would you say you were on top of the situation?'

'This is not a local but a national problem, countered by a national initiative. Anti-terror action is coordinated nationally. We offer whatever help we can, of course, but thankfully anti-terrorism is not my pigeon.'

The last phrase was a mistake; it made Tucker sound complacent. The producer's voice on Gerry Clancy's ear mike told him that there were two minutes of his programme left. He said with a smile and a face full of reason, 'In that case, Chief Superintendent, one is driven to ask why this vastly increased police service cannot deal with the burglary which has spread like a plague over this green and pleasant land. Why, as Adam suggests, police officers cannot at least be more in evidence as a threat to the petty crime which besets us all.' He turned to his audience. 'I'm sure you would want me to thank Adam Cassidy for his presence here today. He has been a joy to talk to, as always. And he has also given us food for thought about some serious issues.'

The closing credits rolled, as the cameras switched away from the discomforted Tucker to the faces of the vigorously applauding audience.

A mile away from the television studio in Manchester, Cassidy's new agent was enduring a difficult phone conversation. Mark Gilbey gazed out at the spectacular view of the Lowry Centre's stainless steel from his fourteenth-storey office and listened carefully, whilst saying as little as possible.

This wasn't a new situation for him. Former agents often cut up rough when their clients transferred their allegiance. Indeed, Gilbey handled very few people who hadn't come to him from someone else. He didn't take unknowns on to his books; he could afford to pick and choose among the people who wanted him to represent them.

Normally the complaints of agents who had been forsaken did not trouble him. He never poached clients, so his conscience as well as the legal situation was clear. Everyone who used the Gilbey agency came to him on his or her own initiative. Mark's only action was to agree to take them on. Any previous business relationships were neither his responsibility nor his concern. Agents who felt they had been betrayed must take up the issue with their former clients, not with him. The legal situation was exactly the same for him in this case as in many others; he had nothing to fear from the law. But he was being very careful not to offer provocation to the angry man at the other end of the phone line.

That was because this man was Tony Valento.

Mark had no idea which of the many tales which were told about Valento were true. The man was certainly of Italian extraction; his dark hair and olive complexion bore witness to that. But he spoke with no trace of an accent other than cockney. How far his reputation for violence was genuine was not clear, and Mark did not intend to research the matter at first hand. Tony Valento was supposed to have Mafia connections and to have made his way in the industry by a mixture of charm and violence. How much violence? There were few facts and a wealth of myth about that. As usual, the rumour-mongers could soon transform a small happening into high-pitched melodrama. Mark Gilbey would stick to his guns, be as firm as he always was, but steer clear of any personal involvement.

Valento was going through the sort of argument Mark had heard many times before. 'I took the bastard on when he was almost unknown. I made thc brand that is now Adam Cassidy. He'd have got nowhere without me.'

'I'm sure you're right, Tony. These people have no loyalty. I'm sure all show business people have a touch of the tart in them.'

'So tell him that. Tell the bugger he'd have got nowhere without me.'

'I'm sure you've already told him that yourself, Tony.'

'I haven't. The first I heard about this was the letter from you today which told me you were taking over his contracts.'

'I'm sorry about that. I am really. But all I got from him was your name as his former agent. It's the normal protocol to write and inform the previous operator that you've been asked to take over. I'm sure you do the same thing yourself.'

'But this is the first I've heard of it! The bloody man hasn't said a word to me.'

'I'm sorry about that. I can see how annoying it must be for you. But you must take that up with Mr Cassidy. All I've done is agree to represent him, in response to a direct request from him. I'm sure you'll agree that I have acted honourably. Indeed, I would have been flouting the unwritten rules of our profession if I had refused a well-established actor services which he considered would be valuable to him. I have fulfilled all the normal protocol. That includes my formal letter advising you of our representation of Mr Cassidy, which you received this morning.'

'I got him the Alec Dawson role. He'd be nothing without that. Now he thinks he's big enough to ditch me and go to Hollywood.'

'He didn't tell me about the way he was treating his previous agent. I didn't even know that was you, Tony. But of course that wasn't my business, was it? If these people come and ask us to act for them, we have to take them on, don't we? I can only presume that he thinks we have the contacts to get him the work he wants. But from an ethical point of view, he should have discussed it with you first. Of course he should.'

There was a pause. Mark could hear the man breathing hard into the mouthpiece of his phone; ethics were probably a novel consideration for Mr Valento. 'You say the bugger's already signed up with you?'

'I'm afraid he has, yes. He should have discussed his intentions with you, but I'm sure you'll agree that I couldn't turn him away when he came to us.'

'Too bloody right you couldn't. Or wouldn't. The slimy sod's going to have to answer to me for this!' The line was abruptly dead.

Mark Gilbey ran a finger round the inside of his collar. He was sweating, despite the calm tone he had preserved for his phone conversation. Adam Cassidy was perfectly within his rights to change his agent. There was no doubt about that. But at the moment Mark was glad that he wasn't in Cassidy's expensive Italian leather shoes.

'You're late!' said Harry Cassidy accusingly to his elder son. As with many an ageing person, his world was growing smaller by the day. And he was increasingly unaware of anyone else's world outside his own.

'It's only twenty past five, Dad. And you know I never arrange to be here at a particular time, because I'm never sure when I'll be able to get away after school. I have things to do after the children have gone home. I was giving a bit of tuition to a couple of sixth formers who are trying to get into Cambridge.'

'You fart about with all kinds of stupid things, you do! You've missed our Adam on the telly.' He spoke as if this were a sin several degrees beyond adultery.

Luke had forgotten all about the chat show appearance, though his father had spoken of little else for almost a week. 'I couldn't have seen it anyway, Dad. I was teaching thirty fourteen-year-olds when the Gerry Clancy show was on.'

'Well, think yourself bloody lucky, then. I've recorded it for you on the Sky Plus.'

'That's good. I'll just put this dinner in the oven for you and then we'll sit down and watch it together.'

'You'll enjoy this,' his father assured him, as Luke pulled up a chair beside him. 'There's some bloody police officer on from Brunton. Our Adam makes a right fool of him.'

Luke decided after watching Thomas Bulstrode Tucker for two minutes that the man was probably a pompous twit. But he plainly didn't realize that he'd been set up as an easy target by his amiable-sounding host. Luke began to have a little more sympathy for Tucker as Clancy weighed into him about the incidence of burglary.

'He's a right bloody twit, this bugger,' said Harry Cassidy.

'He's on a hiding to nothing here, Dad. And he's probably very nervous.'

'Nervous my arse!' Harry's language had become steadily more uninhibited since his wife's death. 'Just you watch what a fool he looks when he tries to argue with a smart lad like our Adam!'

Luke began to wonder how many times his Dad had already played back this recording. He was hugging his thin chest with pleasure, rocking backwards and forwards and silently mouthing words which were clearly already familiar words to him as Adam spoke them. 'He'll mention me in a minute!' he told Luke urgently, then sat back and grinned delightedly as Adam told of his father doing his bit for Queen and country.

'You didn't fight in the war! You were too young for that!' Luke said indignantly. The words were out before he could stop them.

'I did my National Service, didn't I? Two years in bloody

uniform, and don't you forget it! Our Adam doesn't forget it.'
He stopped the recording and wound it back resentfully.
'You're making us miss the best bit! You just listen to Adam
weighing into this copper about all the bloody Pakis in
Brunton.'

He didn't do that, of course. Adam Cassidy would never
involve himself in anything so controversial. But Harry Cassidy
like all bigots heard what he wanted to hear. Luke said rather
feebly, 'The chief superintendent says we've a large number
of Muslims in our town, most of whom are law-abiding citizens, Dad.'

'He says we can't control the bastards, you mean. Just you
listen – you're supposed to be intelligent.'

'No, Dad. He says that there is a small minority amongst
them who could be very dangerous.'

'He says those wankers are working to destroy our country
and the bloody police can do fuck-all about it. And our Adam
tells him where to get off. Just you bloody listen instead of
yapping, lad!' He had paused the recording as the exchanges
with his son grew more heated. Now he switched it on again
and the pair watched the conclusion of the show in silence.
Luke noticed that Tucker wasn't allowed the right of reply to
either his brother's or Clancy's wilder generalizations at the
end of the broadcast. But he didn't point this out to his father,
wisely recognizing that prejudice had gone beyond the point
of hearing reason.

Luke brought in his father's meal on a tray and set it on
his lap, tucking a paper kitchen towel into his collar to prevent
food soiling his clothing. He sat with him for a little while
longer, trying to talk about some of the problems in his own
working life. But Harry was still too excited to talk about
anyone or anything other than his younger son. 'He's a lad,
is our Adam! Pity you haven't got a bit of his go.'

It was intended as a challenge. Harry jutted his chin a little
and waited for a response. Luke wondered why people became
more aggressive with those around them as their physical
powers declined towards helplessness. Or was that just his
dad? Luke said mildly, 'Adam and I are different beings, Dad,
different personalities. Always were and always will be. It
wouldn't do if everyone was the same, would it?'

Harry gazed unseeingly at the news pictures on his television screen. 'He told 'em what was what, didn't he, our Adam?' He pushed his tray aside and hugged himself again, this time in slow motion.

'Pity he couldn't pop in and see you this morning, as he'd promised faithfully to do.' The comment was out before Luke could stop it, a splutter of bile to release the tension of the resentment the old man had roused in him.

Harry Cassidy looked at Luke as if he had been thumped. His previously exultant face filled abruptly with shock and incomprehension. 'He's a busy man, Luke. He's always busy, our Adam. You don't understand the life he has to lead.'

The life he's chosen to lead, thought Luke. 'I expect he is busy, Dad. We all are, for most of the time. But he shouldn't promise to come to see you and then not turn up.'

The old man's face set back into its normal impassive state, and in that moment Luke felt guilty for snatching away the undoubted pleasure the television footage had brought to him. 'He'd have come if he could have,' said Harry stubbornly. 'He's fond of his old Dad, Adam is. Not like some I could mention!'

This time Luke managed to avoid any response. He slid the old man's dinner plate and pudding dish on to the tray and took them into the kitchen to wash. Whilst he waited for the water from the tap to run hot, he looked round at the familiar sink and the familiar kitchen, reviving memories of his boyhood here. He tried to relieve his frustration by reminding himself of the man that querulous old bigot out there had once been and what he owed to him.

Yet the memories brought not the comfort he had sought but a tumbling anger against the man who had been a boy here with him. Why the hell couldn't Adam at least pop in here regularly to see the old man who adored him? Why couldn't he at least keep his promises, instead of leaving others to pick up the pieces? Why should Luke collect only drudgery and contempt whilst Adam cruised through life and picked off its prizes?

# EIGHT

There were others as well as Harry Cassidy who had recorded the afternoon's Gerry Clancy show.

At ten fifteen that night, after DCI Percy Peach had put Tommy Bloody Tucker in his place by watching programmes he considered more important, he sat with the new Mrs Peach and watched his chief's ordeal by interview.

'He's not getting a fair hearing,' said Lucy after a few minutes.

They watched the rest of the show in silence, apart from one or two muffled oaths from Percy. There was a pause at the end before he said, 'Tucker was bloody anxious to get himself on the telly. He couldn't wait to get himself sitting next to the man who plays Alec Dawson.'

'That's probably down to his wife. She's a great fan of the series.'

Peach marvelled anew at the capacity of women to know trivia that would have taken men much effort to discover. 'Well, I hope Brunnhilde Barbara is well pleased with what she's done to the poor sod.'

'I should think she still thinks Adam Cassidy is marvellous. She'll probably think her husband should have stood up for himself better.'

'I'd have to support her on that. It might be the first thing Brunnhilde Barbara and I have ever agreed upon. And probably the last.'

Lucy said thoughtfully, 'He's right about the militant Muslim element. With thirty thousand in the town, there are bound to be a tiny number of fanatics among them. Once an ideology like that gets hold of young men, we're in trouble.'

He glanced quickly sideways at her, then said as casually as he could, 'You making any progress with your investigations?'

She paused, considering her reply carefully; she knew that despite his relaxed manner, he worried about her involvement with ruthless people like this. 'We've identified a couple of cells of militants. The trouble is, we need to find the people

in the background who are pulling the strings. Those men are
both more dangerous and more elusive – like drug barons,
but bent on violence rather than profit. They're probably not
even in the town. Maybe not even in the country.'

'You just go carefully, girl.' It was a fatuous warning, but
he was like an anxious parent, needing to voice his concern.
He watched a politician trying not to answer Jeremy Paxman's
questions about tax cuts and decided that Tommy Bloody
Tucker had had it easy. He let his hand steal slowly across to
Lucy's knee then on to the delicious thigh above it. 'Sometimes
we need to draw the curtains and forget all about the dangerous
world out there.'

She leant against him and dropped her head on to his
shoulder. 'We're pretty good at shutting the world out, aren't
we?'

'We are indeed.' He brought a second hand to the task in
hand: a body like Lucy's definitely warranted both hands. 'A
man has his needs!' he murmured softly into her perfectly
shaped ear.

'And isn't a woman allowed to have hers?' she said drowsily.

'Bloody 'ell, Norah!' said Percy, suddenly sitting bolt
upright. It was his favourite expression of mock outrage. 'If
you're determined to take me again, I can't deny you your
rights, I suppose.'

He was in bed within three minutes, growling his approval
as she disrobed swiftly in the chilly bedroom.

Ten days later, as December moved into its second week, the
big stores watched the rising tide of Christmas trade and
wondered whether the much trumpeted economic recovery
would declare itself in the retail trade figures.

In the studios at Manchester, the final touches had been put
to the last episode of the current Alec Dawson series. There
was no party, as there might have been after a successful stage
production. Many of the cast had already departed to other
assignments; most of the supporting technical staff such as
camera operators and continuity girls were now engaged in
other television work.

In the office of ITV's senior producer, James Walton, an
unexpectedly difficult meeting was in progress. There were
only three people involved: Walton himself, the series director

Joe Hartley, and Adam Cassidy as its star. They had met to confirm the final arrangements for the next series. Walton had expected this to be a matter of the three of them formally approving a series of decisions he had already made about the organization of shooting and the casting of the series. With his long experience and status in television, Walton prided himself on being able to anticipate snags and remedy things quickly, but he hadn't foreseen any of this. A star being prickly was the last thing he needed just now.

It was Joe Hartley who raised the matter of casting, when they had finished their review of the series just completed. 'One of the problems of casting has been the need to find completely different personnel for each episode, except for Alec Dawson himself and one or two minor supporting roles. As you know, we've agreed two major changes which should help to remedy this. The first is to give our leading man a permanent girlfriend, instead of a succession of damsels in distress who are saved from either death itself or a fate which used to be considered much worse than death. The second is to build in a major figure who consistently pits his wits against Dawson's, instead of a series of villains who are outsmarted episode by episode. A sort of Napoleon of crime, like Moriarty in the Sherlock Holmes stories. It will build up the status of our hero to be pitting his own meagre resources against a man who can command huge forces. The implication will be that this monster's fortune and his heavies come from drugs, but that won't be made explicit. Pictures of coke and heroin addicts would be too squalid for a fast-moving, escapist series like this.'

Walton nodded. 'I agree with that. We need to keep the right note in the new series. That isn't easy, when people see realistic policing all the time in programmes like *The Bill*. These moves will also make casting easier, as well as hopefully keeping it within budget.' He couldn't prevent himself glancing quickly at Adam Cassidy, whose agent had secured a major rise in his already astronomical salary for the new series. 'The overall cost of one major villain and one heroine rather than a series of each should make us a saving. And we seem to have competent people already in place for these roles.'

'Really?' Adam, who had been waiting for this moment,

was pleased with his timing as he came in with the single word. The looks of surprise and apprehension on the faces of his companions showed how telling it had been.

'I thought you were happy with Dean Morley for the major villain and Michelle Davies for your regular female lead,' said Walton. He glanced at Joe Hartley. 'I think our director is certainly happy with their work in the series we've just completed.'

'Very happy. Both of them are model professionals. And once I knew what was planned for the future, I've watched them off-shoot as well. They're excellent team players, as far as I can see. That can be as important as acting ability when you're asking people to work together for a whole series.'

Walton nodded. 'I've always been impressed by the ensemble playing in the Alec Dawson episodes. It makes it easier for everyone when you operate as a team.'

'And no one sets greater store by team playing than I do,' said Adam sententiously. 'Nevertheless, I think both these roles need to be cast with great care.'

'I can assure you that great consideration has already been given to them,' said Walton with his first visible sign of irritation.

Adam Cassidy smiled at him, feeling his power and enjoying it. 'I don't remember anyone asking me for my views on these developments.'

Walton looked at Joe Hartley, who said, 'Not formally, perhaps, Adam. But I'm sure you and I have discussed the new series and these two key roles. I got the impression that you were happy enough with Michelle Davies in the leading female role.' He glanced for the merest instant at Cassidy, who did not react. 'And I know that Dean Morley is a very old friend of yours.'

By which he means that I'd never have got started without him, thought Adam. All the more reason to cast him off at this point, then. If I'm going to Hollywood and American television, I don't want anyone from the past clinging to my coat-tails. 'We mustn't cast important roles on the principle of the old pals' act,' he said sanctimoniously.

James Walton knew quite well that he had verbally already offered these parts to the pair he had mentioned. He was also uncomfortably aware that Cassidy had the right of veto, that the bigger the star, the more necessary it was to keep him happy. For the first time, he realized just how big a star Adam Cassidy had become, and cursed himself for not taking note of it earlier. During previous series, the man had seemed happy to have his role and be paid big bucks for it. Now he was flexing his star muscles and asserting himself. This might be a late and wilful, even a mischievous, changing of his views, but there was nothing they could do about it. Walton had seen too many big names stamp their metaphorical feet like spoilt children to think they would be able to argue Cassidy round, but they had to try.

As if he read his producer's mind, Joe Hartley said, 'Dean Morley has a lot of experience. He knows what he's doing. I think he'd play very well opposite you, Adam.'

His star smiled, then tried to speak as if it pained him to be so objective. 'Dean's in a bit of a rut, in my view. It pains me to say it, but we know exactly how he'd play this villain. As an old-fashioned routine heavy rather than a Napoleon of crime, in my view. *Call Alec Dawson* is very big now. We can pick and choose among actors.'

'That is certainly true. But we know Dean and what he can do. If we tell him what we want, he'll rise to the demands of the new role.'

Adam didn't bother to answer that. He turned to Walton. 'Let's have someone completely new to the series. Let's freshen things up.'

It was time to cut losses. James Walton said, 'All right. We'll cast around. People will want the part, as you say, but we'll need to find someone who isn't already committed to other work. I suppose we can always come back to Dean Morely if no one suitable is available.'

Cassidy said with a touch of venom, 'Of course we can, Dean won't be going anywhere.' But all of them knew now that Morley wasn't an option. The star had spoken.

Joe Hartley said, 'What about Michelle Davies? I thought you were happy with her.'

Adam knew from some tiny inflection in his tone that Hartley knew he had bedded her. He said carefully, 'I was perfectly happy with her in the one episode where we used her. It's just that I have doubts about giving her this plum role for a whole series. Once again, I think we should set our sights a little higher.' He produced his most disarming smile. 'But you're the expert, Joe. You've seen everything from the other side of the cameras. You can be objective. Do you think Michelle is the best we can get for this role?'

An old ploy, but none the less effective for that. Ask the opinion of the man in charge of shaping the whole series, of ensuring that his cast produces the best possible effects from the budget allowed to it. Flattering, on the face of it. But the question also implies that if the man sees no fault in a performer, he must be in some way deficient himself. Has he not spotted the limitations which are obvious to others? Is he sloppily going for the easiest option instead of striving for the very best available results?

To do him credit, Joe Hartley stuck to his guns. 'Michelle seemed to make the best of some very forgettable lines in the episode we've just finished. She's got the looks and she doesn't seem to have failed in anything she's tackled so far. I think she's learned her trade and she's now ready for a major tele-vision role. And she's a good ensemble player.'

It was a valuable quality, especially for a director used to struggling to reconcile warring egos. But it was a mistake to conclude on that thought. Adam Cassidy allowed himself a patronizing smile. 'Is that the best we can aspire to, Joe? A good team player? Someone who won't rock the boat, what-ever her other limitations? I didn't suggest Michelle Davies was incompetent. All I'm saying is that we can do a little better. Gentlemen, look at the viewing figures for the last series, and set your sights a little higher for the next one!'

James Walton frowned beneath his silver hair. Not for the first time, he was wondering whether he should consider an honourable retirement from an increasingly sordid working world. He had endured quite enough of modern television drama and the so-called stars who dominated it. Squalid little people, most of them, despite their earnings. For every Dame Judi Dench, there were a score of loud-mouthed braggarts who had fallen lucky and were determined to exploit it.

He allowed himself a sigh before he said, 'We'll need to get on with it. I'll make some phone calls this afternoon. See who's available, for a start.'

Adam beamed his approval, first briefly at Hartley and then

continuously at Walton. Be magnanimous, once you've asserted yourself and they've come into line. 'I'm sure you'll find most people are available, once they find you are offering major roles in the new *Call Alec Dawson* series. With a hefty initial salary, worldwide exposure, and repeat fees stretching ten years ahead, actors tend to find ways of setting aside other commitments.' He was quoting the phrases Tony Valento had used when he'd set up the last series for him, but this pair weren't to know that. Pity he was having to ditch Valento, in many ways, but a world star demanded a world-class agent – a bit of quality.

James Walton was thinking at that moment that quality was exactly what Cassidy lacked. But he knew who was the most important man in the room when it came to making decisions. 'I'll see what I can do. We'd better say nothing more to Dean Morley and Michelle Davies, for the moment.' He tried to load his next sentence with irony, though he doubted if Cassidy would recognize it. 'I'll come back to you with any suggestions before making definite offers.'

'That would be best, I think. Run it past me. And Joe as well, of course.' Adam nodded two or three times, beaming with contentment. 'I'm glad we've had this little meeting. Very productive, I think. Don't you?'

Thirty miles away in Cassidy's native Brunton, DCI Percy Peach was also enduring a difficult meeting.

In Tommy Bloody Tucker's penthouse office, the fitful sun was at its lowest point of the year and it shone into Percy's face. He had been asked to sit down and he had been called Percy by his chief: two warning signs. He gave a cautious account of his team's CID action during the past week, hoping that if he made it sufficiently routine and boring Tucker would not question him about the detail.

The chief superintendent looked at him steadily over his glasses until he ground to a halt. 'Not much doing in the way of serious crime, then.'

'The way it should be, as you have often reminded us, sir. If there is no serious crime afoot, CID must be doing a good job.'

'Indeed you must, Percy. But we must find a proper vehicle for your talents.'

'Must we, sir?'

'Indeed we must. I need to deploy my resources so as to make maximum use of their efficiency. That is part of my job, Percy.'

'Yes, sir. Part of the overview you keep of the crime situation in our area.'

Tucker looked at him suspiciously. When he found his own phrases coming back at him obsequiously from this source, there was usually mischief at hand.

Peach took advantage of his hesitation with an attempt at diversion. 'I thought you might have told Mr Clancy about your overview and the way we worked last week, sir.'

'You saw the way that fellow treated me?' Tucker had maintained a resolute silence at the station in the days since the Gerry Clancy show. He'd been hoping against hope that this man hadn't seen it. He realized now that he should have known better. 'They don't give you a chance, you know. They say the wildest things and don't give you the chance to answer.'

'Yes, sir. Perhaps best not to go on and give them the chance to do that.'

'It's part of the job of senior officers in the service to present our case to the people,' said Tucker loftily.

God help us if we have to rely on the likes of Tommy Bloody Tucker to do that, thought Percy. 'Yes, sir. I haven't got your experience of television and the media, but I didn't think they allowed you to give a very balanced view.'

'You're right there, Peach. I had no chance to state our case. And it wasn't just Clancy. That actor fellow was most offensive. I said so to Barbara, but she thinks the bloody man can do no wrong.'

He was being addressed as Peach again; that was a good sign. And when he thought of the formidable wrath of Brunnhilde Barbara, even Tommy Bloody Tucker compelled in Percy a reluctant sympathy. 'I don't think you were given a fair hearing, sir. I suppose we shouldn't expect it, on a programme like that. They're only interested in entertainment.'

'I got an autographed picture of Adam Cassidy for Barbara. He seemed to have hundreds of them ready to hand out.'

'Really, sir? And I shouldn't think you had one of yourself ready for him to take home for his wife.'

'I could have done with you beside me, Peach, to speak

about our Asian element. I found you quite impressive when we had that community meeting.'

'Thank you, sir. I probably said more than I should have, but it came from the heart. But I don't consider it an area of expertise for me.' He was suddenly afraid that he was to be redeployed on to anti-terrorist work. 'Well, I really mustn't take up any more of your time, sir. I know how busy you always are. It's good of you to fit me in as you do.'

He had been gone two minutes before Tucker remembered that he had intended to switch Peach and his team on to a series of burglaries in the best district of Brunton, where Tucker himself lived. Back in the CID section, Percy was reflecting that this could be only a temporary reprieve from some boring assignment.

What he needed was a high-profile murder case, as quickly as possible. Not that he wished ill on any of his fellow citizens, of course.

As the evening advanced, a white frost was creeping stealthily over the land to the east of the Trough of Bowland. But it was pleasantly warm in the kitchen of the big new house on the edge of the village. Adam Cassidy and his wife were speaking guardedly to each other.

Adam worked in a world where people treated each other with conversational kid gloves. You might trust people you had known for a long time, but you treated even their opinions with suspicion, if they involved professional judgements. Everyone needed constant reassurance in the world of show business, but the fact that it was always at hand and always favourable meant curiously that none of it could be trusted. In a world where you were always wonderful tonight, darling, no assessment could really be taken as genuine. There were the critics, of course, but every actor knew that the critics had no idea of what they were about. You read them of course, but you always claimed that you despised and ignored them.

Jane Cassidy knew all this from her own years in theatre and television, but a house and domesticity and above all children gave you a proper sense of perspective. You couldn't give yourself airs and graces in a maternity ward, even in an expensive private hospital. The business of giving birth was at once degrading and uplifting, but it didn't leave room for any deceits. And now you couldn't pussyfoot with children. Everyone at the school gates knew that.

Jane realized that she was being guarded with Adam, but she wasn't sure that he had noticed that. The bloody man was so preoccupied with himself and his own plans these days that he seemed scarcely aware of her and the children.

She tried a little self-consciously to get closer to him as he stared at the Aga. 'We'll have more time together, now that you've finished the series.'

'What? Oh, yes, I suppose so. I've put off a lot of things, though, whilst we were working so frantically over the last few months. There are a lot of things waiting for my attention.'

'Yes. Your children for a start. They've hardly seen you recently.'

'Yes. Well, I expect we could go for a holiday, if you like.'

'When?'

'Oh, some time in the new year, I suppose, when I've had the chance to wind down and catch up with other things.'

'The children are getting older, Adam. We can't just take them out of school for a fortnight at a time.'

'Let me speak to that snooty head teacher. She needs to understand that I have to take holidays between schedules. I can't just go off when I want like other people.'

Jane gave a sad little smile. 'Other people have problems too, you know. And I'm not just worried about what the head teacher might say. I don't want our kids missing their schooling.'

'We can pay for private tuition. That's not a problem.'

She turned the heat low under the pan and crossed the big kitchen to where Adam sat at the table. 'You can't solve every problem by throwing money at it, Adam. The children want to be like the other children they're with every day. I know that's not always possible, but—'

'It's bloody impossible and you should know it! They've got a famous Dad, who's probably got more money than any other Dad whose kids go to that school. We can't alter that, and personally I wouldn't want to.'

She sat down opposite him and he knew he was in for one of her little holier-than-thou lectures. He noted with a little shock how coarsened her hands had become. He hadn't noticed that before. She gave him a nervous smile before she spoke. 'Money isn't a problem, as you said. Couldn't you use some of it to buy a little time for yourself? They don't need expensive presents from you. What Kate and Damon need is your time and your affection. You don't want them to grow up without you, do you?'

'No, of course I don't. What sort of a question is that? I have a high-pressure job and I need to wind down. I don't always choose to do that with noisy, demanding young kids. OK?'

She looked at the surface of the long rectangular table, at the brilliant deep blue of the piece of Moorcroft pottery he had brought when he had come in late a couple of weeks ago. She knew she should be looking into his face and smiling as she said this, but she could do neither. 'Is your job really so high-pressure? What about the man who's wondering all day whether he'll be working next week? Sometimes I think we give ourselves excuses; sometimes I think the pressures are just different, not greater.'

He resented her including herself alongside him in this. He wanted to tell her that she was small-time as an actress, that he had moved on now, that she couldn't possibly understand what it was like to be a major star, surrounded by all the new strains that brought. He had more sense than to voice the thought. 'I'll find time for them, Jane. After all, Christmas is coming up. You can't get away from children at Christmas!'

He smiled at her, but she wished he hadn't put it like that. She made herself think of Damon and Kate and what their faces would be like on Christmas Day. 'Well, you'll be able to see more of them between series, won't you? Perhaps this weekend, for a start.'

'Yes. Well, perhaps not this weekend. I've already made plans to do other things, this weekend, Jane.' For a moment, his face was a blank in which she could read nothing. Then it brightened abruptly. 'You should come and see what I've bought!'

He sprang up from the table. After a moment of contemplation, she rose and followed him from the room. He was already disappearing up the stairs when she reached the hall. She was getting used to the distances in this house now, but she still found that everything took a little longer. That gave you more time to think, and you didn't always want that. Adam was throwing aside some sort of packing, caressing the dark wooden handle of a new gun, when she entered the room. The stock, you called it; she remembered that. 'Isn't she a beauty?' he asked her, transformed by his excitement from a forty-two-year-old man to a child with a new toy.

He was staring down at the bright, dark metal of a new shotgun. She wanted to share the animation which had transformed him. But she found she could say only, 'It looks very good, yes.' She felt him looking hard into her face, but she could not take her eyes from the thing in his hands. 'I know nothing about guns. You must remember that.'

'This is the best you can get, Jane. Purdey, the classic make. It's a thing of beauty!' He broke the barrel and flexed the gun, showing her how the cartridges were automatically ejected. Then he took swift aim and brought down an imaginary woodcock from high on the bedroom wall. 'Just feel it! Feel the balance of it. Feel how it sits in the crook of your arm!'

She took the weapon, trying to catch some of his boyish pleasure, thrusting away the thought that he had a small daughter he should be cradling in the crook of his arm. 'It's very heavy, isn't it?' She was suddenly conscious how banal that sounded. 'I'm no good with guns. They frighten me. You know that.' She raised it dutifully to her shoulder.

He snatched it away from her. 'Don't do that! You were pointing it at me. You should never, ever, point a weapon at anyone. I'm sure I've told you that before.'

'It's not loaded, is it?' she stared down dumbly at the cold, smooth steel of the barrel.

'No, it's not loaded. But that's not the point. You have to get into the right habits. You never, ever, point a gun at anyone.'

'I'm sorry. I told you, I'm no good with guns. But show me how you fire it.'

'It's obvious enough, surely.' But he put the Purdey back in her hands, then stood behind her and flexed it open and shut. He lifted it until she stared straight down the barrel with the stock against her shoulder, and pressed her finger gently upon the trigger. 'There you are, you've brought down a pheasant!'

Jane couldn't repress a shudder. She would never understand why people had to shoot down living things for nothing but the pleasure of killing. She laid the new toy down in its case. She couldn't think of anything to say.

Adam closed the case on the shotgun carefully, almost reverentially, before he spoke again. 'That's why I won't be around this weekend, you see. I've got the chance of a weekend's shooting in the Scottish borders.'

She said dully, 'Can't you get out of it? I had plans for us to do things round here.'

'Not now, darling, I'm afraid. These chances don't come very often, you know.'

Jane Cassidy said nothing more. Her mind still held the feel of her index finger upon that trigger, still felt the smooth click which the tiniest pressure had brought.

# NINE

In the end, Adam Cassidy left for his weekend's shooting on Friday night. It was the fourteenth of December and the days were the shortest of the year. You needed to be out early to make the most of the light, he told Jane. If you travelled a hundred and fifty miles on Saturday morning, you'd lose most of that day's shooting.

He took the BMW sports car which was his favourite for long distance motoring. He didn't need the extra seating of the Merc or the Jag, because he'd be travelling alone. The rest of the party would already be up there, he explained to Jane. He was only waiting until Friday night so that he could see the children before he went. He would like to collect them from school, but his presence brought so much unwelcome attention from the other parents that he couldn't do that. Much better for the children if they avoided that circus and the nanny Ingrid collected them. Jane wondered uncharitably how long it was since their father had last met them at the school gates.

Adam asked Damon about his day at school, though he didn't seem to give a lot of attention to the six-year-old's account of his reading triumphs and what the teacher had said about them. Kate didn't need to be asked about her day in the nursery class. As usual, she burbled happily about her paintings and how she was now the tallest in her group and was ready for the big school next year. She was very pleased with the doll her father gave her as he left, and Damon seemed almost as happy with his ray-gun. There was no need to worry about all this gender-shaping nonsense when you were buying gifts, Adam assured Jane. She wondered who had been sent out from the studios to buy these things for him.

Damon and Kate were bathed and in their pyjamas when she heard the BMW explode into life in the garage. Jane hurried them down the stairs to wave their daddy off, but by the time they reached the back door he had swung the car rapidly round on the forecourt in front of the garage. He did

not hear the children's shrill cries above the throaty roar of
the engine as the low car zoomed away into the darkness.

The forecast had said there might be snow showers tonight
in this north-eastern part of Lancashire, particularly on high
ground. In any event, there would be the sharpest frost of the
winter so far. The young men and women of Brunton got on
with whatever Friday night activities they had planned for
themselves. Most of the middle-aged adults in the town took
a swift glance at the rising moon and the clear sky, turned up
the heating, and resolved to stay comfortable indoors. There
was a busy weekend of Christmas shopping and preparation
for the great commercial festival creeping up on them. Best
to save themselves for that rather than be out in weather like
this.

The weathermen were right: in the ancient argot of the
region, it was going to be a cold 'un tonight.

One of the middle-aged men who did go out was Adam
Cassidy's elder brother. Luke looked exhausted after a week
of intensive work at school, followed each day by at least an
hour with his father. When he said he fancied an hour at the
pub, his wife was surprised. But she encouraged him to go.
In past years, Luke had been a star of the quiz nights, and a
popular member of the darts and domino teams whenever they
were short. But promotions at school had given him more
work, at the same time as his father became more dependent
on him and Hazel. Luke had neither the time nor the energy
to enjoy himself as he once had.

Tonight, he was out for longer than Hazel expected. But
that was surely a good thing. He must be enjoying himself,
chattering to people he had not met for months, even years
perhaps. It was Friday night and there was no school tomorrow,
so it took her longer than usual to persuade the children into
bed. They'd be teenagers soon, with all the tiresome arguments and contests that would bring, but they were good kids
really, both of them. She was surprised to find it was eleven
o'clock. The heating had switched off and the temperature
was dropping in the lounge. Hazel went upstairs and got ready
for bed. She was glad to creep between the cool sheets and
curl herself into a foetal ball of warmth, but she knew she
would not sleep until Luke was safely in.

At twenty past eleven, she heard him closing the front door softly and going through the hall. He didn't want to disturb her; she called softly through the open door that it was all right, she was still awake. She meant to ask him whether he had enjoyed himself at the pub, but once he was safely back in the house, she relaxed. She was almost asleep when he came into the room. Luke whispered a goodnight to her, told her that it was bloody cold outside, and went to the bathroom. By the time he returned three minutes later, Hazel was sleeping peacefully.

Luke was right about the cold. There was not a breath of air outside and the temperature dropped steadily beneath a cloudless navy sky. By the time old Harry Cassidy's bladder disturbed him at three o'clock, as it invariably did, it was perishing cold, as he muttered to himself. He relieved himself as he did everything else nowadays, fitfully and arthritically. It took a long time for his old bones to warm up, once he was safely back in the valley of the worn-out mattress. He wished his wife was still in the old bed with him. He had always thought that he would go first. For a moment, he had expected her to be there now when he got back into bed; he must be getting more confused, as people said he was. He hadn't known old age would be like this. Perhaps Adam would come this weekend.

It was as well Harry didn't know where Adam was at that moment. The A666 runs between Blackburn and Bolton, and on beyond that to Manchester. It is a busy road by day, though less so since the M66 offered the speed of motorway travel to those making major journeys north and south. The older road is not very busy during the night, and on this freezing one it was almost deserted. Frost like this clamps itself quickly on to metal, as if it were a living fungus, with a preference for the cool smoothness of steel sheeting. In one of the lay-bys beside the highest part of the A666, Adam Cassidy's BMW hard-top sports car was covered with an ever-thickening layer of white frost.

Sixty yards away from it, Adam's eyes stared unseeingly skywards. The face was handsome still, scarcely touched by what had happened beneath it. But the left half of his chest was blown away completely, scattered around his fallen corpse in bloody fragments of bone and sinew.

The devil's number, some call 666. It had been so for Adam Cassidy. At four o'clock in the morning, tiny flakes of snow began to fall. A shower, no more than that; the weathermen were vindicated. But the snow fell steadily over the frozen face of Cassidy and the awful mess of what had been his torso.

# TEN

Many football matches were postponed on that Saturday. But frozen turf was no problem to Brunton Rovers, who played in the English Premier League, and had under-soil heating to allow them a perfect playing surface.

The Rovers were playing Stoke City. This was a match in which both needed points in the perennial fight against relegation. It was a contest without subtleties, with fierce tackling and several bookings. Brunton were a goal down at half-time, but some forthright words from their manager and a couple of substitutions worked magic. The Rovers conducted a prolonged second-half siege of the Stoke goal, equalized after an hour, and scored the decisive goal with ten minutes left, after the stubborn Stoke defenders had twice blocked the ball on the line. The third goal in injury time was, as the local paper put it, merely icing on the Christmas cake.

Wayne Carter was a Stoke City supporter, had been since his birth. He journeyed the eighty miles to the ground in Brunton with three of his companions in a battered Ford Focus with two hundred thousand miles on the clock. They stayed on the motorway until Preston, then turned on to the A59 and took their time over the ten miles to the ground. There was no hurry; they had an hour to spare before kick-off. They passed a spliff of pot round among themselves as they ran into the suburbs of Brunton, then found some other Potteries men in a pub and downed a couple of swift pints before kick-off.

Thus insulated against the cold, they were happy to strip their upper bodies down to their red and white replica Stoke City shirts in the visitors' enclosure. When City took the lead, Wayne was moved to slip his shirt over his shoulders and whirl it around his head in celebration, displaying the delicate skin and less delicate tattoos of a lilywhite physique to an unimpressed Brunton public.

Wayne and his companions had a good day until about twenty past four, when Brunton Rovers scored their first goal.

Things went rapidly downhill after that. The four young men were disappointed but philosophical. They were Stoke City supporters, after all. You were prepared for these things because you had a considerable previous experience of them. They managed a ragged clatter of applause when their captain and a few other members of their team turned briefly and waved to them before trooping disconsolately off the pitch.

At least there was no parking ticket on the Focus when they got back to it in the narrow street near the ground. Wayne proposed that they went back through Bolton and joined the M6 south of Manchester. No doubt they'd be stopping for a pee and a few tinnies on the way home and it was best not to rely on the motorway service stations. They didn't sell booze and they could be thronged with rowdy returning football supporters. You didn't want to meet the Liverpool lot returning from Birmingham – they travelled in much greater numbers than the men of Stoke, and numbers meant strength, if it came to the tribal exchanges of football factions.

The young men stopped in Darwen and picked up a dozen cans of Budweiser in a Co-op supermarket. Enough to dull the pain of defeat until they were back in the sympathetic Potteries. It was ten miles later that Wayne Carter told their driver to pull in to the parking bay beside the road because he needed a leak.

His three companions moaned a little about this early delay in their return journey. But the power of suggestion is strong upon receptive minds and full bladders. Within thirty seconds of their stopping, the other three had followed Wayne out into the low bushes beyond the parking bay, cursing the sudden cold and fumbling urgently with the flies of their jeans.

There was still a thin covering of snow at this height, where it had remained around freezing point all day. It was Wayne who had the torch; there had been ribald comments about the necessity of light to discover his equipment in these temperatures. He moved carefully a little way further away from the car than his fellows; these things demanded a degree of privacy, even from your intimates. He switched off the torch and urinated copiously, examining the stars in the night sky and gasping at the simple pleasure of relief which had been delayed a little too long. He switched the torch on again when he had finished. You had to be careful where you placed your feet in places like this, which had been used by others before you for similar and perhaps worse purposes.

None of his friends mistook his scream for a hoax. There was too sincere a note of terror in it for that. Wayne stared down in horror at all that remained of what had once been a man, at the blood and gore amidst the whiteness of the snow and frost.

Percy Peach had been at the Brunton Rovers–Stoke City match himself that afternoon. He had supported the Rovers since he had been a boy, so that he was much elated by their second-half recovery and went home with a warm glow within him which owed nothing to alcohol.

'Stuffed 'em!' he informed Lucy triumphantly. Then, with a conscientious attempt at objectivity, 'We were a bit flattered by three–one, really. But it was an exciting match.'

'That's good, then. The meal will be ready in twenty minutes. There's a gin and tonic ready for you on the table.' Detective Sergeant Peach, as she was still getting used to calling herself, was enjoying domesticity more than she had expected. It must be the novelty factor, she told herself, as a consciously modern woman.

It was just after six o'clock when the call came through for Detective Chief Inspector Peach. A suspicious death. The body of a male beside the highest and loneliest stretch of the A666, on the other side of Darwen. Been there for some time, by the looks of it. The police surgeon was on his way, for the ridiculous legal formality of confirming death. Percy gave swift, automatic orders. Check the missing persons register for any males reported in the last three days. The scene to be cordoned off immediately, but not investigated until daylight. Even with floodlights, investigators might destroy more than they revealed, if they blundered around before morning. A uniformed PC to be stationed beside it overnight. Two officers in a car, taking turns to keep watch. Poor bloody sods: he hoped they realized what it would be like up there, with the temperature below freezing.

He came back in sober mood to the table, where Lucy produced the meal she had slid back into the oven when he was called to the phone. It was the worst possible point in the week to assemble a scene of crime team. Nowadays they were all civilians and many of them simply wouldn't be available on a Saturday night. As soon as they had finished the main course, he rang his old colleague Jack Chadwick, who had been invalided out of the police service and now ran SOCO teams as a civilian. They agreed that Jack would have a scene of crime team assembled on the site by nine o'clock on Sunday morning.

The sweet was gooseberry crumble, one of his favourites. When he had chomped thoughtfully for several minutes without speaking, Lucy said, 'You'll be up and out bright and early in the morning, then.'

'No. I'll let my new sergeant go out there. Clyde Northcott can take Brendan Murphy with him. Be good experience for the pair of them. I'll have a lie-in with the woman of my dreams. If I have any energy at all at the end of that, I might go and worry Tommy Bloody Tucker with this later in the morning.'

It wasn't like Percy Peach not to visit the scene of crime scene. But for over three years he had always done that with the then Lucy Blake as his DS. Marriage had meant they could no longer work together, even though she was still in the Brunton CID section. Perhaps that was why he had elected to let others do the job this time – not that you ever discovered anything an efficient SOCO team and the forensic labs weren't going to show up for you anyway. Lucy wouldn't ask him why he wasn't going to this one. He would dismiss the idea that he didn't fancy it without her as sentimental rubbish.

But she was grateful to him nevertheless.

Jack Chadwick drove his SOCO team out through Darwen and on to the lonely moorland stretch of the A666 at nine o'clock on Sunday morning.

He took a photographer, a fingerprints man and one non-specialist with him. They would search for the miscellaneous detritus which might offer a clue to whoever else other than the dead man had been in this place at the moment when he died. They were an experienced team; they didn't expect much on a site like this one, but they would do their job and search it minutely, nonetheless. The car was pretty quiet as they drove through Darwen; everyone in it had expected to be still in bed or yawning at breakfast at this time on a Sunday morning. But they knew what to expect and what they were about.

None of them voiced the thought, but there was always the outside chance that one of them would pick up something vital at the scene, something which would lead many months later to a commendation from a judge in the high court on the diligence of the person who had brought this to light and ensured justice. Jack Chadwick knew from long experience that the possibility was remote, but anything which buoyed enthusiasm on a morning like this was valuable.

They were glad to see one thing when they reached the site and saw the ribbons delineating the area of the crime scene. It was some distance from the parking bay. When there were no toilets at a parking place, everyone knew what happened on the ground immediately adjacent to it. The team donned their plastic shoe covers and overalls, looking like a surgical theatre team as they reached the single narrow entrance which had already been marked out at the site.

There had never been more than an inch of snow, but another hard frost had crusted this thin covering over the ground where the body lay, some sixty yards from the tarmac of the parking bay. They made one immediate and satisfying discovery, but they had been at work for no more than ten minutes when they heard an unexpected sound through the clear, cold air.

A powerful motorbike, roaring throatily in the distance, then changing gear as it turned into the parking bay and stopped behind Jack Chadwick's Citroen. The two tall men who climbed off the bike were in black leathers and gauntlets. They did not remove the helmets for a moment, which they spent studying the frost-coated BMW sports car which was cordoned off in the car park. Then they turned and marched carefully to where Chadwick and his team had stopped work to witness their impressive entrance.

The leading figure removed his helmet only when he was two yards short of Jack Chadwick. There were involuntary starts of shock in the three people behind Chadwick, for the features now revealed were almost as black and shiny as the helmet which had concealed them. Everyone who worked at Brunton police station would have already recognized the Yamaha 350. The black face gazed for a moment around the civilian faces, then smiled and said, 'Detective Sergeant Clyde Northcott. And this is DC Brendan Murphy. Anything of interest yet?'

'We have, yes. Percy Peach not coming today?' Chadwick had been looking forward to a few words with his old comrade.

Northcott's smile broadened to a grin. 'Percy sent the poor bloody infantry, didn't he? Too cold for him, I expect. He won't be in church, if I know Percy. He'll be still in bed, with Lucy Blake as was. Lucky sod!'

It was said without bitterness but with genuine envy. Lucy Blake, with her dark red hair, blue-green eyes and ample curves, had been the object of many advances and many more erotic fantasies among the male officers of the Brunton service. It had been an immense surprise and a source of lasting regret among them when she had announced her commitment to the bald, bustling figure with the out of date black toothbrush moustache. Percy Peach was a local detective legend, a figure who excited respect and fear in equal measure among his juniors, but they had not thought of him as a rival for the delectable Detective Sergeant Blake. But all argument and all speculation were over now; she was Mrs Lucy Peach. Not all envy, though; virile young men and the odd woman still clung to their sexual fantasies.

Brendan Murphy, a native Lancastrian despite his Irish name and heritage, rubbed his hands vigorously together and beat his arms rapidly across his chest. 'Last time you'll get me on that damned bike! I had my eyes shut most of the time. And now I'm bloody frozen!'

The four people who had already begun work on the site smiled at him in friendly fashion. When you were dragged out on a morning like this to work in a place like this, it was always good to see someone even colder and more distressed than you were. 'You'll live!' Northcott growled unsympathetically towards the fresh, unlined face which was almost as white as his was black. 'Put another woolly on next time.'

Murphy informed them that he was wearing a thermal vest and long johns, but no one was interested any more. Jack Chadwick had lifted their one indisputable trophy and was holding it out reverently in gloved hands towards Clyde Northcott, as if he were an acolyte in some solemn religious service.

Northcott did not touch it, but studied it for a moment through the transparent plastic which already protected it against contamination. 'You're holding a lot of money there, Jack. That's a Purdey. Is it the murder weapon?'

'Almost certainly, I should think, unless it was left here to divert us. Forensic and the pathology boys will confirm it. But all of us here know enough to be certain that this man died from a shotgun fired at close quarters.'

The two policemen turned towards the white mound they had been conscious of since they came here. They stared down wordlessly for a moment at the shattered torso and the crimson-black spattering on the white ground. Above them, the face was curiously unmarked, frozen into a rictus of surprise, with only two spots of now blackened blood upon it. The sun was rising now, slowly melting the thin layer of whiteness which covered the grisly contents of this cordoned area. On the face of the corpse, only the eyebrows still held their covering of frost.

It was the woman in the team who identified the victim. She gave a quick gasp and said, 'That's Alec Dawson. Or rather the man who plays him, Adam Cassidy.'

Jack Chadwick and the others abandoned their work for a moment and came over to confirm this. It was Chadwick who said, 'You're right, Annette. Never watch that rubbish myself, because it's so far away from real policing.' He was anxious to assert his ex-copper status with the derision he knew would be the police reaction. 'But my wife loves the series.' He glanced round his team. 'This is a local celebrity, the most famous man to come out of Brunton for a long time. The shit's going to hit the fan when this gets out. For God's sake, let's make sure we don't miss anything.'

The two CID men looked round at what they recognized already as an unpromising scene of crime. The photographer had already finished his work here; he was helping a younger woman to conduct a minute examination of the frozen ground. They each had tweezers and sample bags. They had already collected several cigarette ends and a few hairs from a stunted hawthorn. These looked animal rather than human; dogs too felt calls of nature, and their owners usually took them further away from parking areas, in unconscious acknowledgement of man's pre-eminence over the rest of the animal world.

The pair were treating this ground with due care, carefully skirting the dark yellow circle of Wayne Carter's urination before he discovered the corpse. So far, they had found none of the used contraceptives which were too often discarded in places like this. Perhaps this spot was too wintry and exposed for even the hardy fornicators of Lancashire. But they would bag everything they found here, however unsavoury. Ninety per cent, perhaps a hundred per cent, of what they took away would have no relevance to this crime, but there was no means of distinguishing that on site.

'Have you done the car yet?' asked Northcott.

'No. The keys were in his pocket, though. I've opened the door and had a quick look, but we'll move on to it when we've finished here. I don't think we'll find much in the BMW. It's very new: only eight hundred miles on the clock. The passenger seat looks as if it's never been used. Maybe it hasn't.'

Brendan Murphy came back to the one jewel the place had so far offered to its investigators. He looked down at the shotgun, then at the corpse, then back at the most experienced man there. 'Any chance of suicide?'

Jack Chadwick came and stood beside him. When you find the instrument of death near a body, it holds about it a strange wonder. The pair stared at the inanimate object as if it could tell them more, if they only looked at it long enough. Jack eventually said, 'This isn't suicide. At least not in my view, but forensics will confirm it. For a start, suicides normally shoot themselves in the head, especially if they're using a shotgun. And though recoils can do strange things to weapons, the Purdey was lying too far away from the body for this to be self-inflicted.'

'Then why should a killer leave it here for us to find?'

Chadwick glanced at the fresh young face beside him. DC Murphy was eager for knowledge, not afraid to appear naïve if that's what the search for knowledge demanded. 'We don't even know for certain yet that this is the murder weapon. If it is, then it's possible that someone who was shocked by what he had done simply flung away the shotgun in a panic. The more likely reason for it's being here is that your killer didn't care if it was found, because he knew it wouldn't tell you anything about him.' Killers were always male until you knew otherwise, simply because in violent deaths men were overwhelmingly more numerous. 'We've already fingerprinted it and found nothing useful.'

Murphy beat his arms across his chest again. He wasn't looking forward to getting back astride the Yamaha. He glanced at Clyde Northcott, who seemed to be preparing to do just that, then down again at the shotgun in its wrapper. 'Even someone who wasn't contemplating murder when he came here would have been wearing gloves in December, in a place like this.'

'Welcome to the murder team,' said DS Northcott grimly.

Chief Superintendent Thomas Bulstrode Tucker was an enthusiastic but dreadful golfer. This combination exists in all sports, but it is commonest in golf. There are many reasons for that. The commonest is probably the much-lauded handicap system, which allows the abject to play against the proficient, on what should be level terms. The system is more complex for the outsider than the Bible and Koran combined, but basically it means that the duffer is given extra shots to compensate for his dufferdom.

Thomas Bulstrode Tucker disappeared resolutely to the course on Sunday mornings, worshipping at his chosen golfing shrine come sun, rain, hail or frost. Brunnhilde Barbara, who controlled the rest of his social life with a Valkyrean fierceness, indulged him in this. She approved of three things in her husband: his high rank in the police service; his embracement of Freemasonry, where he was in line to become Master of his local lodge; and his participation in the mystic rites of golf. She was under the impression that the latter two had helped him to a series of promotions, that he would not be a chief superintendent without his enthusiastic membership of his local lodge and of Brunton Golf Club.

The only one of the three with which Barbara could claim any personal contact was Freemasonry. Thomas looked good in an evening suit, or even a well-tailored lounge suit; she had judged him against others on ladies' nights at his own and other lodges, and found in his favour. He was quite handsome, with his full, well-groomed head of hair, now attractively silvered at the temples. He could make an adequate speech at the Masons, where the standard of competition was not high. There was ample scope for the conventional, and Thomas could be neither heckled nor questioned.

Because of her husband's perceived success at the lodge, Brunnhilde Barbara had no idea how abject was his failure both as the Head of Brunton CID and as a humble playing member of Brunton Golf Club. Indeed, she was wont to announce with a Wagnerian certainty at coffee mornings that Thomas played golf and that she understood he was quite good at it.

Percy Peach knew that he was not.

He ranked Tommy Bloody Tucker as one of the world's worst golfers. In Percy's not entirely unbiased view, his chief's golf was a reflection of his capacity as a senior police officer. Another question which posed itself to Percy Peach's perennially enquiring mind was why the worst golfers so often seemed intent upon drawing attention to their ineptitude by wearing the most garish golfing attire.

On this bright but bitterly cold morning, Tucker favoured a tight-fitting pale-blue cap with the legend 'Welsh Ryder Cup, 2010' as its badge. His sturdy physique sported a canary yellow roll-neck sweater. His lower limbs carried plus twos in a scarlet and green tartan which even the most colour-blind of Highland chieftains had surely never sanctioned. His knee-length socks were a deeper yellow than his canary sweater; their neatness was marred by the loose threads which bore witness to his frequent sorties into bushes in search of his errant golf ball. The deep scuffing in the leather of his two-tone fawn and white golf shoes also demonstrated heroic endurance rather than expertise.

The chief superintendent was having one of his better golfing mornings. The ball was running long on frozen fairways, so that when he topped his drives, as he habitually did, they were running like startled rabbits over the iron-hard ground. To avoid damage to the regular greens, the few enthusiasts on the course today were forced to use the temporary greens, which on frozen turf made putting a game of chance. The holes on these rough surfaces were six inches in diameter rather than the normal four and a quarter. This lottery was today favouring the duffer Tucker, the man who had long suffered at the unremitting hands of the gods of golf.

The larger holes were gathering in the putts of this peacock practitioner of the sport. Tucker and his three companions had agreed on the first tee that serious golf was impossible. These conditions could offer no more than healthy fresh air and exercise. But as the morning wore on and Tucker's ball disappeared erratically into a succession of the large holes, these same conditions became in his view ones which tested the skills and adaptability of the dedicated golfer.

The three men with him were by now ready to welcome any diversion from his voluble celebrations. They were thus quite happy to see a motionless figure waiting as impassive as the grim reaper beside the tee on the thirteenth hole.

T.B. Tucker was not. He ignored the muffled man in black ostentatiously, insisting that they putt out on the frozen temporary green of the twelfth. It was a move which was in his view immediately justified. His own putt from some six yards was at least a foot wide of the hole when it hit a frozen heel-mark on its second bounce, broke sharply left, and dived into the edge of the large hole. 'Read that one just right!' said Tucker with satisfaction. His companions looked at each other and cast their eyes towards heaven as they followed him glumly. He evidently meant that seriously.

'What the hell do you want?' Tucker enquired aggressively of his chief inspector.

'And a good morning to you, sir!' returned Percy Peach equably. 'Most effective use of the googly, if I may say so. I've never seen a googly turn like that on the second bounce before.'

'This is the one chance in the week I get to relax. And you have to pursue me, even here!'

Percy, conscious of the three men listening expectantly behind his chief, bowed his head reverently for a moment. 'I'm very sorry, sir. I'm merely acting on orders. Your orders.' His smile when he looked up again was splendidly complacent.

'I never ordered you to disturb me and my friends at the golf club.'

Percy had removed his bobble hat as Tucker approached. He now allowed his eyebrows to rise a little towards the whiteness of his bald pate. For an impressive moment, he looked hurt but mute in the face of this injustice. 'You told me you were to be apprised immediately of any serious crime on our patch, sir. With particular attention to high-profile cases.'

Tucker had walked on to the tee. He now teed the ball for his drive, determined to impress his companions with his insouciance in the face of this impertinent interference. 'Well, what is it, then?'

'A suspicious death, sir. A death which in my opinion is almost certainly murder.'

Tucker paused in addressing his ball. 'What sort of murder? Don't tell me you've come here to report some routine domestic incident.'

'Murder is never merely an incident, sir. You said that to me in 2008, sir. I remember thinking what a worthwhile reminder it was for all of us. I treasure your aphorisms, sir.'

Tucker, who was not quite sure what an aphorism was, decided to dispatch his ball whilst he pondered this. It was a mistake. His familiar crouch over the ball translated itself suddenly into the galvanic heave of his backswing. It was a little too much for his worn shoe-studs to handle on this frozen turf. His feet slid swiftly from beneath him and his garish posterior hit the unyielding ground with a thump which seemed to the appreciative onlookers to measure at least four on the Richter scale.

After a few seconds of a silence which throbbed with suppressed hilarity, Tucker's partner in the four-ball managed to enquire whether he had seriously damaged himself. An opponent suggested hopefully that they would quite understand if he wished to abandon golf for the day in view of the farcical conditions. Tucker shrugged their solicitude nobly aside, rolled on to all fours, and rose gingerly to assert his shattered authority. He said with all the sarcasm he could muster, 'And what exactly do you expect me to do about this, Peach?'

Percy studied him for a moment with his head on one side. 'You could shorten your backswing a little, sir. Turn the shoulders by all means, but resist with the hips. Your energy and determination were impressive, but you lost balance, you see. You could try—'

'Not about my golf swing, you fool! What do you expect me to do about this so-called high-profile murder?'

'Ah!' Percy studied the ground for a few seconds; it seemed that the evidence in the frost of his chief's recent fall held a professional interest. Then he said thoughtfully, 'Well, sir, I expect you to do nothing of any consequence. I expect you to maintain your professional overview of the situation, as it is your professed policy to do. I have fulfilled my orders in coming here to apprise you of events.'

The three men behind the chief superintendent in charge of Brunton CID were listening intently, but one of them had his hand over his mouth, whilst the other two were finding the top of a frost-covered fir tree to the left of them of absorbing interest. Apparently their pompous companion's mastery of the local crime scene was not as absolute as he always professed it to be in the clubhouse.

T.B. Tucker strove to assert himself. 'I shall take overall charge of the case, of course. You will direct the day-to-day investigation, Peach. You will start by questioning anyone who had any sort of a grudge against the dead man. Is that clear?'

Percy marvelled at how this man never lost his talent for the blindin' bleedin' obvious. 'Of course, sir.' He produced a notebook and ball-pen from some recess in his heavy clothing and adopted an even more formal tone. 'Could you give me a full account of your movements on Friday night and Saturday morning, please, sir?'

'I was— what the hell do you mean, Peach?'

'I'm obeying orders again, sir. I have reason to think from statements you made to me last week that you had a great dislike of the dead man, as a result of an appearance with him on a television programme called *The Gerry Clancy Show*. If you could just tell me where you were at these times, preferably with the name of a witness who could confirm your statement, I shall probably be able to eliminate you from the initial list of suspects.'

Tucker's jaw dropped to reflect his total bafflement. Peach was glad to note the familiar distressed-goldfish look on these noble features. He had only seen it indoors before, usually in the sanctity of Tommy Bloody Tucker's office. In this more public setting, the look was even more impressive. The chief super managed just two syllables before the vacancy overtook him again. 'You mean—'

'I do indeed, sir. The identity of the victim is yet to be formally confirmed, but we believe it to be one Adam Cassidy. More familiar to some as Alec Dawson, I believe. The man who, according to your own account, made you look a right arse before millions of television viewers. Hence my request for a statement, sir.'

'And I repeat to you, Peach, don't be bloody ridiculous!'

There was steel in the tone at last. It was time to be on his way. Peach addressed an apology to the golfing companions of his chief, as if he had noticed them for the first time. 'Just police routine, gentlemen. Just an attempt to eliminate one person who recently had occasion to dislike the man who is now a murder victim.' He dropped his formal tone and added in a lower voice. 'In my own personal view, I think your golfing chum is not really a dangerous or violent man. I think you should have no fear of completing the rest of your round with him. Sorry to have interrupted your game.'

Tucker had limped painfully away from the tee during this. He brushed his rear carefully free of frost and grass, wincing at the physical hurt as well as the damage to his *amour-propre*. Through gritted teeth he ordered, 'Be on your way, Peach!'

'Yes, sir. Enjoy your game, sir. Hope the fall hasn't affected your googlies.'

# ELEVEN

There could be no doubt that Jane Cassidy was genuinely upset by the news of her husband's death. She burst into tears, and asked if the police were really sure that it was Adam. When told there could be little doubt of that, she sank on to the sofa, and allowed the young woman in police uniform to make her a cup of tea.

PC Nell Hayward recorded these things carefully in her report. It was distressing to have to report sudden deaths like this to the next of kin, but the case was going to be a big one, and she had a career of her own to consider. She gave Mrs Cassidy the few details she had been told to release about the death. Over the tea, she told her that it would be necessary that she answer a few questions for Detective Chief Inspector Peach, who had taken charge of the investigation. Mrs Cassidy said that she certainly couldn't do that today. She had to break the news about Adam to the children and she would be in no state to answer questions after doing that. Tomorrow morning would be quite acceptable, said PC Hayward firmly. They were sorry to intrude at a time like this, but the circumstances demanded it. She was sure that Mrs Cassidy would want to give them all the information she could, to ensure that they arrested someone quickly.

Was this Mr Peach a good man, the widow wanted to know. Very good indeed, said PC Hayward. No, she hadn't worked with him herself, but she was sure he would solve the case quickly and bring the culprit to justice. DCI Peach had a considerable local reputation. Nell just managed to prevent herself from saying formidable. That didn't seem quite the right word, being police code for a right bastard if you riled him.

The mortuary attendant sized up the man carefully. You had to be very careful with the identification of dead bodies, particularly when they followed violent and unexpected deaths; the next of kin could collapse on you. He wondered if this man had been summoned here so quickly because of the fame of the corpse. He fancied so: the powers that be wouldn't want the faintest possibility of error, if they were about to announce to the world that the man who played Alec Dawson was dead.

At least this haste meant you didn't have to disguise the effects of a post-mortem; that could be very tricky. He liked the look of the man who had come here to do the identification. He was white and drawn, but you would expect that. He also looked composed and determined. You could never be sure, but experience told the attendant that this man was unlikely to disintegrate under the weight of emotion when he saw what he had to see.

He took him through the formalities, filling in the boxes on the form for him to sign. He found himself instinctively producing his best script when the man said he was a teacher. 'Relationship to the deceased?'

'I'm his brother. His elder brother by three years.' Luke answered the routine questions, watched the man completing the form for him, told himself that this was reality, not a dream from which he would shortly awake. 'Do you want me to sign that?'

'Not just yet. You can do that after identification. So as to confirm it, you see.'

He watched his man carefully as he took him into the room where the corpse lay. 'We prefer it that you don't touch the deceased, please.' He would explain why if the man queried this; otherwise he wouldn't upset him with the information that there might still be traces of a murderer to be lifted from the flesh, that the passionless butchery of a post-mortem was compulsory once foul play was suspected.

But this man merely nodded and said, 'I shan't need to touch him. I never intended to do that.' He followed the attendant along the corridor, looking straight ahead of him as he had done throughout, as if he was deliberately remaining unaware of his surroundings.

He stopped suddenly and instinctively when he saw the body of his brother. The sheet was drawn tightly up to the chin, so that the awful damage to the chest was quite invisible. The handsome face was pale and spotlessly clean; the eyes had been closed. He might at first sight have been merely asleep. Luke knew that was the kind of banal thing that people often felt in this situation. A few of the wrinkles of early middle age seemed to have dropped away from round the eyes and the features seemed quite relaxed, as if they welcomed this repose. Otherwise, the face was as he remembered it.

A few seconds elapsed whilst he steadied his breathing. Then Luke Cassidy said quietly, 'Yes, that's my brother. That is Adam.'

The person who had so abruptly ended Adam Cassidy's existence waited all weekend for an announcement that the remains had been discovered.

The hours crept by slowly on Saturday, with no word on television, on radio, even on local radio, that a body had been found. But the killer knew that this death was much too big for local radio. The evening news at six o'clock on Radio Four revealed that a famous author had died in Hampshire, and that a movie star of the nineteen fifties and sixties had died in Santa Monica at the age of ninety-four. There were potted biographies of both of them, but no word yet of this much more sensational death.

Surely the body could not be lying up on the moors, still undiscovered? Yet on Sunday morning and at Sunday lunchtime there was still nothing. The Sunday evening bulletin gave lengthy details of the key clash between Manchester United and Arsenal in the Premier League, where there had been goals and a sending off. There was still no mention of Adam Cassidy. Surely the authorities must know by now? They must be deliberately holding back the release of the information. Yet no one had come to the door with questions. That ought to be reassuring.

It was not until Monday morning that the first bald details were announced. A body believed to be that of the television star Adam Cassidy had been discovered on moorland between Darwen and Bolton. Foul play was suspected.

It was almost a relief that it was out at last.

Neither radio nor television was switched on early in the big new house near the Trough of Bowland.

Jane Cassidy had told the children last night that Daddy had met with an accident, that they wouldn't be seeing him again. That was enough; she didn't want them to hear the harsher truths which might be announced to the public. They had cried last night, so that she had eventually pushed Kate's cot into Damon's room and allowed them to sleep together. But they had seemed curiously composed this morning, in that surprising, brittle calmness which seems only available to children. The advice from the policewoman had been to get them back into their normal routine as quickly as possible, and both Damon and Kate seemed happy enough to go to school.

She was glad that she had a nanny available to take them, though. Jane hugged them a little more tightly than usual, then waved to them from the door until they were out of sight. It hurt her a little that they should seem so little affected. Each of them had a hand in Ingrid's; they seemed to be chatting to her quite happily as they disappeared.

Adam should have seen more of them than he did. He would never have the chance now. She switched the radio on and heard the formal police announcement on the nine o'clock bulletin. The calm tones of the newsreader seemed to be talking about someone else entirely. She made herself a beaker of tea and tried to organize her mind, but it did not work. Her usually calm and efficient brain seemed in this crisis to refuse her commands. When she eventually remembered the tea, she found it untouched and cold. She looked at the clock and discovered that it was ten to ten.

The CID people came at exactly ten o'clock, the time they had arranged with her. She watched them get out of the police Ford Mondeo; a shortish, muscular man with a bald head, in an immaculate grey suit, and a very tall black man who had been driving, who had a black roll-neck sweater above navy trousers. They looked up automatically at the front elevation of the house. She could imagine what they were saying to each other: that its harsh modern brick and ostentatious size looked inappropriate in this quiet country setting. Adam had assured her that it would mellow and blend with the landscape in a few years, as the shrubs in the garden matured and the trees at the boundary grew taller.

Ingrid had offered to let the officers in, but Jane preferred to answer the door herself rather than play the grand lady. The shorter man said, 'I am Detective Chief Inspector Peach and this is Detective Sergeant Northcott.' They were polite and apologetic, apologizing for having to intrude at a time like this and promising to be as brief as they could be. She realized after the first minute that they were watching every movement she made. When she herself had commiserated with

people after a bereavement, she fancied she looked at anything
around them rather than their faces, to cover her embarrassment. Yet these men, despite their sympathy, were observing
her intently, noting her every reaction to whatever they asked
her. That was part of detection, she supposed; she found it
unnerving, nonetheless.

They would be able to see that she'd been crying. Deep
within her, a voice said that was a good thing.

Peach said quietly, 'We need to know when you last saw
your husband, Mrs Cassidy. It might help us to fix the time
of his death more clearly, you see. At the moment, we cannot
be certain of that.'

'Why? When was he found?'

He smiled, not unkindly. 'You mustn't answer our questions with questions of your own, I'm afraid. That isn't the
way this works.'

'I'm sorry. Friday night was the last time I saw him. I
brought the children down to say goodbye in their pyjamas.
It must have been between half past seven and eight o'clock,
I think.' She watched the black man making a note. He seemed
to write very quickly, but the ball-pen looked ridiculously
small in his huge and powerful hand.

Peach nodded and said, 'Do you know where he was going?'

'He was going away for the weekend on a shooting party.
I can't tell you exactly where that was to be. The Border
country, I think he said. I – I expect he'd have rung me on
his mobile when he got there.'

Northcott spoke for the first time, his voice deep, brown,
somehow reassuring. 'And did he ring you during the evening,
Mrs Cassidy?'

'No. But he never got there, did he?'

For a moment, Peach thought she was going to break down.
From the puffing around the eyes in the oval, attractive face,
he knew that she had been weeping and that her control was
brittle. He said gently, 'He didn't, no. Weren't you disturbed
by that? Didn't you think of contacting the police when you
didn't hear from him?'

She managed a wan smile. 'Adam didn't always do what
you expected or what he'd said he'd do. I just thought he was
enjoying his weekend and the company up there. He was really
looking forward to it. He'd bought himself a new shotgun and

he was as excited as a kid about it. Men are like that, aren't they? They always keep a bit of the boy inside them – sometimes quite a lot of the boy. Not many women are like that.'

Clyde Northcott said, 'Do you remember the make of this new shotgun?'

She frowned. 'I'm afraid I don't. I'm not very interested in these things. I've never shot things myself and I never will . . . Oh, I think I remember now. A Purdey, I think. I have heard that name before. He told me it was the best you could buy. Did you find – find it with him where he died?'

If she was acting this, she was doing it very well. But Peach remembered ruefully that a highly competent actress was exactly what Jane Cassidy was: he could remember watching her on the box as Jane Webster. 'The Purdey shotgun has been recovered, yes. I'm afraid we will not be able to release it for a considerable time.'

She shook her head sharply, her dark-blonde hair fluttering with the vigour of the movement. 'I don't want ever to see that gun again.'

There was no doubt about her vehemence, but she hadn't asked whether the Purdey had been the instrument of his death. He wondered if she already knew the answer to that. 'This is difficult for me as well as for you, but the situation demands it. I have to ask you about the state of your relationship with your husband at the time of his death.'

She supposed she should have been annoyed, should perhaps have bridled at this intrusion into the intimacy of their marriage. Instead, Jane felt curiously detached. It was the only matter she had thought about before they came here. She said as evenly as she could, 'I understand why you have to ask that. You want to know if I was desperately unhappy, if I had a motive for killing Adam. Well, I'm sorry if it disappoints you, but we were perfectly happy. He was busy, of course. In our business, where so many people are "resting" for long periods, you welcome that. But the more successful you are, the more calls there are upon your time. He couldn't spend as much time with me and the children as we both wanted him to, but as an actress myself, I understood why that was.'

'He'd just finished a series of the Alec Dawson tales, hadn't he?'

She wondered if beneath the studiously neutral tone there

lurked the contempt for the improbabilities in the Alec Dawson tales of derring-do which she'd expect from professional policemen. 'He had, yes. We were hoping to get away for a holiday, some time after Christmas.'

'But you weren't disappointed that he was going to be away for the whole of the weekend?'

He was quietly insistent beneath the politeness. It wouldn't do to underestimate this man, she decided. 'I wasn't, no. I knew how excited he was about the shooting, which is quite a new hobby for him. These opportunities aren't available to you all the time, as he said. He needed to wind down, after a period of hectic work. And he'd have been with us all for Christmas, which is far more important.'

Perhaps the lady doth protest too much, thought Peach. He looked away from her for a moment, round the huge room with its expensive, brand-new furnishings. 'It's a beautiful spot this, and you have built a splendid home here. I walked a lot round here as a boy. Don't you find it a little quiet, after a busy life as an actress?'

Again the wan smile, her face looking even whiter with the golden hair falling across it. 'We built here because it *was* quiet. Adam is – was – a very well-known face. You not only treasure your privacy, you need it. I'm not complaining, and neither did he, because that sort of exposure also makes you very rich. We were able to build this place and have more or less anything we wanted. We chose it because the Trough of Bowland and the whole area to the west of it is, as you said, a beautiful place.'

It was a well-argued explanation. It was delivered so convincingly that Peach could not be sure whether it was prepared to conceal the sort of loneliness he had met before in women isolated with young children after leading a busy professional life. Perhaps it was a reply she had delivered to other people who had asked similar questions. He nodded and said, 'But you've seen very little of your husband over the last few months.'

'No. I didn't expect to. That's the advantage of being in the business, as I said. You understand that there will be periods of intense activity. You are grateful for them, when you see what it brings for you.'

He saw her face closing with her repetition of this sentiment. If she was concealing anything about her own life, he wasn't going to prise it from her today. He said quietly, apolo-

getically, 'Are you aware of any complications in your
husband's life?'

She was quiet for a moment. He had thought she might
allow herself the relief of anger. Instead, she said wearily,
'You mean did he have other women on the go, don't you?
Do you expect me to answer a question like that?'

'I mean did he have anything at all which might compli-
cate what you have already told us was a very busy life. And
yes, I do expect you to answer, because I expect you to want
to give us anything which might eventually lead us to the
person who killed him.'

It was his first direct acknowledgement that this was murder
or manslaughter. You tried to skate round the brutality of
violent death, if you could. But this young widow seemed
unaffected by the idea. She nodded slowly two or three times,
as if accepting the logic of his arguments. 'A handsome,
successful actor like Adam is constantly receiving sexual
offers, from men as well as women. I knew that when I married
him. I don't know where he's been for every minute of the
last six months, but I'm confident that there has been nothing
which threatens – threatened – our marriage.'

Clyde Northcott gave her his first smile. It transformed the
stern, dark features, as he made a note and thanked her for
her frankness. She watched the rapid movement of the pen in
the long fingers, then said rebukingly, 'If you are interested
in his movements, you need to know that Adam had an ageing
father in Brunton, whom he visited regularly.'

Northcott noted the address and that of the deceased's brother,
Luke Cassidy. He was aware that Luke had by now identified
the body, but he thought it better not to remind the widow of
that melancholy necessity. Then he said in that persuasive, dark-
brown voice, 'Do you know of anyone who might have wished
ill against Adam, Mrs Cassidy? Anyone who has had a serious
difference with him in the last year, say?'

They were a good combination, these two, she decided.
They had both given every sign of respecting her grief, but
she was sure that Peach had been probing to detect whether
she had other men in her life and then whether Adam had
been putting it about. Now this man was broadening the field
of suspects. They were determined to take as much as they
could from a meeting which had been put to her as merely a

segment of police routine. 'You'll need to question others about that. As I say, I haven't seen a lot of Adam in the last few months. I know he was planning to change his agent. I know that passions occasionally run high in the theatre and television, when people don't get the parts they want. It's a highly precarious business. Disappointments are accentuated by that. Adam wanted to switch off and enjoy his family life when he was away from the studio or location filming, which I understood. But it also means that I know nothing of any quarrels that might have occurred in the recent past. The people he's been working with might be able to tell you something about that. But I'm sure you'll find nothing which would be serious enough to warrant killing him.'

It was a long speech and she looked at the end of her resources. Peach flicked a look at Northcott, then said, 'Thank you for being so helpful, Mrs Cassidy. We'll keep you in touch with developments. And we shall probably need to speak to you again in a few days, when we know more about this.'

She rose and accompanied them to the front door, where she stood watching until they had swung the car round and disappeared between the high brick gateposts.

Northcott had driven a slow mile through the lanes before Peach said, 'You did well in there, Clyde. The best thing to aim at is to be a complementary team. It's not always just good-cop, bad-cop; you have to play it by ear. I'll need you to be a hard bastard at times – I know you can do that. At other times, like this morning, you need to seem sympathetic. Perhaps even to be genuinely sympathetic, if it helps us to get the information we need.'

Clyde knew that the DCI was thinking of that very different presence which had been beside him the last three years, Lucy Blake. Good to know that the much-feared and much-admired Percy Peach could be a sentimental old sod, at times. But Clyde had far too much sense to voice that thought.

They had gone another half-mile before Peach said, 'The first interview with the spouse of the victim is always difficult. You want to learn everything you can, but you can only push a grieving wife so far. She seemed a nice woman, Jane Cassidy. I wonder how deep her grief really goes.'

# TWELVE

Joe Hartley, the director of the Alec Dawson series, had been in the business for a long time. He had cut his teeth on documentaries, served three years as an assistant director on *Coronation Street*, directed a couple of moderately successful sitcoms, then confirmed his status and greatly increased his salary over the four series of *Call Alec Dawson*. Despite his proven talent, Joe was an unprepossessing figure. He was a little below average height, thin-limbed and scrawny rather than slim. His hair was straight, grey and thinning rapidly and his nose was a little crooked; it had been badly set after an accident in his last year at school forty years ago. His small grey eyes missed very little; they were set deep, behind silver-rimmed spectacles, in a face which was now deeply lined.

Few things in television could surprise Joe Hartley any more. But this was reality, not television. He had never before been interviewed by the police in a murder case. He was nervous and it showed.

Peach did nothing to ease the strain. A man on edge was likely to reveal much more than one who was relaxed and unthreatened – particularly when it came to those things he would rather conceal. The DCI nodded towards an unsmiling Clyde Northcott. 'We're here in connection with the death of your big star. Mr Hartley, I'm told you're the man who can tell us most about his life in the last few months.'

'I know nothing about this awful thing. I'm just a professional associate of Adam's. I stand to lose by this, not gain by it. I don't suppose we'll make another series, without our star.'

Peach's very black eyebrows rose towards the baldness of his pate, more eloquent than any words. 'No one is suggesting you killed him, Mr Hartley. Not yet, anyway. I've merely been directed to you as a source of information. I'm told you are the man with what my chief superintendent calls "an overview" of the situation. You can tell me about who liked Cassidy and who disliked him; about his relationships with you and the rest of your cast. About his sexual preferences and how they manifested themselves.'

Hartley looked very doubtful. 'So long as it's understood that I had nothing to do with this – that I'm just giving you information.'

Peach leaned even closer to him, making Joe wish that the office they had been allocated for this meeting was not so small and cramped. 'Nothing is understood at present, Mr Hartley. Not until we know much more about what happened to your star.' He leaned back again and smiled, making Joe very conscious of a full set of healthy white teeth. 'But if you've nothing to hide, then you've nothing to fear from us. Can't say fairer than that, can I?'

'I suppose not. But are you sure that Adam was murdered?'

'We are, yes. Even though it's not been officially announced yet. There you are, you see! I'm volunteering information to you already, when I should be gathering it in. Sometimes I think I'm too soft-hearted altogether for this job. DS Northcott here often tells me that I am.'

As Joe looked automatically at the big man, the long black face nodded solemnly. The dark eyes studied Hartley for a moment as if he were a specimen beneath a microscope. Then Northcott said, 'When did you last see the victim, Mr Hartley?'

'Last Friday. About three o'clock. But you surely can't think that I had—'

'Did he seem his normal self then, or in any way upset?' Clyde did not even look up from his notebook to reassure his man. DCI Peach congratulated himself on a wise choice in his newly promoted sergeant.

'His normal self, I think. He was looking forward to his weekend. Looking forward to the next few weeks, I think, when he'd have had time to himself before we began filming the new series.'

'Looking forward to his weekend.' Clyde echoed the words slowly as he wrote them down. Then he looked hard into Hartley's eyes. 'Did he tell you what he proposed to do in this weekend he was so looking forward to?'

'No. Not that I can remember.'

'And you surely would remember, as it's so recent and you're a man used to having to remember things.' This was Peach again, just as Joe was priming himself to address the tall man beside him. 'A drama director has a lot of things to remember, I should think. He must get to know the men and women he directs quite intimately, as the weeks become months and the pressure on everyone increases. I think you're the best person to give us the names of the people Cassidy worked with most closely.'

Joe reeled them off, glad to be able to offer something to this formidable pair as evidence of his good faith. DS Northcott wrote seven names down in his notebook, with the odd detail about the importance of their roles which Hartley volunteered to him. Then Peach said sharply, 'Which of these people had cause to dislike Adam Cassidy, Joe?'

Joe tried not to conjecture what this first use of his forename might imply. He licked his lips and said, 'There are always things flying about among a cast working intensively together. We try to foster an ensemble attitude in our actors, because we think team playing is important when they've been brought together for a series. Emotions run high and the degree of friendship varies. But I'm sure no one hated Adam enough to kill him.'

'Did I mention hate, Joe? I think I used the word "dislike". Important that. Briefs don't like you twisting their words, when you're in court. Be best if you just tell us everything you know, and let us worry about the degree of dislike.'

Joe didn't at all like the mention of briefs and courts. 'Yes, I can see what you mean. And I must emphasize that I only saw what went on when we were rehearsing and filming. I make it a policy to know as little as possible about what goes on in people's private lives.'

'Do you, indeed? Pity, that, from our point of view. We'd like you to be able to come straight out and tell us who blew Adam Cassidy almost in two. But I suppose if you can't, you can't.' He made it sound as though it was a highly suspicious omission on the director's part.

Joe was anxious now to offer them everything he could. 'Two of the people I've mentioned had good reason to be . . . well, to be, shall we say, disappointed with Adam.'

'Shall we say "disappointed" or not, Joe? I'm in your hands, here. You're the only one in possession of the facts.'

This man was unlike any policeman in the limited range Joe Hartley had met before. When James Walton had said that these people wanted to speak to him, he had expected it to be quiet and sympathetic. He had half-expected them to be deferential, in view of his status as a major director. Now he was terrified of missing out anything which might prove significant, which might lead this man with the sharp black eyes which never left Joe's face to come back and accuse him of concealment. He said hastily, hearing the tremor in his voice, 'I'd better tell you everything I know, and let you decide what to make of it.'

Now Peach almost purred behind his sudden smile. 'Much the best policy, Joe, as I think I indicated to you at the outset. Let *us* follow up these little disagreements. Let *us* see whether they grew into hate when people were away from the set. We shan't even reveal the source of our information when we speak to the parties involved.'

Hartley took a deep breath. He was now pathetically anxious to convince them that he was being absolutely honest. 'Dean Morley was an old friend of Adam's. He'd appeared in the last episode of the *Call Alec Dawson* series we've just completed. The producer and I had him in mind for a major role in the next series. He was going to be the master-villain who controls all the people operating against Alec. That way he would have been in every episode.'

'Would have been, Joe?'

'Yes. The plans were changed. Dean wasn't going to get that part, after all.'

'I see. And who changed the plans?'

'Adam Cassidy did. Stars don't cast people, but they have the right of veto over casting. Adam asserted that right.'

'I see. Did Morley know about this?'

'Yes. James Walton, our producer, has overall responsibility for casting. He said it was only fair to let people know as quickly as possible that they weren't going to be involved, so as to give them the chance to look for other work.'

'You said "people". Were there others involved in losing parts they thought they'd secured?'

Hartley gave a little sigh, as if lamenting the foolishness of human behaviour. 'There was one. The woman we'd thought ideal for the female lead in the next series, Michelle Davies. Adam suddenly said he didn't want her.'

DS Northcott made a note of this second name, then said,

'From what you say, Cassidy seems to have gone along with these changes initially.'

Joe paused, wanting to get this exactly right; he needed to be rid of this formidable pair, once and for all. 'I don't think he'd given his formal approval. Things don't work that way; actors normally leave the producer to get everything in place for the next series. But a kind of tradition has grown up that the star can intervene if he really objects to someone. No one thinks it's a good system, but it's a fact of life. Everyone knows that once the lead actor in a series becomes a well-known face to the millions who watch it, the whole thing falls apart if he decides to withdraw. So he accumulates powers over casting which he never had at the outset. In the great days of Hollywood, the studio bosses controlled the stars. In British television, it's the star players who have the power – sometimes to make and break careers. For the last two series, Adam Cassidy has had the right to veto casting built into his contract.'

Peach frowned. 'So Mr Walton had to tell both Dean Morley and Michelle Davies that they weren't going to get the leading roles they had expected. Did he tell them that it was Mr Cassidy who had made this decision?'

'I'm sure he did. James was furious with Adam for forcing his hand when we both thought everything was decided. We spoke afterwards and he said that both Dean and Michelle had virtually been told they were in and were delighted about it. James was furious because he felt he'd been undermined. He'd every intention of letting both Dean and Michelle know just who it was who had dumped them.'

'Do you know when he told them?'

'Yes. He said he had to tell them in person and as quickly as possible. He had them both in to his office on Thursday morning of last week.'

Clyde Northcott made a careful note of that, then said thoughtfully, 'About thirty-six hours before Adam Cassidy was last seen alive.'

It was twelve thirty before Jane Cassidy finally managed to make contact. 'I've been trying to get you all morning. Ever since the CID men left.'

Her voice was nervous, resentful, almost accusing. He said,

'Calm down, Jane. I've been out and about on the farm. I told you I would be.'

'You could have taken your mobile with you. You knew they were coming here at ten.'

'I did, yes. But I never take my mobile when I'm working in the fields or in the shippon. My workers know that; they know that I don't like being interrupted on the farm. We have to follow the routines we normally do, until the police arrest someone for this. That's what we agreed. We don't want to attract suspicion. I knew you'd get me on the landline if I came home for lunch. There's only me here.'

A short pause. He could hear her breathing, could picture that look of wide-eyed concentration, that slight furrowing of her forehead which was so attractive to him. Then she said, 'You're right. I'm sorry. It's just that I'm more on edge than I expected to be. It was quite an ordeal. And you're the only one I can talk to.'

'So how did it go?'

Now that she had managed to contact him at last, she realized that she hadn't much to say, beyond the fact that it was over. 'All right, I think. They wanted to know when I last saw him. They'd found his Purdey shotgun – whether in the car or beside his body, they didn't say. I don't think they know yet exactly when he died. But I might be wrong about that: they don't give much away.'

'What else did they ask?'

'If I knew of any enemies he had. I said I wasn't in touch with the people he'd been working with. Which is true enough. He's shut me out of his life pretty effectively over the last year or so.'

'And let me into it.'

'I suppose so. Except that I like to think you'd have been part of my life, however Adam had behaved.'

He was silent for a moment, wondering how far her husband's neglect of her had contributed to her turning towards him. 'Did you tell him that Adam was fond of putting it about?'

'I think I suggested it. But I didn't have to, really. They were looking for anything and anyone who might have had reason to hate him. Don't the police say that sex and money are the motives behind most crimes?'

'I think they do, yes.' He gave a small, mirthless chuckle. 'Which is why we have to be careful, isn't it?'

'I suppose so. I think that at one point they were suggesting I might have been bored here and looking for diversions, but I didn't give them anything.'

'Attagirl! I can just see you looking puzzled and innocent! You're a cracking actress, and you'd do it so much better than I could.'

'It's different when you're acting for real. But I think it was OK. They didn't really press me. But they said they might be back to see me again when they knew more.'

'I expect that's part of their routine. I shouldn't worry about it.'

'I feel very lonely. I'll be glad when the children come home from school and demand my attention.'

'I want to hold you in my arms, my darling, to feel your fingers on my back! But we mustn't see each other for a while.'

'No.' Jane sighed heavily. 'I can see why, but that doesn't make it any easier. Let's hope they arrest someone soon.' She blew a little kiss into the phone. She enjoyed being silly and childish again, with the right person.

'We'll speak again tomorrow. Same time? I'll make sure I'm here.'

Paul Barnes put down the phone and stared at it thoughtfully for a few seconds.

When a citizen becomes a murder victim, lists of his associates are quickly compiled and fed into computers. Principally through cross-referencing, modern technology can throw up matters of interest which in the past might have taken weeks to emerge. When a victim has the public prominence of Adam Cassidy, these lists of people who have connections with the deceased can quickly become so long that there is a danger of careful police work becoming counter-productive.

DCI Peach, scanning a catalogue of names and functions which was lengthening alarmingly, lighted upon one which prompted his immediate attention. He collected Clyde Walcott and drove the thirty miles to Manchester swiftly.

The block letter capitals stretched black and bold across the full width of the frosted glass door. TONY VALENTO.

THEATRICAL AGENT. Peach paused for a moment before he turned the handle. He said in a low voice to his companion, 'You might need to be the hard bastard here, DC Northcott. I need you to protect me from my easy-going nature.'

In the outer office, the PA uncrossed long legs from beneath a very short black skirt and looked at them doubtfully. She said coldly, 'Mr Valento doesn't take people on unless they already have considerable experience in theatre or television. He normally prefers to make his own contacts with people in the profession rather than have people approach him.'

'He'll see an old acquaintance like me, love.' As her mouth opened to protest, Peach brandished his warrant card before her blue-lidded eyes. Clyde Northcott sprang forward on cue to line his own card up beside his chief's. Peach grinned. 'I take DS Northcott around with me in case things get violent. But he's a softy, when people are reasonable. He enjoys his tea and biscuits, when people are kind enough to provide them.'

The PA spoke in a low voice into the intercom. She did not trouble to conceal her disappointment as she said, 'Mr Valento will see you now, Detective Chief Inspector.'

Peach already had his hand upon the door. 'Long time no see, Tony!' he said as he flung it open. 'Can't say that's been a disappointment, though.' His smile said that this sort of meeting was much more to his taste than the one he had conducted with a grieving widow earlier in the day.

'What the hell do you want, Peach?'

'And a good afternoon to you, Tony! I think you know very well what I'm here for.'

'I haven't a bloody clue, mate. And time's money. So spit it out.'

Peach took the seat he had not been offered and gestured to Northcott to take the one beside him. He looked round at the pictures of show business luminaries, past and present, which lined the walls, presumably because they were clients of Valento. Only then did his attention switch back to the big man with the black curly hair and olive skin who sat behind the desk. 'Adam Cassidy. Sometime client of yours. Recently became an ex-client, as you learned a week ago. Now also a murder victim. Are these three things a random series of events, or is there a logical progression in them? That is what I have to ask myself.'

'Don't be fucking daft, Peach!'

Percy's smile grew wider. 'You've written that down, DC Northcott? Not a formal cassette-recorded interview, this, but we might wish to recall Mr Valento's tone and attitude at some future date. As a citizen anxious to help the police with their enquiries, he doesn't seem wholly cooperative.' He glanced at the door to the outer office. 'And we wouldn't want important clients with delicate ears to hear unseemly words, would we? Ah, here comes the tea. What friendly and thoughtful staff you have, Mr Valento!'

Tony Valento glared his disapproval at the girl as she set the tray with china crockery on his desk; Peach and Northcott beamed quietly at the rear view of short skirt and long legs. Percy sprang to his feet as the PA closed the door firmly behind her. 'Shall I be mother, Tony? It's no trouble, really it isn't.' He poured the tea with elaborate care.

Valento glared at the cup and saucer set in front of him and shook his head angrily when offered the biscuits. 'You're wasting your time here, Peach.'

'I'm glad to hear it, Tony. If we could eliminate you from this enquiry, it would be a major step forward.'

'I can tell you exactly where I was at the time of this death.'

Clyde Northcott looked up from his notebook and spoke for the first time. 'And when would that be, Mr Valento?'

The agent realized immediately that he'd made a mistake. Until this moment Peach, the man he'd clashed with years ago, had taken all his attention. Now he looked into the black, unsmiling face with the unblinking brown eyes and the faint scar at the top of the left cheekbone. More the sort of face he was used to dealing with, this, among the heavy muscle he and his associates used when they needed it. He said, 'I'm willing to tell you where I was on Friday night. That's what you want to know about isn't it?'

Clyde allowed himself a slow smile. 'Is it, Mr Valento? You tell us. We haven't established a time of death yet. We're still waiting for the PM report and forensics to tell us that. So how would an innocent man like you know so much more than them?'

'I don't know, you black dumbo! It's just that from what they said on television, it seemed to me—'

'Whoa, Tony! Stop it right there.' Peach's amiable tone was

gone. 'Seems we're going to have to add racialist abuse to obscene epithets and unhelpful attitude. Won't make a good impression on a judge, these things. Not when he takes into account your previous record.'

'It's not going to come in front of any fucking judge, because there won't be any bloody charges, Peach.'

The big man didn't sound as confident of that as he meant to. The olive forehead was now oily with sweat, but he couldn't give the man on the other side of his desk the satisfaction of seeing him wipe it. Peach nibbled a chocolate digestive thoughtfully, took a sip of his tea, and said, 'Tell us how you know when Cassidy died, will you, please? In your own time – wouldn't like to hurry you on something as important as this.'

'I'm sure they said Friday night on radio or television. I'm sure I'm right.'

'Oh, I'm sure you're right as well, Tony. I'd put a week's wages on it being Friday night, now that you've told us. But none of the bulletins included that information, because we didn't know it ourselves when they were issued.'

Valento said from beneath a thunderous brow, 'I must have just assumed it. It must have seemed the likeliest time, from what I heard. I wasn't paying a lot of attention.'

Peach's amusement returned to him with that remark. 'Not paying a lot of attention, Tony? When hearing about the death of your most valuable and high-profile client? Or rather, ex-client. You didn't take kindly to his switch of agents, did you?'

Valento silently cursed himself for the threats against Cassidy he had issued in his phone conversation with that smooth bugger Mark Gilbey, who had poached Cassidy from him. He said sullenly, 'I can get along without Cassidy. I got the bastard everything he had and he sold himself on without even consulting me. But we're big enough not to need him.'

'Maybe, but treachery hurts, doesn't it? And you're not used to it, are you, Tony? You're used to responding with violence when anyone upsets you; we know that from our previous dealings with you. This killing will certainly encourage others to think twice before deserting you, won't it?'

'You never proved anything against me, Peach! Never even got me into court.'

'But we could have proved it, and you knew it. Cost you

best part of a million pounds to prevent those two giving evidence against you six years ago, I'm told.'

'They're in Marbella now, having a good laugh at you.'

'Must be quite an unsavoury place, Marbella, with the number of villains sitting beside those expensive swimming pools. I expect you'd feel at home there.'

'I didn't kill Adam Cassidy. I can account for my movements for the whole of Friday night and Saturday, so I'm out of the frame whenever he died.'

'Can you, indeed? Almost suspicious that, a man having an alibi for such a long period. Doesn't often happen with innocent people. But I'm sure you're right about it, Tony, if you say so. Doesn't get you off the hook, though, does it?'

'Of course it does. I'm telling you that I can demonstrate that I couldn't possibly have done this killing.'

Peach set his cup and saucer back on the tray, then wiped his mouth delicately on the paper napkin provided. He smiled contentedly. 'That's not your way, though, is it? We know from previous experience that you don't do anything as sordid and obvious as killing for yourself. You employ people to do that sort of work for you.'

'I didn't use a hit man on Cassidy.'

'I'm glad to hear it, Tony. But I'm sure you wouldn't expect us simply to accept that. Not from a man with your record. We'll get a formal statement from you about your whereabouts at the time of this death, once it's definitely established. But we shall also investigate the whereabouts and the movements of people you have employed in the past to eliminate men who have displeased you. Hit men, as professionals like you and me call them. Don't leave the area without letting us know your new address, will you?'

They departed as abruptly as they had arrived. Tony Valento was more shaken than he cared to admit to his PA. He took a few minutes to collect himself before he picked up the phone.

The death of Adam Cassidy was the lead item on the six o'clock news bulletins on both television and radio. There were snippets of scenes from his work, most of them showing him as the man-of-action hero, triumphing over evil against the odds.

The word 'murder' was used for the first time. Chief

Superintendent Tucker, the man in charge of Brunton CID, said that although no one was at present helping police with their enquiries, he was confident of an early arrest, in what he recognized was a case of national, even international, interest. He jutted his chin towards the camera and said that he was determined that the man or woman responsible for this despicable crime would not get away with the brutal murder of a well-loved national figure.

Tucker's image was a little undermined by the news editor, who chose to follow his statement with a clip from a recent edition of the *The Gerry Clancy Show* on afternoon television. This purported to show the dead actor's sense of humour and his concern with the wider issues of life. In reality, the item had a nice, understated paradox for any viewer who chose to see it. Adam Cassidy was making a fool of Tucker, the same senior policeman who was now directing the investigation into his sudden and violent death.

The irony was not lost on the person who had killed Cassidy. But more important to the murderer was the fact that as yet the police had clearly come upon nothing vital.

# THIRTEEN

Dean Morley looked more than his forty-seven years. Perhaps that was because he was nervous, Clyde Northcott thought. In his early days in CID, he had considered anxiety a possible indication of guilt. Now he realized that everyone who is interviewed in connection with a serious crime is nervous and that sometimes the most innocent people are the most nervous of all. But perhaps it might just be that actors were naturally nervous at nine fifteen in the morning, being more naturally creatures of the evening and the night.

If Percy Peach was given to such esoteric musings, he gave no sign of it on the steps of the big late-Victorian house. 'Dean Morley? I'm Detective Chief Inspector Peach and this is Detective Sergeant Northcott.'

Morley glanced at his watch. 'You come most carefully upon your hour.'

'Even a minute or two early, I suspect,' said Peach affably. 'We don't often get greeted with the opening of *Hamlet*.'

'You must forgive me. My first few lines in the theatre were as a sentry in *Hamlet*.' If Morley was surprised by a policeman who recognized his quotation, he gave no sign of it. He led them through a shabby hall with a strip of worn carpet down the middle and opened a wide oak door. The room beyond it was a surprise to the CID men. It was beautifully decorated, in a combination of very pale green and cream which not many people would have selected but which seemed to fit perfectly with the high walls and spacious dimensions. With its wide Yorkshire stone bay window, the room now recalled the Victorian heyday of this house. A large white glass light-fitting was adorned with delicate pink flowers. There was a print of Monet's garden over the big fireplace. The other paintings in the room looked like originals; there were three oil paintings and five smaller watercolours.

Peach surveyed the room automatically, looking as always for anything it might say about its occupants. He said conventionally, 'Nice room, this,' and meant it.

'You can compliment Keith on that,' said Morley. 'The paintings are his, apart from the print, and he decorated the place a fortnight ago.'

He had spoken with genuine pride. As if entering on cue, a man emerged from a door on the other side of the room and stood awkwardly, like a child accepting praise but not sure how to react to it. His diffidence seemed more ridiculous as he was six feet tall, with rapidly receding hair and shiny black leather jacket. He said, 'They were good houses, these, when they were built. They've gone downhill since they were split up into flats. I'm Keith Arnold, by the way; I live here with Dean.' He looked from Peach to Northcott, and actually recoiled a few inches as he confronted the big man. Then he said to Morley, 'I must be off to the gallery, Dean. I'm on duty at ten.' He nodded briefly to Peach, ignored Northcott completely, and disappeared into the hall. They heard the front door close behind him and watched him march quickly past the police Mondeo outside.

'Doesn't like cops,' said Peach thoughtfully. 'I wonder what he has to hide.'

'Cops don't like us,' said Morley in prompt defence of his partner. 'They don't have much time for puffs. Some of them are not averse to the odd kicking to declare it.' He glanced speculatively at the formidable figure who towered above him and Peach.

'A prejudice from the past, Mr Morley. And you shouldn't use that word, you know. Leastways, I suppose you can call yourselves whatever you like, but we mustn't use it. If it's of any interest to you, the only time I've seen DS Northcott use violence recently was in making the arrest of four yobboes who were beating up three men outside a gay club. He's a hard bastard – don't make any mistake about that. But he's generally on the right side, nowadays.'

Clyde, who thought it was high time he was allowed to speak for himself, said briskly, 'We're here because we're investigating the death of Adam Cassidy.'

'Yes. And I'm anxious to answer your questions and be done with it,' said Dean firmly.

'Friend of yours, was he, Mr Cassidy?' said Peach.

Dean didn't hurry into his reply. Anyone of his sexual persuasion had brushed often with the police over the last thirty years; one of the things he had taught himself was not to rush into hasty statements. 'Yes. I suppose you could say he was, until quite recently. I helped him to get his first part in the theatre and recommended him for others. Took what you might call a fatherly interest in him, until his looks and his luck took him out of my sphere.'

Not his talent, Peach noticed: Morley hadn't mentioned that. 'You must have been gratified to watch his progress?'

Dean smiled, recognizing the guarded nature of the question as a response to his own caution. 'I was. It's always good to see people you've known as youngsters doing well. Ours is a precarious business, but we all know that and accept it, I suppose. More fool us for staying in it, as Keith tells me when I go on about it.'

Peach glanced round at the paintings. 'Your partner is an artist. Another overcrowded profession.'

'And full of even more phoneys. Keith has a part-time job as curator at the art gallery, but he earns a pittance. He's a good painter, as far as I can tell. Other people who know a lot more than me about art tell me that he is. But getting established in art is even more difficult than in the theatre. You need to mount your own exhibition, and unless you have money or a rich patron, it's almost impossible to do that.'

He was eager to talk about his partner. Peach pulled him back to the reason why they were here. 'But you're doing quite well in your own profession. That must be a help to you.'

Dean was immediately cautious. 'I suppose I've done well enough, over the last ten or fifteen years. Television's been good for me. I've never had a star part, but I've had a series of small roles, which means that I've been able to keep working. But there's no guarantee those parts won't dry up. There's always another generation of young actors coming along. Always someone anxious to take the part you thought was yours. Dog-eat-dog is the nature of the business, now that the old repertory theatres have closed down. Not many of us can aspire to the National Theatre or the Royal Shakespeare Company, where subsidy gives them a little more latitude.'

He was talking too much, trying to postpone the questions he must surely know were coming to him. Peach said bluntly, 'But you thought you had a big role lined up in the next series of *Call Alec Dawson*, didn't you?'

Morley's face set itself into a cautious mask. 'I thought I

had the part nailed down, yes. But as I said, you learn to take nothing for granted in our game.'

There was a pause whilst DS Northcott made his first note. He looked up at Morley and said, 'Tell us about your relationship with Adam Cassidy, please.'

Dean was more intimidated by the big black man than he cared to acknowledge, even to himself. Perhaps that made him give them more than he had intended. 'As I say, I'd known Adam since he started in the business. I was only five years older than him, but I fancy it felt much more than that to both of us then. Once I'd got him his first part, I helped him through his first months in a theatre. They can be pretty hard when you're the new boy.'

'Was Cassidy gay?'

'No.' His face set again, but as the seconds stretched, it was he who had to speak. 'All right, I sounded him out. He was quite a looker, and even more so when he was twenty-two.' For a moment, he pictured Adam's brusque late-night rejection of the pass he had made, when they were the last ones left in the green room after a performance. Such incidents seemed to him now that he had Keith in his life to belong to a different and more tawdry world. 'It didn't upset Adam – there are lots of gays in the profession and I'm sure he'd choked off plenty of others before me.'

Peach came in again now; Dean was sure that they were working as a partnership against him, but he couldn't work out quite how. 'You're telling us that you went on helping Adam Cassidy, despite finding he wasn't of your sexual persuasion.'

Dean forced a smile. 'You work all the time with people who are not "of your sexual persuasion", as you put it. Work is probably easier when you haven't got emotional attachments. It didn't stop me giving Adam all the help I could, in his early years.'

'But only in those early years?'

Dean smiled ruefully. 'Not at all, Mr Peach. It's no use trying to trip me up that way. We remained close friends, but after those first few years, Adam had little further need of my assistance. The work was there for him, the parts got bigger. I gave him advice when he asked for it, but he didn't need me to speak up for him to get work any more.'

'I see. And by the time of his death, he was in a position to return a few favours, I believe.'

'I didn't think of it like that. I knew I could do the part of this major villain who would oppose him throughout the next series. It was the director and the producer who wanted me for it, and they know their business. I knew I was right for the role, but it gives you confidence when hardened professionals like Joe Hartley and James Walton say they want you.'

'It was a big break for you, wasn't it, this part?'

Dean, who had told Keith last night that he was going to give the CID as little as he could, found now that he wanted to explain himself. 'It was a big part in a successful series. The one I needed. At forty-seven, I may not get another chance of something as big as this.'

'Big money?'

'It would have paid five times as much for each episode as I've ever been paid before. Plus repeat fees around the world.' He looked at the door through which his partner had disappeared, then at the two very different but equally attentive faces. 'You pretend that money doesn't matter, when you're starting in the business. But that attitude gets worn down over the years. When you come here, you see a couple of ageing queers making the best of things in a rundown flat. But Keith Arnold is the love of my life, DCI Peach. I don't think either of us will want anyone else for the rest of our lives. But money is more important as you get older and Keith earns very little. I believe in him as an artist and I want him to go on trying to sell his paintings. This part would have made us secure. The role would have guaranteed us money and removed any uncertainties about our future together.'

He spoke defiantly, like a man proud to assert his allegiance to Keith Arnold. Probably he had not had many opportunities to proclaim it publicly before. It was left to Peach to say quietly, 'You do realize that you are declaring a perfect motive for murder?'

Dean Morley forced a smile he could not feel. He had not intended to declare anything of the sort. He had intended to keep this interview low-key and unemotional, to behave as if the loss of this role was no more than par for the course, the sort of thing he had met many times before. Well, it was out now; at least he hadn't been mealy-mouthed or evasive with them. He felt a strange need to make everything clear, to tell them exactly how strongly this had affected him and how badly he felt about Cassidy's part in it. 'The part was mine, you know. Not only was it right up my street, but I'd had it confirmed by Joe Hartley and James Walton, the people doing the casting, that the job was mine. It was Cassidy who changed everything, when he asserted his right of veto over casting.'

'Have you any idea why he did that? Had you had some sort of row with him?'

'No. We got on as well as we'd always done.' He paused for a moment, motivated again by the need to make the justice of his case clear to them. 'Adam did say a week or two ago that I shouldn't take things for granted. Perhaps it was just a power thing. Actors can be very childish, you know. When they become stars – which Adam certainly had done – they sometimes want to stamp their feet and assert themselves, to see how far their new power extends. It's childish, but the effects on smaller people like me can be dire.'

Clyde Northcott cleared his throat, then said quietly, 'Where were you overnight on Friday, Mr Morley?'

'Was that when he was killed? I was here with Keith. Throughout the evening and through the night. We often go out on a Friday, but he wanted to finish a painting – he'd not been able to get on with it because he'd been busy decorating this room.'

Too much detail, perhaps. The answer had come very promptly, as if Morley had been anticipating the question. But perhaps he just wished to tell them about the deeds of his partner; people who supported partners financially were often anxious to convince you that they worked hard and earned their keep. Northcott made a note of these details: it would be necessary to check out the alibi with the absent Keith Arnold. This was going to be like a wife's corroboration of a suspect's whereabouts: not necessarily believed by the police, but very difficult to disprove.

Peach studied his man intently for a moment, digesting the fact that what had always seemed likely to be a puzzling case now had an extra layer of complexity added to it by the fact that many of the people involved were professional actors. 'Did you kill Adam Cassidy, Mr Morley? If you did, it would be less harrowing for all of us if you admitted it this morning.'

Dean replied as calmly as the question had been put. 'No. I hear what you're saying about motive, but I'm not the murdering type.'

Sitting in the middle of this unexpectedly elegant room, with the original art on the walls, this slight, oddly dignified figure certainly seemed an unlikely killer. But he had been frank about his passion for his partner and his determination to make that secure. And passion often drives men to murder. Peach gave his man a small smile, inviting him for a moment to be on his side in the puzzle. 'Then who do you think did kill him?'

Morley did not give him the blank refusal which was the usual answer to this. 'I don't know. I've thought about it, not just to preserve my own skin, but because I was still quite fond of Adam, despite what he was doing to me. I know his wife, because she's in the business, but I've scarcely seen her for years. As you would guess from his looks and his success, Adam had lots of offers from other women, and he didn't refuse all of them. I can't give you any recent details, because as you've seen heterosexual affairs are not an interest of mine.' He paused for a moment, as if savouring this phrasing. 'How Jane would react to his playing away, you must decide for yourselves. Or how any women he used and discarded might react, for that matter. I'm afraid a man who rises as fast and as ruthlessly as Adam did in our profession makes many enemies, Mr Peach.'

He picked his words very carefully, his lips framing a little preciously what he had to deliver. They gave him the usual direction to get in touch with the Brunton CID if anything further occurred to him and left. Dean Morley stood in the big stone bay window and watched them go, as cool and unrevealing as he had been for most of the interview.

He would have been surprised if he had heard what the Detective Sergeant he had seen as an archetypal homophobic said as the pair drove away. Clyde Northcott negotiated a badly parked van at the corner of the road, then said to Peach, 'I know we have to keep an open mind about all the people we see, but I hope Dean Morley didn't do this. He seems a pretty decent man to me.'

The post-mortem and forensic reports gave the team what they had expected, plus a special precious piece of evidence which they hadn't.

The progress of rigor mortis in the corpse had been affected by the extremely low temperatures in which it had lain from the moment of death until its eventual discovery by the returning Stoke City football supporters on Saturday evening. However, the pathologist was satisfied that the fatal wound had been delivered some time between six p.m. and midnight on the night of Friday, the fourteenth of December. Police questioning had already established that Cassidy had been waved away from his home by his wife and children at around half past seven on that night. He could not have arrived at the lay-by beside which he was killed before nine o'clock. This left a time of death between nine and midnight. Assuming that he had driven straight to the site and been killed shortly afterwards, he had probably died between nine and nine thirty p.m.

This meant that the remains had lain undiscovered for around twenty-one hours after death. This was a result of two factors: first, the extreme weather conditions prevailing, which meant that many fewer vehicles than usual had used the parking bay; secondly, the fact that death had taken place some fifty-seven yards from the edge of the tarmac, more than most people would have cared to venture in frost and snow.

Peach looked up from the copies of the report which he and his two chosen colleagues from the team, DS Northcott and DC Murphy, had been reading. 'First question: did Cassidy pick up someone and take them to that place – almost certainly his killer – or did he meet someone there?'

Brendan Murphy, flattered to be selected as a member of this elect trio, was anxious to contribute. 'I think it's unlikely that if he'd picked someone up he'd have driven to that particular spot with them – unless of course he was forced at gunpoint to do so. I think it's much more likely that he'd arranged to meet someone there.'

Northcott said, 'I agree. Forensic say that whilst they can't be absolutely certain, they think it unlikely that anyone had sat in the passenger seat of the BMW on that night. The only material they have gathered from the vehicle is older than that.'

Peach nodded. 'Let's assume for the moment that our victim had arranged to meet someone there, or that someone contacted him whilst he was driving and asked for the meeting – the BMW like his other cars is equipped with a hands-free device, though his mobile was missing when forensic examined the car. That means he was almost certainly killed at nine o'clock or soon afterwards. And he was killed with his own shotgun. The Purdey was found within yards of him.'

'But the PM says no chance of suicide.'

'No. But we didn't expect that, did we, DC Murphy? Did you ever hear of a suicide blasting his chest apart with a shotgun? They invariably put the muzzle either in the mouth or against the temple. In any case, the weapon was too far away from the body for this to be self-administered. It's good that forensic are satisfied this was the weapon – it's not always easy with shotguns. But the SOCO found the cartridge case, and forensic are satisfied from the imprint of the firing-head on it that it came from the Purdey.'

Northcott said, 'Doesn't this eliminate hit men from the enquiry? They like to use their own weapons. The quick, anonymous bullet in the city back-alley is more their method.'

Peach smiled. No CID man wanted a killing by a hit man. They were the most expert and most anonymous of killers; experienced, unemotional and professional. You might know it was the crime of such a killer, might even suspect an actual culprit, but you very rarely secured the evidence to bring a hit man to court. 'We can't rule out a hit man – probably employed by Tony Valento, who we know has used such men before. A hit man is a clear-sighted opportunist. If he saw the chance of killing Cassidy with his own weapon, he would take it, whatever he had previously planned. That way there isn't even a bullet we can trace to a weapon. He leaves nothing of himself at the scene.'

Brendan Murphy said glumly, 'Whoever did this has left nothing of himself at the scene, it seems to me.'

Peach smiled again. At least he had two people working with him who were delighted to be at the heart of a murder case, rather than part of the more peripheral team, as they had been previously. 'Spoken with all the optimism of Tommy Bloody Tucker, that. You need to watch these Tucker tendencies, Brendan. This is the most high-profile victim we've ever had in a case, and our esteemed leader is duly shitting himself. Whereas we can be positive. We have a much more exact time of death than usual, and the instrument of that death in our hands. And forensic have come up with one unexpected gem for us.'

'The group of hairs from the BMW,' said Clyde Northcott.

'Yes. Several long dark hairs from the same scalp, found on the carpet beside the passenger seat in the BMW. Gathered together, as if someone had cleaned out the contents of a comb. Probably female. And an indication that you shouldn't be so anxious to assume our killer is a male, DC Murphy!'

'You think the wife is still in the frame for this?'

'I think we still need to check out the exact state of the fragrant Jane's relationship with her husband at the time of his death, yes. But there are other women awaiting our most urgent efforts, are there not, DS Northcott?'

'The car is ready to transport you, *mein Fuehrer*! Do you think we might snatch a flying sandwich in the canteen on our way to it?'

Northcott reversed the police Mondeo expertly into the visitors' section of the car park. They glanced automatically at the very regular elevation of the neat block of modern flats, but saw no watcher at any of the windows.

Nevertheless, their arrival must have been observed, for the door of the flat nearest to the entrance opened almost before the double doors had shut behind them. Peach recognized the cool, oval face with its frame of dark hair from television, before she said, 'I'm Michelle Davies. Please come in,' and led them into the sitting room of her flat.

A neat room, with a small bowl of fresh fruit on a low table in front of the sofa; a modern, brightly coloured print of a harbour with small craft at their moorings and the open sea in the background; a single photograph of a stiffly posed wedding couple, probably the actress's mother and father. Conventional, comfortable, but not much 'lived-in', not telling you much about the occupant.

As if she saw their scrutiny and divined their conclusion, Michelle Davies said, 'I'm not here all that much, when I'm working. Which is most of the time, fortunately.'

'You may be here a little more in the coming year than you had anticipated,' said Peach evenly. He was quite ready to ruffle her, if he could. So far, the members of the acting fraternity were proving rather too good at masking their real feelings.

Her reaction merely confirmed this. Michelle was in fact a little shaken by his directness, by the lack of any polite

preamble, but she did not much show it. Like an actor denied
the proper cue, she improvised and covered her excitement.
'I presume you mean that I wasn't going to get the part I'd
been promised. You're right about that. James Walton made
it clear that it was no decision of his. But he couldn't go
against Adam's wishes. Losing that role was a disappointment
and I won't deny it. Playing Alec Dawson's regular girlfriend
in the new series would have opened up lots of other possibilities, as well as being lucrative in itself. But no doubt something will turn up.'

'It didn't for Mr Micawber.'

'No. And Dickens was a real ham – he'd love to have
worked in the theatre. But television wasn't around in
Dickens's day, or Mr Micawber might have had offers.' A
capable return from a challenging serve, Michelle thought.

'How much money did you lose when this part was withdrawn?' said Peach. Try the real shock for an Englishwoman,
the financial one. British people would answer all kinds of
questions about their sex lives, but pry into the state of their
finances and they would be really shocked. And amongst the
British, the English were prickliest of all.

'I don't think that's any of your business.'

The predictable, automatic reaction. Peach smiled, almost
as if she had walked into his trap. 'Everything's our business
in a murder enquiry, Ms Davies. But we can get the answer
from someone else, if you want to be cagey.'

'I never saw the full details of the contract, because we
never reached the signing stage. But I was reckoning upon a
quarter of a million; perhaps all told a little more, with repeat
fees and worldwide sales virtually guaranteed.'

Peach whistled softly at his DS. 'Tidy sum that. Worth
killing for, if it's suddenly whipped away from you on the
mere whim of your star.'

Michelle realized now that this strange man was deliberately trying to nettle her. The tall black officer had looked to
her much more dangerous, but he hadn't spoken since the intro-
ductions; all the aggression was coming from this stocky ball
of energy who was in charge. She could handle it, she told
herself. She said coldly, 'You obviously get your standards
from the criminal fraternity, DCI Peach. I was disappointed
when the part was withdrawn. I should have told Adam exactly

what I thought of him, no doubt with the addition of a few
unladylike words to underline my feelings. I never entertained
the thought of murder.'

Peach nodded calmly, as if he had expected exactly this
reply. 'Could you describe your relationship with Mr Cassidy
for us, please? Take your time; it's important that you get this
right.'

The last instruction was put in purely to increase her tension,
she thought. Michelle was infuriated to find that it had
succeeded in doing that. The words she had prepared before
they came here seemed suddenly inadequate and she felt
herself fumbling for others to make herself convincing. 'We
were close colleagues.'

'Even though you'd only been together for the final episode
of the last series of *Call Alec Dawson*?'

'Yes. We knew each other longer than that. Theatre and
television are both still fairly small worlds, as far as actors
are concerned. We'd done small scenes together in other things
a few years ago. And even a single episode of a series can
involve a lot of work. There were two or three weeks of studio
work and several days' shooting on location.'

'So you would say a close professional relationship?'

'Yes. And a friendly one.'

'I see. And how far did friendship spread beyond the confines
of your professional closeness?'

Michelle felt the blood was rushing to her face and wondered
if it could be seen. She hadn't been troubled by blushing since
she was a teenager, but this odious man might have prompted
it. 'You get close together as actors. I was his girlfriend, the
damsel in distress he was rescuing, so we were acting together
in most of my scenes.'

Peach sat with his head a little on one side and let the
seconds stretch. Then he smiled and said, 'That is a politician's answer, Ms Davies. In other words, no answer at all.
I'll rephrase my question: did you see much of Adam Cassidy
off-screen?'

Michelle told herself not to be so on edge. She'd anticipated this, hadn't she? You never knew how much gossip was
going on among the rest of the cast, particularly during those
long periods when they had to sit around waiting to be called.
She'd really no idea what had been said about her and Adam

among the bit-part players, and how much the team of police
officers had discovered in the last couple of days as they took
statements from everyone in the cast. She was in too vulnerable a position to be caught out in a lie. 'We were lovers.'
She glanced automatically towards the door of the bedroom.
'He came here, after a day's location shooting in the Pennines.
It happens, DCI Peach. More often among actors than among
the rest of the public. It's the peculiar nature of the work we
do, I suppose.'

'I'm not here to take any particular moral stance, Ms Davies.
I'm interested in facts, and how those facts relate to the death
of Adam Cassidy.'

'And I've been very frank about those facts. Now I'll give
you another one: I had nothing to do with Adam's death.'

Peach merely nodded. 'You've told me that you were lovers.
Which I presume means that you had sex with him. I have to
ask you how far beyond the sexual act your term "lovers"
extends. How deeply were you emotionally involved?'

Michelle felt her fingernails digging into her palms. She
wasn't going to let this man see how much he was annoying
her. It was, she decided reluctantly, a reasonable question, if
you put yourself in his place. She said evenly, 'I don't leap
in and out of bed with people all the time. For some reason,
I'd like you to know that, even if you're not planning to adopt
any particular moral stance.'

Peach ignored the ring of sarcasm in her repetition of his
phrase. 'So how did you feel about Adam Cassidy – before
you heard the news that he was cutting you out of his next
series, I mean?'

'We were attracted to each other. I didn't see it as long-
term and I don't suppose he did – he had a fair trail of deserted
females behind him, as well as a wife and family. And I'm
not a marriage-wrecker by nature. All right, we were playing
with fire, but we both knew the score. We worked very closely
together in the Alec Dawson episode and we both knew that
not everything was simulated in the clinches we enjoyed there.
It seemed natural to take it a little further off-screen. I'm sure
you'd understand that if you'd ever worked in the theatre.'

'I'm sure I would, yes,' said Peach dryly. 'When did you
find out that your lover had vetoed further clinches in another
series?'

'Last Thursday morning. James Walton told me; he also made it very clear that it was none of his doing. It was all down to Adam.'

'Why do you think Adam did it?'

'I don't know. I was planning to ask him that myself. He wouldn't have enjoyed the meeting.'

'You must have given some thought to this. Do you think that he merely wished to be rid of a liaison with you which might have complicated life for him?'

'No, I don't. We weren't in deep with each other. Either of us could have said we didn't want to take things any further at any time. There wouldn't have been any recriminations.'

'Then why dispense with you? Have you any other theory?'

'Yes. I rather think James Walton might be right about this. He says people like Adam just get too far too quickly. They can't really believe that they're stars, despite all the money and all the attention. An inferiority complex, if you like. It makes them throw tantrums and assert themselves every so often, just to prove to themselves and others that they really are stars.'

This was very close to what Dean Morley had said about Cassidy. But Peach had the policeman's habitual distrust of psychology and its practitioners, who too often were recruited by unscrupulous lawyers to enable villains to escape justice. He said tersely, 'Do you buy that?'

Unexpectedly, the woman he had been trying to rile was as sceptical as he was. Michelle Davies gave a rueful smile and said, 'At that moment, I wasn't interested in Adam's psyche. I wanted to know why the bastard was snatching away a part which was made for me and which I thought I'd already secured.'

Peach answered her smile with a grim one of his own. 'So you decided the bastard in question deserved to be killed.'

'I probably did, yes. But that doesn't mean I made any plans to kill him. I didn't shed too many tears when I heard the news, but it wasn't me who killed Adam.'

Peach looked round again at the comfortable, unrevealing room. He brought his dark eyes back to the pale, determined face, which looked like that of an old-masters' Madonna in this very modern setting. 'He died within ten miles of here. You live nearer to the spot than anyone else we're interviewing about this.'

'Does that make me the leading suspect? These days everyone has a car, DCI Peach. If you're saying the proximity of my home to the place where he died makes me the leading suspect, you must be pretty desperate!'

Peach nodded calmly. There was no way this spirited woman was going to discover from him whether he was desperate or otherwise. 'Probably Cassidy arranged to meet someone up there. I'm merely suggesting it would have been a very convenient point for the two of you to meet, whatever the purpose of such a meeting.'

'I didn't arrange to meet Adam up there on Friday night and I don't know who did.'

Clyde Northcott said quietly, 'When did you last see Adam Cassidy, Ms Davies?'

She switched her attention to the man taking notes. At least she had established some sort of contact with Peach as he had sparked her antagonism. This dark, unyielding face could have belonged to an automaton. 'At the beginning of last week. Tuesday. Certainly before he had announced any intention of ditching me from the next series.'

'Where were you last Friday night, please?'

'Here.' She watched his pen move over the page like the quill of a recording angel. 'I can give you the details of the television programmes I watched, if you like.'

'I'm sure you could do that. Were you alone throughout the evening?'

'I was, yes.' She resisted the impulse to give him some reason why that might have been.

'And have you any thoughts on who might have killed Mr Cassidy?'

That title rang oddly in her ears. She couldn't remember Adam ever having been referred to as 'Mister' before. 'No. I've already told you that I don't. I've thought about it since I heard. Of course I have – I assume that's only natural.' She glanced at Peach and contrived a final barb. 'But at the moment I'm as baffled about who did this as you seem to be.'

# FOURTEEN

'When's the funeral?' Harry Cassidy spoke for the first time in many minutes.

'Not yet, Dad. The police can't release the body yet.'

'And why's that?'

Luke knew from his father's tone that he didn't trust him. When you were old and confused, you felt that the whole world was likely to lie to you, even the son who tried to shield you from the worst of it. He tried not to resent it, fought against the idea that a dying man was distrusting the one person in the world who still loved him. He couldn't tell him what the policeman had explained to him, that they had to retain the body because at some future stage a murderer's defending counsel might demand a second post-mortem examination with a different pathologist. So he said limply, 'Murder isn't like other deaths, Dad. They just don't allow immediate funerals.'

The old man's face was the pallid grey it had been ever since he heard the news. The features were set like a death mask and just about as responsive. There was no method of knowing whether he had understood what you said to him. It was a long time before Harry said, 'They used to lay them out in the front parlour, you know.'

'Yes, Dad. That's a long time ago, though.'

'Don't seem long. Not to me. I saw my granddad laid out like that. On two trestles, they had the coffin. For two days. Everyone came in to see him. In the front parlour.'

'They were simpler days, Dad.'

'That they were. Simpler and better days. You didn't meet wogs round every corner then.'

'You shouldn't call them that, Dad. They're men and women, like the rest of us.'

But the old man had switched off, had retreated thankfully into the days of his boyhood, when the last clogs were still clattering to the mills and King Cotton had ruled over a simpler world. It was five minutes before Luke said, 'You've let your dinner go cold again, Dad.'

'Don't want it. Don't need it. Not hungry.'

'You must eat, Dad. You've had practically nothing since . . . since this happened.'

'Not hungry. Don't want it.'

And why, indeed, should Luke struggle each night to get him to take the food his wife had so assiduously prepared? To preserve what life was in the old body, of course. But what sort of life was it? What was left for Harry Cassidy, now that the son he doted on was gone? A world which he hated because it was so changed; a town he could no longer move about in even had he wished to do so. It was the love in his own heart which made the pain of his father's plight so sharp to him.

He was clearing away the waste of the uneaten dinner when the phone shrilled unexpectedly by his father's chair. The old man started, but made no attempt to answer it. When his son picked it up, the voice was official, slightly apologetic. 'Luke Cassidy? Sorry to disturb you, but your wife said we'd get you at this number. Detective Chief Inspector Peach and his sergeant need to see you, in connection with your brother's death. Could we fix a time tomorrow, please?'

They offered to come to the house, but he arranged it for lunchtime at the school. He didn't want the police coming into the house and speaking to Hazel or the children. He didn't want bloody Adam soiling his life even now.

Detective Constable Brendan Murphy didn't want his companion to see that he was nervous about this meeting. She wasn't to know that this was the first time he'd been trusted to lead in an interview. It was her first month as a DC, so she would be grateful for any guidance she could get. She was also very attractive, with soft blonde hair and what he thought remarkable blue eyes. But that of course was irrelevant.

The farmer was only in his mid-thirties, but he seemed very mature and experienced to twenty-three-year-old Brendan Murphy. He said stiffly, 'Are you Mr Paul Barnes, sir?'

'Indeed I am. I was told to expect you. You'd better come inside.'

'I'm DC Brendan Murphy and this is DC Alison Freeman.' They followed the farmer through the wide, low hall of a two-hundred-year-old stone farmhouse, into a room with a huge Turkish carpet with a deep-red ground. They were invited to sit on a leather three-piece suite, which was large, old and seemingly indestructible, the way Alison's grandfather told her that leather furniture always used to be. She said conventionally, 'Nice building, this.'

Barnes glanced round the room as if appraising its comfortable opulence anew. 'This was always the best farm in the area. On the rich floor of the valley, you see. There used to be a lot of small farms around us, with poor tenants striving desperately to make a living. As most of them failed, my father and grandfather took them over and absorbed the land into ours. We're one of the few mixed farms left in the county. It's a big building for two adults – only I, my sister and my eight-year-old boy live here now. At least Liz and I are able to have completely self-contained sections in the place.'

At other times, the history of the farmhouse would have interested Brendan. At this moment, he was impatient to get on with the interview, to show Alison how brisk and efficient he could be. 'You will appreciate that in a murder interview, we take statements from all sorts of people, even those on the periphery of the case.'

'I do. I was interviewed along with other parents because I met Adam Cassidy very occasionally outside the gates when I delivered my boy to the school. Usually it was their mother or the children's nanny who delivered and collected his two, but I recall Adam being there once or twice.'

'I understand from your statement that you met the deceased also at weekend shooting parties,' said Brendan tersely. Don't let them get away with anything. Keep them on the back foot whenever you could. Percy Peach's mantra for interviews rang insistently at the back of Murphy's brain. 'Perhaps you got to know him rather better there.'

Paul Barnes smiled in the face of this earnestness. 'Yes. I've never thought of our weekend meetings as "shooting parties", but I suppose that is exactly what they are. Sounds very Edwardian, somehow. I've shot woodcock and grouse up on the moor since I was a lad – it just seems like part of the rural life to me. I did chat to Adam a little up there, but other people seemed anxious to monopolize him at lunch – they like to chat to show-business people.' He'd almost said that

that was the only reason why Cassidy had been invited along, which would have sounded petty rather than the neutral he was aiming at. 'Adam was quite new to shooting, but he seemed enthusiastic about it.'

Murphy felt as though he was being outgunned with words, in which this confident, fresh-faced man with the slightly unruly brown hair seemed so much more proficient than he was. Somehow you didn't expect a man with a Lancashire accent to be so adept with the language. Brendan flicked a look at Alison Freeman, who said, 'You seem to be telling us that you didn't know Adam very well.'

'Exactly. I'm a bit shy in those circumstances – I didn't want it to seem as if I was cultivating him just because he was a celebrity. No doubt I'd have got to know him better in the next year or two, but that pleasure will now be denied to me.'

'Perhaps you got to know Mrs Cassidy rather better than her husband.'

Paul took his time. He'd known when the CID wanted to see him again that he should expect this. The more lightly he could handle it, the better. He smiled. 'That sounds quite sinister, when you phrase it like that. Well, it's a plain fact that I do know Jane better than I knew Adam, because of meetings outside the village school. I deliver and collect Thomas whenever I can, and Jane is there far more often than Adam ever was with Damon and Kate.'

DC Murphy decided that it was time to assert himself. 'There has been a suggestion that your friendship extended beyond that of fellow-parents meeting at the school gates.'

For the first time, Barnes's fresh features registered annoyance. 'Has there, indeed? Well that sort of tittle-tattle is inevitable, I suppose, when people have drab lives and too much time for gossip.'

'I'm sure you will understand that we cannot reveal our sources,' said Murphy stiffly.

'Not very reliable sources, I'm afraid. Look, I'm thirty-five, divorced, with a prosperous farm which I own myself. In terms of the rural life, that makes me highly eligible, I suppose. And thus a candidate for gossip. And Jane is an attractive woman of about the same age and also a successful professional actress. But she is – was – married and happily settled, with two children and a very rich and famous husband. I couldn't have competed with that, even if I'd wanted to.'

'You're saying that there is nothing between you and Mrs Cassidy?'

'There is what I'd describe as an easy friendship. Nothing more.'

'Do you know anything else about either Mr or Mrs Cassidy which might have a bearing on his death?'

'No. I don't indulge in gossip at the school gates. I'm a working farmer, with a full life to fit in around my eight-year-old son.'

Alison Freeman spoke as calmly as she could, not wishing to reveal that this was the first time she'd asked this question in a murder case. 'Where were you last Friday night, Mr Barnes?'

In other circumstances, he would have smiled at her earnestness. But this was too serious for that. 'I was here. Throughout the evening and throughout the night.'

'Is there anyone who can confirm that for us?'

'My sister could. But as I say, we have self-contained accommodation within this rambling building. She probably wouldn't know if I'd gone out, as I wouldn't know if she had. We lead separate lives; we find that is much the best way to exist together.'

'Thank you for being so frank, Mr Barnes. If you hear or think of anything which might be relevant to this case, please ring this number immediately.'

Paul waited impatiently with his hand on the phone until the police car turned into the lane and disappeared. It rang only twice before it was answered. He said without preamble, 'It was two youngsters, not the big man in charge and his sidekick, who spoke to you. The very fact that they were sent here might be significant, but I think I stonewalled quite effectively.'

The man wore a charcoal-grey suit and an immaculate white shirt. He examined the chair offered to him and brushed the seat of it before smoothly piloting his elegant backside on to it. He plucked each of his cuffs half an inch forward and announced, 'This is a delicate matter, Detective Chief Inspector Peach.'

'It had better be a speedy one also,' said Percy, who had observed these preliminaries with diminishing patience.

'I see. Well, my name is Percival Spencer. I am the manager and principal partner in the Ghyllside Hotel, Grasmere. A particularly beautiful village in the English Lakes.'

'I know Grasmere. Very pretty, as you say. Gets very over-crowded in the tourist season. I don't know your hotel.'

Spencer's patronizing smile said that it would be quite unthinkable for an oik like this to defile the rooms of the Ghyllside. 'As an exclusive hotel, we are a little off the beaten track. Away from those vulgar throngs of tourists who crowd the village at weekends, as you say.'

'Mr Spencer, you asked to see the man in charge of the Cassidy murder investigation. I am he. But unless you can come to the point very quickly, I shall have to pass you on to one of my sergeants.'

Percival Spencer's shocked countenance was worthy of Lady Bracknell. 'I see. Well, it's a delicate matter, as I said. We don't normally disclose bookings, but—'

'But you think you should tell me about one booking in particular.'

Spencer looked as crestfallen as an actor whose best speech has been cut. 'Yes.'

'Would this booking have been for last Friday night, by any chance?'

'It would, yes. A double room for Friday and Saturday nights. With dinner on Saturday and full English breakfast on Saturday and Sunday.'

'In whose name?'

'Ah! This is where the matter becomes very delicate.' Percival made an effort to resume his lofty demeanour. 'The booking was made in the name of Jackson.'

'Better than Smith, I suppose. Just. Must be the upmarket version. What was the real name of the customer?'

'Normally we would never disclose this.'

'I'll bear that in mind, next time I fancy a dirty weekend at the Ghyllside. Name, please.'

'Well, it was Mr Adam Cassidy. One of our most valued clients. That's why I felt I should come here in person, Detective Inspector Peach.'

'Detective Chief Inspector Peach – as we're being so deli-cate. Had Mr Cassidy used your services before?'

'I'm happy to say that Mr Cassidy had spent several happy

weekends with us. We regarded his extended custom as the best possible evidence that we had given good service.'

'I'm sure you did. Were these happy weekends with a succession of different partners?'

Spencer looked at Peach as if he had just dropped a piece of fine china in his kitchen. 'We regard these details as confidential. It is our duty to protect the privacy of our guests.'

'And it is our duty to find who blew this particular guest apart. I wouldn't wish to find you attempting to frustrate the police in the course of their enquiries.'

Percival looked down at his highly polished black shoes. He told himself that he was fortunate in not having to deal with odious oiks like this very often. 'I think Mr Cassidy was accompanied by a different lady on each of his visits to us.'

'And have you any thoughts on the real identity of the lady who should have visited you as "Mrs Jackson" this weekend?'

'None whatsoever.' Percival delivered those two words with considerable satisfaction.

Percy Peach stood up and allowed himself a closing beam of satisfaction. 'Thank you for this information, Mr Spencer. I do hope that your exclusive establishment does not appear in a court case as a seedy refuge for adulterers. But I fear that will be out of my hands.'

'Just follow me. I've arranged that we won't be disturbed.'

Luke Cassidy led the CID men rapidly past a few hundred curious young eyes, along a wide corridor, and then through an empty classroom to an ancillary room with the words HISTORY SEMINAR on the door. There were about ten upright chairs in here. A large map of England during the Civil War dominated the wall opposite the entrance, with Van Dyke's flattering portrait of Charles I on one side of it and Cromwell, warts and all, on the other. Cassidy ushered them to the two chairs he had set ready for them and took a third chair opposite them himself. He sat rather awkwardly for a moment with arms folded, then dropped them stiffly to his sides, as if he had read the rules of body language and was determined to heed them.

The teacher looked very tired, Peach thought. He had an indoor pallor about him. He looked in dire need of a holiday in a sunnier part of the world. In the silence which hung in this windowless room, the sound of children's voices came faintly to them, a mixture of the shrill and the raucous. Luke Cassidy said with needless apology, 'They're all a bit excited at this time of year. We finish for the Christmas break tomorrow.'

Peach said, 'The biggest problem with murders is that we cannot interview the victim. We always have to build up a picture of a person we didn't know at all before his death. We've spoken to Jane Cassidy; we normally see the spouse first in the case of a suspicious death. But other than her, you're the first person we've spoken to who can give us an accurate account of Adam's family life.'

Luke Cassidy said almost eagerly, 'My mother's been dead for years. My father's got bad rheumatoid arthritis and is failing badly. We're trying to keep him in his own house and out of the home he doesn't want to go to.'

Clyde Northcott said quietly, 'Who is "we", Mr Cassidy?'

A faint, strained smile. 'My wife and I. Hazel cooks a meal for him on most days and I take it round for him. I get my two children to pop in and see him whenever I can, but in all truth there isn't much for them there. Dad's legs have more or less gone, so he won't come round to our place, even in the car. He can't do much for himself any more, and frankly he cares less and less about whatever life is left to him.'

This summary of lonely, confined old age had come tumbling out as though he'd prepared it, but he could scarcely have done that. It was more likely the account of his father's situation and his own part in it which he had grown used to offering as a response to polite queries about old Harry Cassidy's health. Peach said quietly, 'Your father had two sons, Mr Cassidy. Tell us about his relationship with Adam.'

The long, pale face winced instinctively. Whatever the cause of it, this man was under a lot of strain. 'Dad doted on Adam. He's gone downhill quickly in the few days since my brother's death. He was never a bad dad to me, but Adam was always his favourite, even when we were kids.'

'And Adam responded to this?'

There was a long pause, as though Luke was fighting to be fair and finding it difficult. 'Sometimes I felt that Adam wasn't really capable of deep attachments. He scarcely bothered to keep in touch with the two children of his first marriage, and

he had difficulty even remembering the names of my two –
his only niece and nephew. His response to Dad's decline was
to pretend it didn't exist until he was forced to confront it,
and then to throw money at it. What Dad really wanted was
to see Adam, to talk to him and hear about this glamorous
world where he'd become such a hit. It couldn't have been
more different from his father's world, but that in itself would
have made it interesting for Dad.'

'Did he see Harry very often?'

'No. That was a bone of contention between Adam and me.
He would promise to come and then not turn up. I used to
watch the disappointment gathering in Dad's face as the hours
passed and he realized he wasn't going to see Adam after all.
He always made excuses for him, but I knew how much he
was hurting.'

'You must have resented this. Particularly when Harry was
taking up so much of your own life.'

'I don't begrudge the hours I have to spend with Dad. He
was a good husband to Mum and he misses her now. He's
been a good father to me, in his own way. I can still see him
at forty, playing cricket with us and encouraging us at school,
generous with his love and his time. I owe him for that, and
I'm happy to give him my love now, when he's just the shell
of the man he was.'

Luke Cassidy was clearly a man in whom feelings ran deep.
A passionate man, but one under considerable strain; that was
often a combination which erupted into unforeseen violence.
Peach wondered about the influence upon him of the wife he
had seemed so anxious to keep away from them. Peach
suggested quietly, insidiously, 'But Adam did not feel a similar
impulse to repay your father's years of care?'

It was as if he had broken a dam and released the pent-up
waters behind it. 'Adam didn't seem to feel anything at all,
most of the time! Dad had indulged him, the way he would
never have indulged me, when he wanted to become an actor.
All right, it was justified, in the end, because Adam was a
success. But for a man of Dad's background, his support must
have cost him a lot. I know Dad's friends made fun of Adam's
show-business pretensions, but Harry never wavered; I think
he was the only one in the family who really believed that
Adam could make a go of it.'

'That must have made Adam's neglect over the last few years hard for Harry to bear.'

Luke shook his head violently. 'No. It never did that. Dad would never admit to the slightest fault in Adam. It was always someone else's fault when he didn't see him for months.'

'Yours, perhaps.'

A wan, bitter smile. 'Sometimes. As the world closes in on old people, logic deserts them, and they tend to lash out at the ones nearest to them, don't they?'

'Which makes life very hard for people like you.'

He shook his head again, more gently this time. 'I try not to resent it in Dad. He can't help it, any more than he can help his bigotry against the Asians in the town or indeed against most things new. But I used to get furious with bloody Adam, who could have given Dad so much pleasure so easily and yet chose not to.'

'This must have soured your own relationship with your brother.'

Again that sad, reluctant smile. 'I sometimes felt we'd been growing steadily further apart since we were about eighteen. But it was his neglect of Dad which made me feel really bitter against him. Sometimes it felt as if Adam chose to withhold himself simply on a whim, as if he wished to demonstrate how precious his presence and his attention were to Dad. He behaved as if he was above ordinary, human emotion – as if that were something he despised in himself and others. I'd begun to feel over these last few months that Dad would be better without him altogether. At least that way he wouldn't be perpetually disappointed.'

Peach let that last sentiment hang in the air for what seemed to Luke a long, significant moment. Then he said quietly, 'You sound as if you are happy to be rid of him.'

Luke gave them such a measured reply that it seemed as if he had been waiting through the rest of the interview for this very question. 'I'm not glad Adam's dead. Death brings with it memories of happier times in the past and thoughts of chances missed. And this has hit Dad really hard. He's behaving as if he has nothing left to live for now. I don't think he'll last long.'

Peach nodded to Clyde Northcott, who said formally, 'Did you kill your brother, Mr Cassidy?'

There was no outrage. Just that sad, pensive smile again. 'No. There were times when I felt like doing that; I expect you come across that quite often within families. But it wasn't me who killed him.'

'Then have you any idea who did?'

'No. But I wasn't involved in Adam's life, apart from the small, intimate part which concerned Dad. I know Adam's wife and his children. Our two families have met up, but not often. I think it was Boxing Day when we last saw them, so it's virtually a year ago. So the only bit of Adam's life I've been concerned with over that period is his relationship – or rather his non-relationship – with Dad, which I've told you about.'

There was something a little pedantic in his determination to get the details right. But that is plainly what he was: a careful, conscientious man, doing his best for a father who did not appreciate his efforts. DS Northcott finished his note and asked, 'Where were you last Friday night, Mr Cassidy?'

'I went out to the pub at about eight o'clock – at my wife's insistence – intending to stay for only an hour or so. She knew I'd had a trying week at school and with Dad, and she felt I needed a break. In the event, Hazel was right. I saw friends in the White Hart whom I hadn't seen for months and spent more like three hours than one with them. It was after eleven when I got home. About twenty past, I should think.'

Again it seemed important to him that he gave them all the detail he could. CID officers shouldn't mock that quality, thought Clyde; so often people weren't able or weren't willing to give them the degree of detail they needed. He smiled at Luke Cassidy and said, 'Thank you. We can check this out easily enough at the pub, I expect.'

'The pub gets very crowded on Friday night. The landlord and his staff might not remember exact times. But Hazel will certainly confirm them for you.'

They took a quiet leave of this quiet man. But Peach said after they had made their way through a corridor of curious young eyes to the car, 'We'll check out Friday night with the clientele of the White Hart, not his missus, I think.'

They had driven over a mile and were almost back at Brunton nick before he spoke again. 'Yesterday morning you said you hoped our killer wouldn't prove to be the man we'd just interviewed because he was what you called a "decent man".'

Northcott allowed himself a rueful smile. 'Dean Morley, sir. You gave me a bollocking and said I couldn't pick and choose like that among suspects.'

'Not a bollocking, DS Northcott. When I give you a bollocking, you'll be quite certain that's what it is. I merely reminded you that it is a CID officer's duty to remain objective.'

'Yes, sir.' Clyde said nothing further until he was negotiating the sharp turn into the police car park, when curiosity twitched his tongue. 'Why do you raise that now, sir?'

'Because, DS Northcott, I fear I may be due a bollocking from you. Or rather, a reminder that I must be clear-sighted and objective and concentrate on facts, not feelings.'

'And why would that be?'

'I think your soft contours and constantly smiling face must be unearthing a dangerous weakness in me, DS Northcott. I see in Luke Cassidy a man under immense strain, who is passionate about the things he holds dear. And thus a man who might well be our killer. And I find myself thinking that he is a thoroughly decent man and hoping that he isn't a murderer.'

# FIFTEEN

'You need to get your finger out, Peach!'

'Yes, sir.' If Tommy Bloody Tucker was in disciplinary mode, Percy would just let the torrent of abuse flow freely. Occasionally, that was the best strategy. Sooner or later, and usually sooner, the man would run out of insults and the torrent would be reduced to a trickle. Or better still, it might be turned back to flow in his direction.

'Never mind "Yes, sir". I want results. Do you hear me?'

'Yes, sir. Sorry, sir. I mean, you don't want "Yes, sir", do you? You just told me that.'

Tucker was looking pleasingly puzzled already. He said severely. 'Don't piss me about, Peach. This isn't bloody good enough, do you hear me?'

'I hear you, sir.'

'It's Wednesday afternoon already and you've produced bugger all. A man who is a national figure was murdered last Friday night, and you still—'

'But not discovered until Saturday night, sir, as you reminded the nation in your excellent television piece yesterday.'

'Stop pissing me about, Peach! Just because I defended you as best I could to the media yesterday, don't presume that I'm going to tolerate laziness in my team. Is that clear?'

'Yes, sir. Have to point out that we haven't been idle, sir. In fact, we've been buzzing about like blue-arsed flies ever since this crime was discovered.' Percy had never worked out why blue-reared insects should be considered the most active; perhaps it was the police weakness for alliteration that made blue-arsed flies buzz more actively than others.

Tucker leaned forward threateningly over his massive desk and said heavily, 'I see no evidence of that, Peach. No fucking evidence at all!' He had largely eschewed the f-word since he became a chief superintendent, so as to set himself above the common herd of policemen. He hoped it carried extra emphasis now as a result of his normal economy.

Percy did comprehensive work on looking hurt. 'Everyone

on the team has been working long hours since the corpse was discovered, sir.'

'I hope you've not been hammering the overtime budget.'

Non sequiturs were a perpetual problem when you dealt with Tommy Bloody Tucker. The notion that working flat out might demand a bit of overtime had not troubled that unique brain. Percy chose not to react to this contradiction, save with a long-suffering sigh. 'Perhaps it would be best if I gave you a verbal summary of the progress of the investigation, sir.'

'I think it's high time you did.'

'The widow, sir, Jane Cassidy. Formerly Jane Webster, an actress of some standing. It is difficult to be certain about the exact state of their marriage at the time of Cassidy's death.'

'Difficult but not impossible, Peach. You should have pinned this down by now.'

'Do you know, sir, I rather agree with you.' Peach spoke in wonderment, as if he had just stumbled upon a modern Wonder of the World. 'Steps are already in hand to do just that.'

'Don't give me this "steps are in hand" nonsense, Peach. That's what we use to fob off the public when we've nothing to tell them.'

'Yes, sir. I seem to remember the phrase featuring frequently in your media briefings. But in this case steps really are in hand. I shall be speaking to the lady myself later this afternoon.'

'I'm glad to hear it!' Tucker leaned forward confidentially. 'Two thirds of murders are committed by people within the close family.'

It was almost reassuring to Percy to see the blindin', bleedin' bloody obvious resurfacing in his chief. 'Rather more than that, actually, sir. But it's good to have your overview.'

'What about this theatrical agent you mentioned in your memo to me yesterday?'

'Tony Valento, sir. A man with a previous record of violence, but as slippery as an eel in Vaseline. Greater Manchester CID think he's employed a hit man to remove enemies in the past, but have never been able to bring him to court for it. Valento lost the deceased's custom shortly before his death. Cassidy transferred himself to a new agent to pursue international stardom. To try to get to Hollywood, to be precise.'

'Really? Cassidy struck me as a bit of a bounder.'

What a wonderfully old-fashioned term for a senior policeman to use, thought Percy. And strangely enough, fairly accurate, from what he'd so far learned of Adam Cassidy. 'I'm told being a bounder doesn't always pre-empt the right to stardom, sir. DS Murphy has come up with a possible liaison for Mrs Cassidy, which I shall explore further. A man who has the best farm in the area. Sounds quite posh – shoots with the county set, apparently.'

'Tread carefully, then. Tact, Peach, tact.'

'You don't think we should get this chap in and give him the third degree, sir? Rough him up a bit, shine lights into his face?' If Tommy Bloody Tucker chose to talk about bounders, there was every reason to recall an earlier age of policing. Percy's face lit up as a delightful thought struck him. 'You could interview him yourself, sir, whilst I turned a blind eye!'

'PEACH! You will proceed with extreme care here. Is that clear?'

'Yes, sir. Pity, that. There's a brother: Luke Cassidy. Spends a lot of time looking after his old dad, whom Adam Cassidy severely neglected. Seems a decent sort of bloke, to me.'

'Treat him with suspicion. Remember, most murderers come from within the family.'

'Yes, sir. It's good to have your overview of criminal trends in the nation offering us such valuable insights.'

Tucker glared at him suspiciously over his rimless glasses. 'Has this Luke Cassidy got himself a good alibi?'

'Good, sir, but not yet cast-iron. We shall check even more carefully, now that we have your views.' Peach leaned confidentially towards the man behind the big desk, as if offering a clinching piece of confidence. 'He's a highly respected history teacher at the comp.'

Tucker looked with distaste into the round, eager face beneath the baldness. 'Who else?'

'The others are mostly actors from the *Call Alec Dawson* series.'

'I'll bet they're a rum lot! Actors are, you know.'

Another epithet from the past. Peach nodded. 'Decidedly rum, sir. And bounders too, some of them, I should think!'

He waited for a reaction, but all he got from Tucker was, 'Motives?'

'Indeed, sir. Two of them had just lost big parts in the next series of *Call Alec Dawson*. And with them remuneration which would make even a chief superintendent's income seem puny.' He paused to allow the magnitude of this anomaly to be processed by the slowly moving abacus which was Tucker's brain. 'One of them is an actor who knew Cassidy right from his early days in the theatre until his death. Chap by the name of Dean Morley. He was to be the main villain opposing Alec Dawson throughout the series, until Cassidy stamped on the idea.'

'Alibi?'

'Morley has an alibi, of sorts. It's as suspect as the old wifely assurance that a villain was at home with her at the crucial time – and just as difficult to disprove. He claims to have been at home with his male partner when Cassidy died.'

'This man Morley is queer?' Tucker's tortoise speed of comprehension had been restored.

'Bent as a hairpin, sir. But he—'

'They're devious, those people. I've always found them devious.'

But nothing like as devious as some senior CID men in pursuit of promotions and pensions, thought Peach. 'I'll bear that in mind, sir. But we have to be careful to treat gay people in the same way as heterosexuals, don't we, sir?'

'Eh? Oh yes, I suppose we do. This bloody political correctness is a damned nuisance. But you and I are old-fashioned policemen, Peach. We know the score.'

'Yes, sir. For what it's worth, DS Northcott, a man not prone to the sentimental view, thought that Dean Morley was a decent sort of chap.'

Apparently it wasn't worth much. Tucker looked thoroughly bemused for a moment, then said, 'Isn't Northcott that tall black officer?'

'That's the one, sir. The man you'd want to have beside you if and when things turn ugly.'

Tucker shook his head in a bemused fashion and muttered, 'Political correctness gone mad!' It wasn't clear whether he disapproved of Northcott's height or his colour.

Peach said hastily, 'There's also an actress exciting our attention, sir. Attractive, dark-haired woman – you may have seen her on screen. Name of Michelle Davies.'

'*Cherchez la femme*, Peach!'

Tucker looked as satisfied as if he had produced an original thought. But that might have needed a Caesarean, thought Percy. 'Like Mr Morley, Ms Davies had a highly lucrative role in the next series snatched away on what seems to have been little more than Cassidy's whim.'

Tucker shook his silvering head sagely. 'She could well have done this.'

'We thought it a distinct possibility, sir.' The man's now forcing me to be a Jeeves to his Wooster, Percy realized with a shock. He said hastily, 'She had been to bed with Cassidy, sir. On how regular a basis, we are still not sure.'

'Well, make yourselves sure, Peach! Do I have to do everything for you? Surely you can complete the straightforward legwork for yourselves.'

'Indeed we can, sir. And it's high time I was about it!'

Percy Peach went briskly back down the staircase from the ivory tower. He told himself firmly that he couldn't exclude Michelle Davies from suspicion just because Chief Superintendent Tommy Bloody Tucker thought she was a killer.

'I apologize that this meeting had to be at five o'clock. I know it's an awkward time, but I know also that you want the mystery of your husband's death solved as quickly as possible.'

Peach watched Jane Cassidy's face closely for her reaction to this, but she gave him nothing. The winter darkness had dropped thickly over the countryside outside, but the light in the hall of the big new mansion was bright and clear. The widow's face held the welcome of conventional, automatic hospitality, but showed no reaction to his mention of Cassidy's murder. She said, 'The time is no inconvenience to me, Detective Chief Inspector. I've been relieved over the last few days that we decided to employ a nanny – I was in two minds about it when Adam suggested it, but it's been a boon since he died.'

She looked much better than she had on Monday. Her dark-blonde hair had been neatly cut and the colour was back in her cheeks. She was lightly but expertly made up. Her clear blue eyes had now no sign of the puffiness which tears had brought to them in the aftermath of her husband's death. She looked if anything younger than her thirty-seven years. She had made a remarkable recovery from her initial grief. Or perhaps that grief had not been so deep after all, thought Percy Peach; policemen were paid to think uncharitably.

There was a pot of tea and rich fruit cake on the table between her armchair and the sofa where she had invited them to sit. She poured the tea with a steady hand and handed them plates and cake. She could have been an actress playing out a scene in a comedy of manners, thought Peach. Maybe she was doing exactly that. She made a comfortable, composed remark about life having to go on when there were children around. He was emboldened to ask her, 'Will we see you on our screens again, as the children grow up?'

'I always intended to take up my career again. Now I might do it sooner rather than later. Curiously enough, my agent rang me today. The strange thing is that what has happened might make it easier for me to get parts.'

Peach thought he knew what she meant, but he wanted her to talk about herself, wanted to see just how far she had recovered from the death of the man who had been her husband and her children's father. 'In what way would it be easier, Mrs Cassidy?'

She smiled sadly. It seemed to him that she knew just what he was doing but was content to play along with it. 'Adam's death has brought me back into public notice. Every account I've seen mentions "the actress Jane Webster" as the wife of the victim. There will be a certain ghoulish curiosity about whatever roles I undertake. The people who cast for television are aware of such things. They realize the publicity which I would get would help to kick-start audience figures.'

'That old saw about there being no such thing as bad publicity.'

'Precisely. Although I'm sure casting directors and producers would prefer to say they were harnessing public sympathy.'

'You've already thought this through pretty thoroughly.'

She looked at him for a moment. She had a more quizzical smile now, with her head a little on one side. He wondered how many hundreds of men over the years had been influenced by those glistening light-blue eyes. She picked her words carefully as she said, 'I've been forced to do that by circumstances,

Mr Peach. I expect Adam will have left me comfortable for
money, but that isn't the point. Hopefully, I have up to fifty
years left to live and I need to make a start on that. I always
intended to act again: this merely brings forward the date when
it will happen.'

'How are the children coping with this?'

'Very well. We had a nasty incident on Monday when a
press photographer turned up as they were coming out of
school – hoping to get a shot of grieving widow and children
together, I suppose. The rest of the parents were pretty angry
about it. But the headmistress told me how resilient children
are and she was right. They've chatted to me at nights, as
you'd expect, but they seem to have taken it pretty well. It's
proved to be a blessing in disguise that they'd seen so little
of Adam in the months before his death.'

'Yes. You mentioned that on Monday. Has that been a help
to you as well?'

It was startlingly direct after the preliminary fencing. Jane
tried not to be affected by the way the man's black pupils
never seemed to leave her face. 'I suppose it has, really. The
manner of the death was an awful shock, but the fact that
we've almost led separate lives in the last year or so must
have been a help, I suppose.'

She seemed to be inviting him to push this further, almost
willing him to press for details of her own life. Instead, he
said, 'Would you care to tell us more about the people Adam
associated with during the last year of his life?'

'I told you almost as much as I know on Monday. I'd seen
very little of him during the filming of the latest *Call Alec
Dawson* series. I'm sure Adam wasn't lonely when he wasn't
on the set. He never had to work hard to get women. Once
you achieve fame, it's easier than ever. It's the way the world
works, as I'm sure you must be aware.'

Peach nodded, enjoying as he always did the challenge of
a woman who wished to meet him head on rather than retreat
into the conventional banalities. 'You don't seem to be very
resentful about that.'

'It was a fact of life if you chose to live with Adam. If he
went beyond a certain point with other women, he knew I
wouldn't tolerate it.'

'You must have been lonely whilst he was so busy. You

were at home with two children in this beautiful but rather isolated setting.'

'I'm lucky. We could afford whatever help we needed. The nanny in particular has given me independence and freedom. As I say, I was doubtful whether we needed her at first, but Ingrid is a friend as well as an employee now.'

'And her presence has allowed you to make your own friendships.'

He had the feeling that she was gently contesting the control of the interview with him. She paused, then said, 'You must have some particular friendship in mind.'

This time it was Peach who allowed himself the small, enigmatic smile which was a replica of hers. 'Two of our DCs talked to a Mr Paul Barnes this morning. DC Brendan Murphy is very keen. He has his own version of shorthand, which enables him to keep a very full record of his interviews.'

'How enterprising of him! And for some reason you obviously find that significant.'

'I was struck by one thing in his report. When you were mentioned, Mr Barnes denied more than a casual friendship at the school gates. But he knew the names of both of your children. In my experience, other women might know those names, but very few men would remember such details, from the casual and surface acquaintance he claimed.'

'Very perceptive of you. I hardly think you could make it stand up in a court of law.'

'I'm sure I couldn't. But fortunately, I am not in a court of law, but discussing these things informally with a woman who is anxious to give every assistance to police enquiries.'

'Of course you are.' She offered them more cake, refilled Northcott's cup for him; the delicate china seemed ridiculously fragile in those large, careful hands. Having given herself time to think, she said, 'You're right, of course. I should have known we couldn't conceal it, but Paul was anxious to protect my reputation. Paul and I did meet at the school gates, exactly as you've heard. But I was lonely, as you've suggested, and Paul is divorced, with custody of his son. The friendship grew rapidly. For the last three months, we've been lovers. I told you how convenient it is to have a nanny!'

It seemed characteristic of this very direct woman that once she had made up her mind to tell them, she not only gave them the full details but made a sharp joke against herself. Peach said, 'You should have told us this on Monday, Mrs Cassidy. But better late than never.'

'I'm sorry. You can appreciate that we didn't fancy being the subject of everyone's gossip. But you did say there couldn't be secrets, when murder was the crime.'

Peach looked at her grimly for a moment; he couldn't condone concealing facts, however understandable the wish for privacy might be. 'I think we'd better have anything else you were holding back from us, hadn't we?'

'I don't think there is anything else. I was genuinely upset on Monday, whatever you might think: I loved Adam, however confused my feelings might have been about him at the time of his death. Perhaps if you recall to me whatever it is that is puzzling you, I can confirm or deny it for you.'

Peach looked at her steadily for a moment, then gave the briefest of nods to his companion, who already had his notes ready to hand. Northcott's calm, deep voice said, 'You told us that on Friday night you came back into this house after waving goodbye to your husband at about seven thirty and did not leave it again. Your nanny, Ingrid Lundberg, has confirmed that. Would you like to assure us now that you did not leave your house again?'

That small, involuntary smile flashed quickly across the light-skinned face. She took a deep, measured breath. 'Ingrid is very loyal; I think she would say whatever I wanted her to. But I don't think she lied to you: she no doubt believed I was here, particularly when she was told that that was what I had said. Her room is at the other end of the house from the garage; she probably didn't hear me driving out.'

Clyde Northcott's ebony features showed no sign of surprise. 'What time would this be?'

'The children were already in their pyjamas when they waved goodbye to their daddy. I saw them into bed and left Ingrid to read their stories. I must have been away by quarter to eight, or ten to eight at the latest.'

'And where did you go?'

'You can probably guess that. I went to Paul's farm.'

'And were you there overnight?'

'Oh, no! We don't do overnight. We don't want the children to know about us.' She was suddenly careful of her children's sensibilities, where her own conduct had seemed to concern her not a jot. But that was quite a normal convolution: people became more sensitive when children were involved. And in any case, cynical CID men thought, once a young son and daughter were aware of an affair, Adam Cassidy would have learned of it very quickly.

'So you left Mr Barnes's residence at what time?'

'It must have been around eleven. I was back here before half past.'

Northcott made a careful note of the times. There was a cutting edge to Peach's voice as he said, 'Is there anything else in your previous statement which you wish to revise, Mrs Cassidy?'

'No.' For the first time, Jane Cassidy looked a trifle embarrassed. 'I take your point that I should have told you this at first. I'm sorry I acted so foolishly. But will it be possible to keep it confidential that I was with Paul on Friday night? I don't want Damon and Kate to find out about it through gossiping neighbours.'

Peach gave her the standard reply with his face as inscrutable as a Buddha's. 'We treat all information as confidential, Mrs Cassidy. Of course, if it becomes evidence in a court case, the matter passes out of our hands.'

# SIXTEEN

Peach drove as they made their way back to Brunton from Jane Cassidy's house. He had an intimate knowledge of the lanes around here, which were little changed from the days when he had walked and cycled over them as a boy. These roads were actually easier to negotiate at nights, when the headlights of approaching vehicles gave notice of their arrival on blind bends.

It was not until they were running into Clitheroe on the B road, that he said thoughtfully, 'I'm beginning to see things about this case. But through a glass darkly; I'm not sure what they mean as yet.'

Clyde Northcott waited for him to enlarge upon this rather gnomic thought, but nothing else came from his DCI. So Clyde checked his mobile phone messages and decided one of them was significant enough to demand an immediate response. 'Delroy? Clyde Northcott here. What have you got for me?'

'Not on the phone, Mr Northcott.'

'Where, then? Behind the *Fox and Pheasant*?'

'No. You'll need to come here. Back door, through the yard.' There was a sudden fear in the thin voice that Northcott would ring off. 'I've got something worth your while.'

'OK, Delroy. What time?'

'Tonight. Nine o'clock.'

'You got it.' He rang off, stared at the road ahead through the windscreen for thirty seconds, then responded to Peach's unspoken query. 'A snout. About this case.'

'Tread carefully, lad. There are some nasty sods involved in this case.' The warning was as near as Percy Peach would come to voicing affection for his new DS bagman.

Unless he is very new and very junior, every CID officer has his snouts. These are usually pathetically small fish, swimming in the dangerous pools of the criminal underworld, supplementing the income they make there with useful but erratic payments from police officers for information they pick up and retail. For a man in his mid-twenties, Detective Sergeant Clyde

Northcott had a surprisingly extensive range of snouts. It was a range which would only have been available to a man who had once been among the villains himself.

Five years ago, Clyde had been a small-time dealer in illicit drugs with a reliable source of supply. In those days, given forty-eight hours, he could get his hands on heroin, cocaine, LSD, ecstasy and even Rohypnol, the sex drug which was in constant demand. With his physique and the talent for violence he had developed through his teenage years, he had been able to look after himself on the dangerous paths he chose to tread.

Then, before he had any serious criminal record, he had become a murder suspect in a case handled by the then Detective Inspector Peach. He was totally innocent, but things looked bad for him for a while. At the conclusion of the case, Peach, recognizing his qualities as well as his talent for the wrong sort of company, had encouraged him to join the police force. Two years later, Percy had recruited him to his CID team. When marriage necessitated the departure of DS Lucy Blake from this elite group, Clyde Northcott, who had shown many more talents than the 'hard bastard' ones which Peach always instanced, was promoted to detective sergeant alongside his mentor.

The best of snouts have a nose for information and make considerable sums from the police budget allocated to them. But it is a hazardous trade, for they are divulging information about very dangerous men. Only the most shrewd and cautious of snouts survive for long. Delroy Flecker was moderately shrewd and immensely cautious. He also had the snout's talent for hoovering up information from a multitude of different sources.

Three hours after he had spoken to Flecker on his mobile, Clyde Northcott, in jeans, trainers and a black polo-neck sweater, moved cautiously through the shadows towards the back entrance of a terraced house in the oldest part of Brunton. There were not many of these houses left now, with flagged stone back-yards leading down to heavily bolted wooden gates beside what had originally been outside privies. He flashed his small torch briefly and checked the number twenty-three which was crudely painted in grey upon the green of the door.

The bolts were not drawn. The door squeaked softly as he inched it back on its worn hinges. He listened for a moment, then slid through and moved towards the rear of the house, where light spilled thinly through the crack in the shut curtains.

A cat flew suddenly and silently from somewhere near his feet, over the six feet high brick wall to his left and into the blackness beyond it. He was pleased to see the flash of its silhouette for a moment on the top of the wall; he had thought at first it must be a rat.

The door opened immediately to his quiet tap. The man whom he now followed through the battered kitchen and into the room beyond it was a foot shorter than him and half his weight. He sat Clyde down on a dining chair beside the scratched table and took the other one himself. Delroy Flecker was in his fifties, with flecks of white in his frizzy hair and eyes which seemed never to rest anywhere for longer than a second. He was even blacker than Northcott, but where the younger man's features were as smooth as those of a carved Egyptian deity, Flecker's were as heavily lined as those of a man twenty years older than himself.

He said, 'It's big stuff, this, Mr Northcott. But dangerous for me.' He glanced nervously over his shoulder, as if fearing that there might be listeners, even in this empty house.

Clyde gave him a brief, encouraging smile. 'Spit it out, Delroy. Then we'll decide how big it is.'

'Charlie Ford.' Flecker spoke as if the name itself should be impressive, then glanced at Northcott to see if it was.

Charlie Ford was a contract killer, known to have dispatched half a dozen people in the last two years. Like most of his trade, he was impossible to pin down. Those who could have given the evidence which might have brought him to justice were far too frightened to do so. He operated in different parts of the country, under three names, and had almost certainly committed several more killings than the six which the police had assigned to him.

Northcott, professionally impassive, said, 'It's a name, Delroy. No more than a name, until you're prepared to make it more. Can you tell me his target?'

'No. But I can tell you who was using him and how much he paid.'

'Let's have it then.'

Flecker put a gaunt hand on the table, advanced it for a moment towards his visitor, then thought better of the move. 'I need the money up front, Mr Northcott.'

'Do you, indeed? Well, I'm afraid you can piss off on that one, Delroy. You know the rules as well as I do. I hear what you have to say; I decide its value, if any. It's a one-sided world, Delroy, but no one ever told you it was fair.'

'All right, Mr Northcott. I trust you.' His voice rose to a whine as he forsook demand and attempted conciliation. 'This is good, though. You'll be glad you came here tonight.'

'I've had a long day. I get impatient when I'm tired, Delroy.'

'It was Tony Valento who used Charlie Ford. He paid him three thousand.' The facts Flecker had meant to string out tumbled out swiftly under threat.

Three thousand wasn't enough for a killing. It would be a down payment, the first instalment of a transaction to be completed after the target had been dispatched. 'When was this?'

'Thursday night last week. My man saw it happen.'

'It's not enough for a killing, Delroy. Has the balance been attended to?'

'Can't tell you that, Mr Northcott. I'll keep my ear to the ground.'

Northcott slid ten twenty pound notes across the table in his closed hand. Flecker's thin, bony fingers looked like a hen's scratching foot as he gathered in his payment. A free-range hen, thought Clyde, roaming far and gathering valuable information. He didn't question the accuracy of what he had been told; Flecker had proved himself over the years as a snapper-up of unconsidered trifles. Percy Peach would have known who first said that, thought Northcott; probably bloody Shakespeare. Peach seemed to Clyde to know everything.

'There's more where that came from, if you can get more details. How dangerous is it for you?' He hadn't asked earlier; that would have been an invitation to Flecker to press for higher payment.

'It's always dangerous, Mr Northcott.'

'Of course it is, Delroy, and you're St George on a white charger, slaying the dragon of evil. So cut the bullshit and tell me whether you're taking big risks over this.'

'No, not really – not by my standards.' The thin chest bulged like a pouter pigeon's for a moment, but the look on Clyde's face cast him straight back to whining mode. 'I know the score, Mr Northcott. You don't piss about with contract killers. But I listen 'ard, see. Keep my ears open all the time in the pub. Once people have 'ad a couple, they speak louder than they fink they do. That's where I picked this up; two of Valento's 'eavies 'aving a chat.'

'Find whether the transaction's now been completed, Delroy. And when. If it gives us a conviction, there'll be double what you've got there.'

The door shut quickly and softly behind him as Clyde Northcott slid into the welcome cool of the darkness outside. He looked up and down the unlit alley outside the wooden door at the bottom of the yard, then kept close to the wall as he moved over two hundred yards of uneven cobblestones and back to the Yamaha. It was bitterly cold on the short ride to his home. But better the cold than the danger of those scum-laden pools which Delroy Flecker trawled for him.

On Thursday morning, thin flakes of snow drifted slowly across Brunton. The days of Lowry's mills and chimneys were long gone, and the town was crowded with shoppers, but there were enough grimy brick buildings left in the old cotton town for it to retain a shabby air, as the snow turned to sleet and the pavements glistened beneath the Christmas lights.

Clyde Northcott had fed his snout's revelation into the team's briefing meeting at eight thirty. It was much the most interesting of the dozen morsels of information which might or might not be relevant to this case. He felt already well into his day when he knocked at the door of Dean Morley's flat, but Peach beside him was as bouncy and energetic as a Labrador on its morning walk.

Dean Morley's face fell when he opened the door and saw them beneath the stone steps of the Victorian house. 'We've only just finished breakfast,' he said accusingly.

'That's how the other half lives,' said Peach to his companion. 'If you want the soft life, DS Northcott, you should get yourself a job in acting. I should think you'd do well as a Hard Bastard. There seems to be a call for them, in all these unrealistic police series – and there can't be much competition, amongst the acting fraternity.'

Dean looked with some distaste from the big black man to the much smaller white one beside him; perhaps he could not decide which one represented the greater danger to him and the life he had built for himself. 'I suppose you'd better come in.'

He led them into the high, pleasant, nineteenth-century room with the big bay window and the numerous original paintings. Both of the occupants were in shirt sleeves and Dean felt the

need to explain what he obviously felt was a state of *déshabillé*.
'Keith is painting today. And I was just beginning to wash up.
I told you, we've only just finished breakfast; you should really
have told us you were coming here this morning.'

'Should we, indeed? You sound almost as though you have
something to hide, Mr Morley. Doesn't he, Keith?' Peach's
question was addressed to Keith Arnold, who was now standing
awkwardly in the doorway at the far side of the room, his six-
feet frame looking more bony and awkward than ever beneath
the paint-stained old shirt he was using as a smock.

He started like a nervous deer when he was addressed. Then
he said with an attempt at dignity, 'If you come here un-
announced, you must take us as you find us.'

'And we shall do just that, Keith.' Peach divined correctly
that a gay man as nervous of police harassment as Arnold
obviously was would be more intimidated by the use of his
first name. It brought to him memories of past mockings and
ancient brutalities. 'Don't let me keep you from your painting,
Keith.' Then, as Arnold turned away in relief, he said, 'If you
could just tell us where you were between eight and midnight
last Friday night, I don't think we'll need you any more.'

The last line was delivered with an actor's timing, designed
to strike Arnold just at the moment when he was thinking that
he had been dismissed and his ordeal was over. Dean Morley
realized that, but his partner didn't. Arnold turned and stared
panic-stricken at his partner for a significant second before
he spoke to Peach. 'Last Friday? I'm not sure I can recall it
instantly. I—'

'He was here with me. Weren't you, Keith?' Arnold nodded,
not trusting himself to speak immediately. Morley turned back
to Peach. 'I've already answered that for you. I told you when
you were here on Tuesday that Keith and I spent the evening
here together.'

Percy beamed at him, apparently delighted with their joint
discomfiture. 'Of course you did, Dean. And the very efficient
DS Northcott has recorded exactly that. But we needed to
have it confirmed for us, you see. By Mr Arnold himself.
Without anyone pulling his strings.'

Dean told himself to keep calm. 'Did you make a resolu-
tion to be insolent before you ever set foot in our home this
morning, DCI Peach?'

Peach made a good attempt at looking hurt. 'We need to check things out, Mr Morley. Make sure the other party's recall of certain events is exactly the same as yours. You'd be surprised how often that isn't the case.'

'I was here on Friday night. So was Dean. We were here together at the times you specified.' Keith Arnold was still standing awkwardly in the doorway. He rapped the words out quickly, as if he needed them over with. 'I'd been decorating this room all week. I needed time to catch up with my painting.' His nervousness made the innocent words emerge as if he had carefully memorized them beforehand.

Percy gave him a reassuring beam. 'Well, that's all right then, isn't it? DS Northcott can put a big tick against what Mr Morley told us about that and we can move on.'

Arnold hesitated for a moment, balancing unsteadily on one leg. Then he said, 'I'll be in the next room if you need me. I have paints mixed and ready to go on the canvas.'

Peach watched him depart fondly, as if he were a favourite but rather backward child. His smile faded as he turned back to Morley. 'We now need to check whether you were completely honest with us about events at the television studio and on location, in the weeks immediately before Mr Cassidy's death.'

'I told you no lies about that.'

'But you might have withheld certain information, which would amount to the same thing.'

'I don't think I did. And if I did, it was unwitting.'

'Unwitting. Interesting word, that, don't you think, Mr Morley? If you withheld certain facts about the deceased's relationships, you would be failing to provide the police with the assistance to be expected when they were investigating a serious crime. If the import of what you withheld was significant, you might even be accused of obstructing the police in the course of their enquiries.'

'What is it you want to know?'

'Ah! The apparently innocent question which may or may not constitute a shrewd evasion! I don't know what I want to know, do I? I merely want Mr Dean Morley, a close associate of the deceased for twenty years and more, to be completely frank with me.'

Dean sighed wearily – almost theatrically, Percy thought uncharitably. 'I've told you all about my relationship with Adam. I thought we were close; then he shafted me over my part in the new series. I was devastated by that. But I didn't kill him. End of story.'

'Oh, if only it were, Mr Morley. If only it were!' Peach's sigh replicated that of the man opposite him. 'But even if that's the end of it for you, I still have a murder to solve. And I'm certain you can help me with that.' He leaned forward until his face was within four feet of Morley's. 'If we discount for the moment your own close friendship and its disintegration, what other serious relationships did you discern in the last few weeks of Cassidy's life?'

Dean was acutely conscious of two things. First, of the face he could not escape in front of him, round and bald and threatening, like a child's simple but disturbing drawing. And secondly of his partner's anxious ears, as he stood before his easel in the adjoining room. He licked his lips and put his head down. 'Michelle Davies. Adam had a thing going with her. The other girls on the set were beginning to rib her about it. From hints she let drop to them, I'm pretty sure Adam was planning to take her away on the weekend he died.'

Peach and Northcott stood on either side of Mark Gilbey and looked out over Salford Quays. With the Lowry Centre dominating the architecture and the sun glinting on wide expanses of water around it, it was the most impressive demonstration available of the transformation of the former slum landscapes of Salford and Manchester to a breathtaking view of the future. The twenty-first century equivalent of Oxford's dreaming spires in the nineteenth, perhaps. Neither policeman had seen the view from this height before. From the fourteenth storey of the skyscraper, distance lent not enchantment but a kind of detachment to the view. So tiny and so silent were the people and cars which moved below them, that it seemed that they could observe the movements in this Lilliputian world without being part of it.

'Impressive,' said Peach conventionally.

'It's what you pay for,' said the man the newspapers called 'the agent to the stars'.

'I'm more your Lake District man when it comes to views,' said Percy. 'Helvellyn and Striding Edge are more my taste.'

'They don't build offices there,' said Gilbey with a smile.

'Not yet they don't. But they're edging into the green belt.'

'You said you wanted to see me about Adam Cassidy,' said
Mark. The name signified the end of the preliminaries and
the beginning of business. The two CID men went and sat in
the comfortable chairs set out for them and Mark resumed his
accustomed seat behind his desk.

'How long had you had Cassidy's custom, Mr Gilbey?' said
Northcott.

'Not long enough to negotiate anything for him, unfortun-
ately, though we had begun our efforts to do so. Adam had
been with us for less than two weeks at the time of his death.'

'Which robbed you of his custom and a nice little earner,'
said Peach.

Gilbey was not at all put out by this vulgar mention of
money. He plucked at his immaculate cuffs and smiled his
professional smile. 'Indeed. But we shall no doubt make
respectable profits from the sales and re-sales around the world
of the five series of *Call Adam Cassidy* which Mr Cassidy
had already completed. He passed all existing rights over to
us when he signed his new contract.'

'Very nice for you.'

'I suppose so. And human nature being what it is, there'll
be interest in a star who has just been sensationally murdered.
There'll be a demand from around the world. It will be short-
term, but it should last long enough for us to secure some
lucrative sales for the Cassidy estate and some useful commis-
sion for us.' Mark Gilbey didn't seem disappointed that human
nature should be so flawed. He looked more like a cat presented
with a bowl of cream.

'All of which must add to Mr Valento's chagrin.'

'I don't suppose he'd know the meaning of that word. Tony
Valento's troubles don't concern me. He's a rogue and I hope
he suffers for it.'

'A rogue capable of murder, Mr Gilbey?'

'Capable of it certainly. Guilty of it in the past, I'm sure,
though not with his own greasy hands. But you would know
more about that than I do.'

'Very probably. The question is: did he have Adam Cassidy
killed?'

'I don't know and I'm glad it's not my job to find out. I
do know that he so much resented Adam's decision to change
his agent that he was considering violence.'

Peach raised his expressive black eyebrows. 'When and where, Mr Gilbey?'

'In a phone call he made to me last week. The Tuesday before Adam Cassidy was killed, I think. He'd just heard that we were to be Adam's new agents.'

'Can you tell us exactly what he said?'

Mark gave them the professional smile which comes from supreme competence. 'I can do more than that, gentlemen. It is our policy to retain tapes. Sometimes the exact words people say are highly important, as I'm sure you find yourselves.' He reached into the top drawer of his desk, produced the cassette he had kept there ever since he heard about his new client's death, and slipped it into the player.

They heard the rising notes of Valento's wrath at his client's defection and the counterpoint of Gilbey's coolly scornful replies. They heard the rival agent's final, frustrated words, 'The slimy sod's going to have to answer to me for this!' Clyde Northcott recorded them gleefully in his notebook and the CID prepared to leave this spectacular eyrie.

They were on their feet when Mark Gilbey said, 'I've been reading about your considerable reputation in the national press, Detective Chief Inspector Peach.' He indicated the *Daily Mail* and the *Sun* and some lurid headlines about the case. 'If you decide you'd like to publish your memoirs, we'd be interested in acting for you. When you finally retire and become plain "Mister Peach", perhaps. We can always find you a ghostwriter.'

'I'll bear that in mind,' said Percy, with a last look at Salford Quays.

There was one highly interesting piece of information awaiting them when they got back to the nick at Brunton.

The forensic labs had compared DNA in the sample of human hair retrieved from the passenger seat of Cassidy's BMW 110 with the samples volunteered by the people who had worked with the deceased in the last weeks of his life. There were several hairs in the sample, which had all come from the same scalp: they appeared to have been extracted from the teeth of a comb.

There was a definite and indisputable match with the DNA sample given by one of Cassidy's acting colleagues. Michelle Davies.

# SEVENTEEN

The person who had killed Adam Cassidy was feeling unnaturally calm. That seemed odd, but when everything seemed to be going your way, it was surely natural. There was nothing on the one o'clock television news about the case; that was probably the first time it hadn't merited a mention. Tomorrow night, it would be seven days since the killing. Didn't they say that murders unsolved within a week tended to remain unsolved?

This Chief Superintendent Tucker, who was fronting up the television and radio releases, was a self-righteous prick, and no danger. He was plainly just a front man for the police. That Peach fellow was the real enemy. He knew what he was about and it wouldn't do to underestimate him. Detective Chief Inspector Peach would probably be back again, throwing his weight about and trying to give the impression that he was on the verge of solving the case. But from the other side, you knew better; you knew that he was up against it and just putting on a brave face.

Roast in hell, Adam Cassidy! No one's going down for you. Confidence, but not over-confidence, that's the tactic. Calmness will have its reward.

James Walton told Michelle Davies she could use his office when he heard that the CID officers were coming to the studios to see her. He still felt guilty about having to go back on the offer he had made to her in good faith of the role in the *Call Alec Dawson* series. It might give her a little lift with her fellow-actors to be offered the senior producer's quarters for her interview.

Michelle forced herself to sit in the leather chair behind the big desk. It felt as if she was an upstart usurping the master's position, but it also felt reassuring to have this solid expanse of wood between her and her interrogators. Peach and DS Northcott settled themselves unhurriedly, looking round the walls at the stills of scenes from the studio's most memorable series of the past thirty years, letting the tense silence in the room stretch another few telling seconds.

Then Peach looked hard at her and said evenly, 'We needed to see you again, Ms Davies. As I warned you on Tuesday, new issues always emerge as we gather more knowledge about the murder victim and the people whom he most closely associated with. This shouldn't take very long, if you are completely frank with us. Which I have to advise you will be much the best strategy for you.'

'I've cooperated very fully with this investigation. I've done everything asked of me. Like most of the other people involved in the *Call Alec Dawson* series, I've even given a voluntary DNA sample.'

'Yes. Useful thing, DNA. Very difficult to argue with it; even the bloody lawyers find that. Kind of blackmail about it, too, don't you think? You're asked to volunteer a sample, but you feel that if you refuse, you will inevitably be suspected of having something to hide. Hardly voluntary, is it, in those circumstances? Still, the law hedges us poor policemen about with all kinds of unreasonable restrictions. We deserve to have the odd thing running in our favour.'

Michelle, who had felt exactly the dilemma he had outlined when asked to provide a saliva sample, said primly, 'I gave a sample because I had nothing to fear – because I felt it could only eliminate me from suspicion.'

Peach looked at her with his head on one side, like an intelligent and slightly surprised cocker spaniel. 'Really? Well, I must say that is a refreshing attitude. And a commendably brave one also!'

'No, not brave. I gave a sample because I knew it could only help to clear me from suspicion.'

'Which it has failed to do. Indeed, it seems to have had the reverse effect. Ms Davies, a sample of head hair which was found in Mr Cassidy's BMW sports car at the scene of his death has now been analyzed. I have to tell you that there is a match with the sample you volunteered to our murder team on Tuesday.'

There was no acting needed now. She felt the blood draining from her face as she said dully, 'I've never been in that car. There must be some mistake.'

'There is no mistake, Ms Davies, except on your part.

Any court would accept that the hairs recovered from the passenger seat of the BMW came from your head.'

'But I've never been in that car. The only car of Adam's I was ever in was the maroon Mercedes.' She looked at the closed door behind them and spoke like one in a hypnotic trance.

'Then how do you explain the findings of our forensic analysts?'

'I cannot do that. And I'm not mistaken. I was never in that BMW.'

'Is that your last word on the matter?'

'It is.' Michelle gave herself a tiny but perceptible physical shake, as if emerging from a trance. She knew that she wasn't behaving with her normal confidence. She told herself firmly that the proper strategy in this crisis was to assert herself, to show them that she must not be condemned, however inescapable the evidence might seem. She leaned forward and drummed her small fingers on the big desk, trying to recapture and enjoy her moment of playing the tycoon. 'You said this wouldn't take long, Mr Peach. We're doing the first read-through of a new drama downstairs in the studio. I can't afford to be away for long without disrupting things.'

Peach smiled slowly as he looked at her. He seemed to enjoy the spectacle of this medieval Madonna, with her long black hair and her smooth pale skin, attempting to play the modern industrial mogul. 'I said it wouldn't take long with just one proviso, Ms Davies. That was that you were perfectly frank with us. Which means much more so than you were on Tuesday.'

She withdrew her hands from their slightly ridiculous position on the big desk and folded her arms, trying now to simulate a calmness she did not feel. 'I told you the truth on Tuesday. You cannot instance a single lie!'

Instead of being confounded, Peach leapt eagerly upon her words; the spaniel had found a bone. 'Some truth, indeed, Ms Davies. But not the whole truth and nothing but the truth, as the immortal legal phrase has it. You chose to withhold certain things, which in our view is as damaging as the lie direct. Sometimes more so.'

Michelle felt her arms tightening across her breast, her fingers digging hard into the soft flesh at the top of them. It was like being in one of the hoary old thrillers the older actors said used to be played regularly in rep. Except that this was grim reality. 'I didn't kill Adam Cassidy. I had nothing to do with his death.'

'Difficult for us to accept, that is. Especially now we have the DNA evidence. Had it not been for you, I don't believe he would have been in the lonely place where he met his death last Friday night.'

'I don't know what you mean.'

But she did; it showed for a moment in her face as well as in her voice. It was Clyde Northcott who spoke, deep-voiced and inescapable. 'You told us on Tuesday that you and Mr Cassidy were lovers. You did not tell us that you were planning to go to the Lake District with him on the evening when he died. That was what you chose to withhold.'

'Someone told you about that?' Michelle spoke dully, her brain still struggling to work out the implications of this for her.

'We have Mr Cassidy's phone and its messages.' They would protect Dean Morley, who had confirmed this. Confidentiality mattered, and murder investigations left behind quite enough scars without needless additions. That was assuming that neither Morley nor Davies had committed murder, Clyde Northcott reminded himself wryly.

Peach, sensing that Davies was now at her most vulnerable, said softly, 'Did you arrange to meet him eight miles up the road from here, Michelle? On that lay-by beside the A666?'

'No, I know exactly where it is. I've used it myself.' It was suddenly important to her to give them that curious, irrelevant detail, as if it might help to establish her innocence.

'Then how were you to meet?'

'He was to pick me up here. About half past nine. We weren't going earlier because he said he couldn't get away in time for dinner. But we'd have been in Grasmere by eleven, he said, and then we'd have the rest of the weekend to ourselves.' Again she was giving them every detail she could think of, as if that might add substance to her tale.

'Did he know you'd been told you were out of the next series of *Call Alec Dawson*?'

'I don't know. I presumed he wouldn't have arranged the weekend if he had. But I knew by then that Adam was a strange man. I was planning to have an almighty row with him. If I'm honest, I think I also believed that I might somehow persuade him to reinstate me during the weekend.'

'Much better to be honest, Ms Davies, as you now realize. We'd be more willing to take your statements at face value, if you'd been fully honest with us on Tuesday.'

'I'd have been telling you that I had an assignation with Adam on the very night he was killed. At almost the very time he was killed, as I now understand it.'

'And we'd have been able to accept more easily that you had that assignation but didn't kill him, if you'd told us about it from the start. As it is, we have to ask you again, did you in fact meet him up on that moor and blow him into the next world with his own shotgun?'

She winced at that image, but seemed now to have recovered from the shock she had shown two minutes earlier. 'No. I waited here for him to arrive. When it got to half past ten, I decided he definitely wasn't coming. I'd tried his mobile, but there was no reply. I thought he must have realized I'd been told I was losing the part in his next series and just didn't want to confront me. I could understand that. The longer I waited, the more determined I was to have that matter out with him.'

Northcott's quiet basso profundo voice, which rang in her ears with a curiously comforting tone, said, 'If you didn't kill Cassidy last Friday night, you must have some idea who did.'

'No. I've thought about it, because it would get me off the hook. But I can't think it would be anyone who'd worked with him on the last series. I know I had a motive and I felt when I first heard about his treachery that I could cheerfully kill him for it. But I couldn't and I didn't. Dean Morley had much more to lose than me; he felt his whole existence, the way of life he's only recently established for himself, was threatened by the loss of his role as leading villain in the new series. But Dean doesn't strike me as a man who could plan and execute murder.'

'Then who else?'

'I don't know. Adam told me a couple of weeks ago that he was planning to change his agent because he wanted to break into Hollywood. I told him to think hard about it, because Tony Valento would cut up rough. Did he change his agent?'

\*       \*       \*

Old Harry Cassidy was failing badly. His elder son Luke had never witnessed the lengthy process of dying before. His mother had died suddenly, passing away with the minimum of fuss which had characterized her life of quiet but sturdy labour and virtue. Now he was finding his father's slow, inevitable and now accelerating decline more harrowing than he would have believed possible.

'You need to eat something, Dad.'

'Why do I?'

'You can't bring Adam back by punishing yourself.'

'Who did it? They got anyone for it yet?'

'Not yet, Dad. But the police are working hard on it.'

'Be those bloody Pakis, shouldn't wonder.'

Luke came and stood in front of his father, where the old bigot could see his face. 'Dad, I think one of the few things the police know for certain is that it was probably one of the people who'd been working with him.' Or one of his family; he couldn't tell the old man that his other son and Adam's only brother was still under suspicion.

Harry Cassidy hacked a cough which seemed to shake every bone in his upper body. 'Bloody police don't know what they're bloody doing, nowadays.'

'Dad, you really should eat something, you know. Give it a try, before it goes cold.'

'Don't want it. Don't bloody need it.'

The old man's lips set in sullen rejection. Luke was reminded against his will of Shakespeare's seven ages of man. Harry was now at the 'lean and slipper'd pantaloon' stage, querulous of aid and sullenly rejecting all argument. Luke wasn't sure he could cope with that final stage, the one the remorseless Shakespearean eye saw as:

'Second childishness and mere oblivion,
Sans teeth, sans eyes, sans taste, sans everything.'

Would it come to that? In the years to come, would he still be able to remember that other man, who had swung young Luke high above his head on summer walks, who had taught him marbles and football and how to catch a cricket ball? Would this earlier and happier image survive after Harry was reduced to that living death where he did not even recognize the people who loved him?

Perhaps he shouldn't keep insisting that the old man should eat.

'You can take the lead in this one,' said Peach. 'It was your snout who gave us the information. You're the sort of hard bastard who might frighten even a wrong'un like Tony Valento.'

Coming from Percy Peach, that was probably a sort of compliment, Clyde Northcott told himself. Or at any rate the nearest thing to a compliment he was likely to get.

'CID. Mr Valento is expecting us,' Clyde said to the PA who rose to greet them. He waved his warrant card under her nose and was at her boss's door whilst Peach was still visiting his most cheerful smile upon the bewildered lady.

Perhaps Cassidy's ex-agent had always intended to be aggressive, or perhaps he decided to meet fire with fire. Either way, it was a mistake.

'I won't ask you to sit down, because I don't expect you to be here long,' Tony Valento said.

He was a large, formidably muscled man, but at fifty he was running a little to fat. Clyde Northcott advanced so quickly upon him that he recoiled a pace backwards. Unexpectedly, Northcott's formidable features formed a smile, but it was plainly a smile of contempt at his quarry's retreat. 'We're busy people, Mr Valento. We don't intend wasting much time with the likes of you. The question is whether we depart here as the twosome who came to question you or as a trio, with you in handcuffs.' There was no doubt from the set of the ebony features which alternative DS Northcott would prefer.

Like most men who employ serious muscle to do their dirty work for them, Valento was a coward at heart. It was also many years since he had felt himself threatened with physical violence. He told himself that the British police couldn't beat people up, that the whole weight of the law was nowadays against it. But with Northcott's face three inches higher than his and only a foot away, he wasn't convinced of that. He said, 'There's really no need for this attitude, you know. I've nothing to hide from you. Perhaps after all we'd better sit down.'

He sank into the chair behind his desk. DCI Peach, who had witnessed the exchanges so far with the delight of a sadist in a ringside seat, dusted the immaculate leather of the indicated chair with the flat of his hand, sat down, and crossed his legs to await further developments. Only when he saw both of them sitting did Clyde Northcott accept the third chair in the room. He did so with obvious reluctance, sitting on the front of it, testing it for size, then pulling it forward to the very edge of the desk, so that his uncompromising features were still within three feet of his prey. He evinced every intention of leaping across those three feet, if he did not receive the responses he required from the hapless occupant of this room.

In his apprehension, Valento made the mistake of looking towards Percy Peach for some sort of relief, an error which would have been scarcely credible to the Brunton criminal fraternity. But this was Manchester, and a man not used to Peach's idiosyncrasies. Valento felt an irresistible need to break the silence. 'I've nothing to hide. You've got nothing on me.'

Clyde Northcott paused briefly to examine his immaculate nails and fingers, as if indicating what a shame it would be to contaminate them by violent contact with this recalcitrant subject. 'Lies, Mr Valento, lies. I thought we were agreed that we weren't going to waste time on this?'

'I didn't kill that bastard Cassidy and there's no way you're going to pin it on me.'

'You hired someone to kill him. You don't sully your delicate paws with the nasty stuff.' Clyde looked at the rather pudgy hands in question with some distaste and saw them instantly withdrawn from the top of the desk.

Valento licked his lips, made himself look into the stern black face, and said, 'Prove it! Prove your bloody fantasy or take it back!'

Clyde took his time over his trump card, allowing himself a smile, savouring the apprehension he could scent like a raw stink around the man opposite him.

'Charlie Ford.'

'Never heard of him.' But Tony Valento was not a good liar once he was frightened. The phrase carried no conviction.

'You've used him in the past. Used him as a hit man to eliminate Dangerous Dave Wall four years ago.'

'That was never proved.'

'Precisely. The first time we can agree on something,

Mr Valento. You were never charged, because the Crown Prosecution Service did not have the proof to bring you to court. But they and everyone else involved knew exactly what had happened. We still have the details. Perhaps Mr Ford will give us the proof in the Dangerous Dave case as a bargaining plea, when we arrest him on this one.'

'This is harassment. You've no more proof now than you had then.'

'Three thousand pounds, Mr Valento.'

'What?'

'That is the sum you paid to Charlie Ford on Wednesday December the eleventh. Two days before Charlie fulfilled the contract and blew Adam Cassidy out of your life.'

'Who told you this?'

'Manchester CID keep tabs on Charlie Ford. It takes time, but we get contract killers in the end, you see.' You protected your snouts at all costs; Clyde was determined that this should never be traced back to the hapless Delroy Flecker. 'You should have chosen a different hit man for this killing, you see. But hindsight is a wonderful thing, is it not?'

'Three thousand isn't the price to kill a man.'

'Know all about that, do you?'

'I listen around. You pick these things up.'

'Indeed you do. And we do as well, Mr Valento. We know just as well as you do that three thousand is a deposit. A down payment, with the rest of the price to be paid on completion. Another seven thousand or so. When did you deliver that to Charlie Ford?'

'I didn't. He didn't kill Adam Cassidy.' But Valento was staring hard at his desk now, unable to look into the wide dark eyes which seemed to move ever nearer to him.

Peach had taken an undisguised pleasure in the exchange so far. He now spoke for the first time, saying quietly, 'Much better to tell us now, Tony. Unless you want to run the risk of Charlie Ford turning Queen's evidence and sliding you into a high-security cell beside him.'

'Charlie Ford didn't kill Adam Cassidy.' Valento's dull tone made him sound as if he did not expect to be believed.

Peach raised his eyebrows high and smiled at the same time, a phenomenon which was a new horror for the man on the other side of the desk. 'You're saying Ford didn't deliver on the contract you'd taken out with him? It's a sad thing, when there isn't even honour among thieves.'

'I'm saying nothing.'

'Much the best policy, in your place. Don't think it will save you, though.'

'Charlie Ford didn't kill Adam Cassidy.'

'And how would you know that, Mr Valento?'

He shook his head, as if he could not think straight in the face of this joint attack. 'I'm saying nothing. I want a brief before I say anything else.'

'Very wise, that. Feels to me as though you're slamming the stable door long after the contract killer has bolted, but we're just simple policemen. Don't leave the area without letting us know all about it, will you, Tony? I think we'd better leave it there, DS Northcott. For the moment, that is.'

Throughout his exchanges with Peach, Clyde Northcott had continued to eye Valento like a Rottweiler who has discovered an unexpectedly juicy bone. He now rose with every sign of reluctance, keeping his dark brown eyes unblinkingly upon Valento as he backed reluctantly towards the door.

The two had climbed into the police car before Peach said, 'I thought you did quite well in there, Clyde. You probably went a bit too soft on the bugger, but that will be the effect of working with me and my peaceful pussycat nature.'

# EIGHTEEN

The children were excited as they came out of the village school. They had finished for the Christmas break and they carried Christmas cards for their parents. These exhibited the usual wide range of childish expertise, but they had been compiled with a universal degree of enthusiasm and were received accordingly by the parents at the gates.

Jane Cassidy was a little apprehensive about the names on the trophies which six-year-old Damon and four-year-old Kate would brandish, but she need not have feared. A thoughtful teacher had ensured that only 'Mummy' was afforded the Christmas greeting, that only 'Mummy' featured in the garishly coloured portraits within. Five yards away from them, eight-year-old Thomas Barnes was presenting a relatively much more sophisticated effort to his duly grateful father.

'Have you a few minutes to spare, Paul?' asked Jane, conscious of the eager adult ears around them and trying to sound casual. 'If you have, I'd like your advice on our new lawn. An awful lot of moss seems to have appeared since winter arrived.'

Barnes glanced ostentatiously at his watch. 'I'm sure I can fit that in. I'll have a look at the moss, certainly, but you're probably better to leave any treatment until the spring.'

His response had sounded stagey and contrived, thought Jane. But he wasn't an actor like her, and she found she delighted in the clumsiness of his effort. When you loved someone, even their weaknesses were attractive to you. Or perhaps she just loved the things in him which were so completely different from the life she had previously known. It was reassuring to see his Land Rover following her car up the narrow lane towards her house.

In a few months, they wouldn't need to play these games at the school gates, but for the present it was better not to provide scandal for the gossips. Once the folk round here had got used to the fact of Adam's death, it would seem only natural for two lonely people like her and Paul to be drawn together. She suspected she would always be an exotic creature from the outside as far as these likeable, conservative country folk were concerned. But she would rather be seen as someone who had opted for the rural life with Paul than a scarlet woman with predatory sexual appetites.

They took the children into the playroom. Both of them were pleased to see how Thomas enjoyed his role as the senior and treated little Kate as if she were a fragile piece of human china, rather than the boisterous four-year-old tomboy Jane saw most of the time. She shut the door soundlessly upon the three and flung herself impulsively into Paul's arms. 'I needed that!' she said, when they separated lips and limbs a full minute later.

Paul Barnes nodded, smiled, but was unable to delay his need for information any longer. 'Tell me about last night!'

'It was OK, I think. The CID are still treating me with kid gloves, but they managed to ask about everything they want to know.'

'What about us?'

'They made me tell them about Friday night. I made it so that they had to worm it out of me. I told them I'd come to you. That we'd been together through the evening.' His tense-ness had got through to her. She found herself speaking in terse phrases, wanting to get out what she had to tell him as quickly as possible.

'Didn't they want to know why you hadn't told them that at first? Why you'd changed your story?'

'I think they accepted that it would have been embarrassing for me to confess that I'd been with another man when Adam died. When they saw me this time, they'd already questioned you and found out that there was something between us. If I'd tried to brazen it out and say I'd been here all through last Friday night, they wouldn't have believed me anyway, would they? They don't say much, but I think they just accepted that I was now telling them the truth.'

'Good.' He glanced at the clock on the wall in the kitchen where they were speaking. 'I'd better collect Thomas and be on my way. It's best that we keep things as low-key as possible as far as the public are concerned.'

Hazel Cassidy studied her husband's grey face anxiously. Luke looked exhausted; she felt a sudden, overwhelming surge of tenderness for him. 'I can't think they'll have much to say to you. I've already told the young policewoman who took my statement that I sent you out to the pub last Friday. I'll talk to them with you, if you like.' Adam Cassidy had given Luke quite enough trouble when he was alive. It was cruel that even after his death he should be bringing them problems.

'No. I'll take them into the front room. Where are the children?'

'Upstairs in their rooms. No homework now that they've finished for Christmas. No doubt they're texting their friends with a view to festive mayhem!' In the moment of silence which followed, they could hear the steady, muted bass rhythms which constituted the inevitable background to most teenage activities.

'Make sure they don't interrupt us in the front room. It shouldn't take long, as you say.' It was suddenly very important to Luke Cassidy that neither his wife nor his children should be involved in his exchanges with CID; he didn't want them contaminated by any such contact. He went into the front room and sat nervously watching the clock, trying in vain to get his tired brain to work out tactics for this meeting.

It was eight o'clock in the evening when he answered the door and showed DCI Peach and DS Northcott into the front room. At the end of what had presumably been a long day for them, neither of them looked at all tired. Indeed, Peach, looking curiously round what was obviously a little-used dining room, seemed positively eager to engage with him. Luke felt resentful of the man already, in view of his own weariness.

'Have you made much progress?' he said nervously.

'Discrepancies,' announced Peach gravely. 'Bane of our life, discrepancies are. But in answer to your question, they also represent a kind of progress. We investigate discrepancies and find out things we didn't know. And in our job, new information always means progress.'

'I see.'

'Do you, Mr Cassidy? Then perhaps you can help us to unravel the discrepancies in your own statements to us.'

'I wasn't aware of any discrepancies. What I said seemed straightforward enough to me.'

Peach's eyebrows rose with a slowness which was almost stately. Then he smiled sadly. 'Straightforward does not necessarily mean correct, though, does it? Any more than simplicity means honesty.'

Luke felt an immense lassitude seeping through his body. Wasn't it better just to let this man have his way? It would certainly be much easier than fighting on. He said heavily, 'Perhaps you had better just tell me what the problem is.'

'I think that would indeed be much the best thing to do. DS Northcott, would you recall to us the section of Mr Cassidy's statement which was problematical?'

Clyde opened his notebook and launched into the sentences he had been waiting to deliver. '"I went out to the pub at about eight o'clock – at my wife's insistence . . . I saw friends I hadn't seen for months and spent more like three hours than one with them. It was after eleven when I got home. About twenty past, I should think."'

Peach let the silence hang heavy for a moment. Then he said very quietly, 'Not wholly true, that account, is it, Mr Cassidy?'

'I don't know what you mean. Hazel has told you when I went out. And I'm sure people can confirm to you that I was in the pub, if you need that.'

'They already have confirmed it, Mr Cassidy. The interesting thing from our point of view is when you got there.'

Luke knew now what was coming, but he could see no way of deviating from the course he had set for himself. He said with weary inevitability, 'The people in the White Hart might have a little difficulty in giving you exact times. The place was crowded and noisy – on a Friday evening, it usually is.'

'Yes. I think you were relying on that.' Peach sounded almost sympathetic.

'They know me there, even though I haven't been in much lately. I was greeted by old friends. I even played darts.'

'In other words, you did everything possible to remind people of your presence.'

'I don't know what you mean.' But Luke knew exactly what the man meant; he just couldn't see any loophole left for an escape.

'You played darts to make people very much aware of your presence. You spoke to lots of people. You tried to give the impression that you'd been in the White Hart for much longer than you actually had. Several people remember seeing you in the pub. None of them remembers seeing you before ten o'clock. Indeed, one of them remembers your coming into the pub at about ten.'

'He's mistaken, then, isn't he? I told you the place was crowded and—'

'Where were you between eight and ten o'clock last Friday night, Mr Cassidy?'

For a moment, he considered stubbornly continuing his defiance. But he knew it was pointless. He said dully, 'I went round to Dad's house. I think I wanted to argue with him about Adam, to tell him that he should try to stop doting on his every promise, because he was never going to be reliable. But when I got there and parked, I knew it would be hopeless and I couldn't bring myself to go into the house.'

He was silent then, wondering how he could have spent so long before he went to the pub, wondering how he was ever going to convince them without contriving a better story than he had prepared. Peach said softly, 'You don't get much help with your father, do you, Luke?'

He hadn't expected this. He couldn't see where it was going. He said loyally, 'That isn't true. Hazel cooks a meal for him almost every day. She's been a good daughter-in-law to Dad.'

'But you bear the brunt of his decline, don't you. You're the one who sees him every day. You're the one who had to listen to him perpetually praising Adam, when Adam rarely chose to come near him.'

Luke felt his love for the woman in the rear part of the house like a physical pain. 'Hazel does everything she can for Dad. She won't go and see him any more because she can't stand his bigotry, his racism and his narrowness, and most of all how he insists on going on about Adam and denigrating me. She doesn't like our children seeing him, for the same reasons. It's different for me. I know that Dad's not always been like this; I know the way he used to be when we were young.'

Peach's voice was as gentle as a therapist's. 'But it's not easy for you. Not easy for you to keep things in perspective. Luke, you said on Wednesday that there were times when you could have killed Adam. Did you in fact drive up on to the A666 last Friday night and do just that?'

'No.'

'Perhaps without ever intending to harm him, until you found his shotgun in your hands?'

'No.' He lifted his hands to the level of his chest in an attempt at denial, then let them drop back hopelessly to his sides. 'I didn't go up there. I'd no idea where Adam was. I rang to try to speak to him but Jane said he was away for the weekend. Then I drove up to Revidge Road and sat looking out over the town, trying to get my head into some sort of order.'

It was the road at the highest point in Brunton. It commanded a view over the park and the old cotton town below it; where once there had been scores of mill and foundry chimneys, now there were four. Peach said, 'Are you telling us you were up there for two hours?'

'For the best part of two hours, if you say I didn't get to the White Hart until ten. I sat outside Dad's house for a few minutes, then I drove up there. I remember watching the lights of the town, and for some reason finding it consoling that they didn't change, apart from those of the cars moving along the streets.' He sounded as if he found his conduct as strange as they did. He said feebly, 'I was very tired, I suppose, after a busy week at school and all the troubles with Dad. I wasn't thinking very straight; I think I just wanted to be on my own. Eventually I pulled myself together and told myself that if Hazel had been good enough to send me out to the pub I ought to go there and make the best of things. That's why I put myself about so much when I got there. And it was good for me, I think. Old friends help you to get a better perspective on life, don't you think?'

'Have you any idea who killed Adam?'

'No. I know his wife and children, of course, but I know scarcely any of his friends, and none of the people he'd been working with.'

Clyde Northcott waited until they were safely back in the privacy of the police Mondeo before he said, 'Luke Cassidy strikes me as a man at the end of his resources.'

'Yes. People like that commit murder sometimes. Losing all sense of perspective can be highly dangerous.'

'He's no real alibi for the time of the killing.'

'No. I think if I'd planned murder, I'd have made sure I had something more solid to offer than he had. But this killing might have been completely unplanned, of course. There might have been an argument which erupted into violence, with a shotgun at hand.'

Clyde Northcott negotiated the Mondeo past a group of

office party revellers lurching into the road outside a pub. 'Do you think Luke Cassidy killed him?'

'No. But I've now got a very good idea who did.'

It was just after nine when Percy Peach got home at the end of a long and eventful day. He looked forward to getting back to his rather shabby house now as he had never done when he lived alone in it. He had a new wife. And not only a wife, but a woman who was the subject of male fantasies around the Brunton nick. He still couldn't quite believe his luck. And it was all down to Tommy Bloody Tucker, who four years ago had assigned Lucy Blake to him as his sergeant, in the belief that he would be outraged by being teamed with a woman.

'I'm home, love,' he called down the hall as he hung his coat on the hook in the porch.

Lucy came out and decided that despite his brave show of energy he was allowed to be tired. 'The gin and tonic's ready for you.' She looked at him nervously. 'And mother's here.'

A man at the end of a thirteen-hour working day has every right to be disappointed when he arrives home and finds his mother-in-law encamped there. Indeed, for many men, 'disappointed' would be a mild word. But Percy Peach was no ordinary man. And his mother-in-law was no ordinary woman. Perhaps that is why there had been such a bond between them, from the moment when the then Lucy Blake had taken home her new boyfriend, bald, divorced, and almost ten years older than her.

'Haven't seen you for weeks!' said Percy as he gave Agnes Blake her customary hug. He held her for a moment at arm's length. 'Do you think your daughter is trying to come between us? Do you think she's jealous of our relationship?'

'Get on with yer!' said Agnes Blake delightedly. 'But it's good to see you. Haven't seen you since that community meeting in the Paki quarter. I thought you were great, that night.'

'Not as great as you, young lady. You got things going, you know, when you weighed in with Fazal Mahmood and cricket.'

'I didn't know I was going to speak until I was on my feet. But you spoke your piece after that. And people listened to you.'

Lucy stepped firmly between them. 'I am interrupting this mutual admiration society to announce that there is food available for you, Percy Peach. We've already eaten, but there's a quiche in the oven and some fresh bread and salad to go with it, if you want them.'

'That would be wonderful, my dear wife,' said Percy with the beginnings of a bow. As an aside to Agnes as Lucy turned away, he whispered, 'I'm no longer allowed to use the chip shop, now that I've been rescued by marriage.'

'And a good thing too!' said Agnes emphatically. 'A man working as hard as you needs a proper diet, not all this junk food. I only hope her cooking's improving. You tell me she's a good copper, but she was never much cop at that!' She giggled delightedly; she had thought up this witticism a week ago and stored it up for this occasion.

'So how's the village?' he asked as they subsided into armchairs.

'Getting over your marriage. I still get enquiries about that best man of yours from the girls in the supermarket, you know.'

'Clyde Northcott? He's my right-hand man now, you know. He's taken the place of Lucy – in a manner of speaking. And you can tell them he's still unattached.'

'So how's working life without my Lucy beside you, D.C.S.?'

With the possible exception of her daughter, she was the only person in the world who knew and remembered that Percy's real forenames were Denis Charles Scott, that a sports-mad father who was now long dead had named him after Denis Charles Scott Compton, one of the most popular of all English cricketers and the favourite batsman of Agnes Blake, who had been taken as a girl to see him play against the Australians at Old Trafford.

'Busy but interesting, at the moment.'

'Lucy says you're working on this Adam Cassidy case that's hit all the headlines.' Agnes was far too well-trained by her daughter to ask what progress he was making. 'You should still be playing cricket at the weekends. You need to get away from work. You left the game much too early.'

It was a recurrent theme of hers. She had numerous cuttings and photographs of him as a quick-footed batsman for East Lancs, the Brunton team in the Lancashire League.

'I wouldn't be getting much cricket in December, Mrs B,' Percy pointed out mildly.

Further exchanges on the subject were prevented by the arrival of Lucy with a tray of Percy's food. She had made tea for all three. The three of them made easy, unforced conversation whilst he ate. He hadn't realized how little he'd eaten during the day or how hungry he was until he began to demolish the food on the tray.

'Right! I'm off now,' said Agnes, finishing her tea and downing her cup purposefully.

'There's really no need,' said Percy gallantly.

'There's every need. You've both had a long working day and you need to relax and compare notes. And I'd already said my piece about grandchildren before you got home, Percy Peach!'

'What a sensible woman you are, Mrs B!' said Percy. Lucy was only twenty-nine, but her mother was seventy now, and anxious to have bairns about her whilst she could still be an energetic granny. 'Between the two of us, we'll talk some sense into the girl.'

'The girl is a woman. A woman with a career to think of,' said Lucy firmly. But she feared that her resistance was steadily weakening under the combined assault of this formidable duo.

They watched Agnes drive her Fiesta carefully away into the darkness, then went back into the house. Percy was silent for so long on the sofa beside her that Lucy thought he must indeed be very tired. Then, just when she thought he might have dozed off, he said thoughtfully, 'You need people like your mum around, when you do the work we do.'

'And why would that be?'

'You get tarnished, if you spend the whole of your life in crime. You lose a proper sense of perspective.'

'And one woman of seventy helps you with that?'

'Yes. You need to be reminded that the real world is full of genuine people, good people. They're the people we're working for in the end, aren't they?'

'Yes, I suppose they are. I think I see what you mean. Now that I'm working with the anti-terrorism security people, I see mainly Muslims. I have to remind myself constantly that the great mass of them are friendly, because the minority we're concerned with are sinister and dangerous. If you're not careful, you end up thinking everyone with an Asian face is a potential suspect. Innocence isn't a thing that we see all that often, because it's not what concerns us.'

'I've been dealing with the cheaters and the beaters and the killers for a long time now. I see the illegal drugs trade sweeping over us like an incoming tide, whatever our small successes. It's easy to throw up your hands and say it's not worth bothering, or to be like Tommy Bloody Tucker and think only of PR and your pension. You need passion, if you're going to succeed when evil seems all around you.'

Lucy leaned across and kissed him on the forehead, then on the lips. 'You're quite a philosopher, Percy Peach, underneath all that aggression.'

'No. I'm just a copper, fighting villains and trying to maintain a sense of proportion.'

'You're a little more than that.' There was a pause. When he didn't respond, she said quietly, 'Passion, you said.'

'Yes, I did, didn't I? Speaking of which, I've had a busy day and it's high time I was in bed.' But he showed no immediate sign of moving from the sofa. His hands actively explored the curves and recesses which were so warm and so willing beside him. After a few minutes of increasing delight, he murmured into the ear beneath his lips, 'She has a lot of good ideas, your Mum, doesn't she?'

Alarm bells she did not wish to heed tinkled at the back of Lucy's brain. She forced herself to sit upright. 'And what particular ideas would you be thinking of?'

'High time she was made a granny, she said. Very understandable, that, in a woman of her years.' Percy nodded enthusiastically.

'Very understandable, but there are other considerations as well.'

'I prefer to defer to the wisdom of age. There isn't enough heed given to that in our society.' And he led her firmly up the stairs to pursue this philosophy.

# NINETEEN

The big living room of the old farmhouse had a ten-foot ceiling, but the top of the Christmas tree reached to within six inches of it. Once it had its lights and all of its decorations, it would certainly impress the three children who would focus on it and the presents at the foot of it on Christmas Day.

'It's going to look really good,' said Jane Cassidy.

'I shan't do anything more with it at the moment. Thomas will want to help me with all the trimmings.'

'I'm glad we're coming round here on Christmas Day. Damon and Kate will be less likely to miss Adam if they're not at home.'

'Liz will be here to chaperone us. But don't worry, my sister's good with children. She was a big help with Thomas when Jessica left.' Paul Barnes reached across and took her hands in his. 'Do you think Christmas will be a big problem for the children?'

Jane had already given that a lot of thought. 'No, I don't think so. Adam had seen so little of them over the last few months that they're not as distraught as I'd expected. They seem to have taken it almost too well. I expect there'll be the odd tear when they're going to bed, but not a lot more than that. A small part of me wants there to be more, wants them to feel the loss of their father.'

Paul had too much sense to say anything in response to that thought. After a few moments, he said, 'It will be good to spend Christmas together. It will be another step towards getting the kids used to us being together.'

'Kate asked about you, last night. Asked whether we were good friends. I said yes. She didn't seem to make any connection with Adam.'

'Thomas asked me about us, too. He likes you; I think he's quite looking forward to our being together. Of course, it's different for him; he scarcely remembers Jessica now.'

'The counsellor came to see me yesterday. I imagine the

police arrange it. I talked to her mainly about the children. She said children accept things quickly and easily, so long as you make it seem natural to them. They're remarkably adaptable.'

'It's good that Thomas gets on so well with your two. I think he enjoys feeling in charge, having the responsibility for the younger ones.'

'They're great together. Ingrid was quite happy to have the three of them for the morning. She's planning to take them out for a walk, when the sun gets a bit higher in the sky.'

'It's a lovely day. But we'd getter get on with wrapping these presents if we're to justify your nanny's gallant efforts.' They proceeded to do just that, working in companionable silence, apart from comments about the presents and how they would be received in five days' time.

The rambling old stone building had thick walls, but the irregular windows had not been double-glazed, so that exterior sounds penetrated fairly easily when things within were quiet. Barnes's sharp ears caught the sound of the vehicle as it turned off the lane and began the half-mile journey up the paved track to his farm. Jane Cassidy caught the note later, as the engine changed gear and climbed the last two hundred yards. The pair were at the window by the time the police car turned into the cobbled farmyard and parked unhurriedly near the door.

Detective Chief Inspector Peach, dapper in a light-grey suit, and the much taller Detective Sergeant Northcott, black and menacing in a navy-blue roll-neck sweater. They looked up at the window of the living room for a moment, and caused Jane and Paul to recoil like guilty things, staring at each other with a wild surmise.

Barnes had composed himself by the time he ushered the two men into the room. He said a little awkwardly, 'It's the CID, Jane. Here to ask us a few more questions, though I don't see what we can add to what we've already told them.'

He stood in a light-blue V-neck sweater beside Clyde Northcott, almost as tall as the policeman, looking in that moment almost as white as Northcott was black. Paul seemed almost rooted to the spot after his introduction, so that Jane said hurriedly, 'We were just about to have coffee, gentlemen. Would you care to join us?'

Rather to her surprise, Peach accepted the invitation, once

she had given her assurance that the kettle was already on the Aga and it wouldn't take long. She didn't realize that he was content to assess the situation, to take the pulse of the relationship between these two, to assess the degree of collusion there had been between them and where they planned to go from here. It was also the first time that Northcott had been involved with him in a situation like this, where you needed to play the cards you held with skill, if you were to secure the further evidence you needed.

Peach looked round the big room, taking in the impressive half-decorated Christmas tree and the gaudy Christmas paper upon the floor. He stared for a moment without comment at the space rocket which was destined for Thomas and the paint-set Paul had just begun to wrap for young Kate. It felt to Barnes like a violation. He wanted to hustle these things away from prying police eyes, to protest against the smearing of childish innocence which this CID study seemed to him to imply.

Instead, he went and sat down awkwardly on the edge of the old red leather sofa which was normally so comfortable and waited for Jane to return with the coffee. The visitors seemed much happier with the silence than he was. Paul's first thought was that they had already made a mistake; by offering to make the coffee, Jane had showed them how familiar she was with the geography of his house, how much she already felt at home here. Then he realized that they had already admitted an affair, that the discretion they tried to exercise with the rest of the public had no place here.

As if he had read these thoughts, Peach took up that idea when Jane had handed round the coffee and biscuits, with the lithe assistance of DS Northcott. Only when Jane was sitting on the leather sofa beside Barnes did Percy break the silence, which seemed to Barnes to have stretched him to breaking point. Peach said with typical pugnacity, 'How long have you two been lovers?'

There was a silence in which Northcott, poised with notebook open beside his mentor, felt he could almost feel the electrical charge. Peach watched the pair glance at each other in alarm, then added, 'It's just as well that the two of you are together, don't you think? That way, you won't be likely to contradict each other.'

It was Jane who recovered first. She said, 'Do you set out to be objectionable as a tactic, or does it just come naturally to you, DCI Peach?'

Peach was not at all put out. He allowed himself a half-smile. 'Perhaps I just don't take kindly to people trying to deceive me. Particularly when a man has been brutally murdered.'

'It wasn't like that!' The words were out before Paul could prevent them, his tongue frozen too late by the sudden look of horror on Jane's face.

Jane tried to rescue him. 'Paul means our affair wasn't like that – wasn't something tawdry. To answer your question, we've been lovers for just over three months. That's if your question is when did we first have sex together, as I presume it is. If you really mean love, it would be a little while before that.'

Peach noted the precision of her reply. A woman to whom this relationship was important, who might perhaps kill or accept killing to further its progress. 'Did Adam Cassidy know about this?'

'No. He took plenty of lovers himself, you know.'

'We do know, yes. You did your best to draw our attention to it. But his lovers are not relevant to this case. Whereas your affair with Mr Barnes most certainly is.'

'We would dispute that. And I would ask you not to publicize our relationship at this point. It will leak out soon enough, I'm sure – country folk love the latest gossip. But we both have children to think of. It is no business of yours, but this isn't a casual bit of sex on the side. We shall get married in due course, when people have had time to get used to the idea. Maybe in the autumn.'

She was talking too much, probably because she was afraid of Barnes speaking at all. Peach said grimly, 'You will certainly not be marrying this autumn, Mrs Cassidy. Both of you may well be in prison then.'

She tossed her fair hair angrily in the warm air. 'This is ridiculous! You cannot possibly substantiate that statement.' She could feel Paul's eyes upon her, but she forced herself not to look at him. Turning desperation into fury, she said to Peach, 'Why are you doing this to me? Why do you hate me so?'

She had expected him to deny it, but he did not trouble to do so. He said with distaste rather than admiration, 'You proved your credentials as an actress on Wednesday, Mrs Cassidy. You sold us the tale about being here last Friday night with considerable skill.'

'I don't know what you mean. I was here on Friday with Paul. I'm sorry I deceived you about it in the first place, but I apologized for that when you saw me on Wednesday.'

'You did indeed. You told us on Monday that you'd been in your own home at the time when your husband was being killed, then confessed with some embarrassment on Wednesday that you'd been deceiving us, that instead you'd been here for the evening. You acted out your charade with great skill. I think that at the time both DS Northcott and I believed you.'

'I'm flattered that you think I was acting so well. But my account was convincing because I was telling you the truth.' Jane was conscious now of the horror on Paul's face, but still she would not turn to look at him, sensing that the action might bring words from him which they could not afford.

Peach insisted quietly, 'You were at your own house throughout the evening. You answered the phone when Luke Cassidy rang to try to speak to Adam.'

Jane opened her mouth to bluster her way out of it, but suddenly no words would come. Her brain forced her to accept that there was no escape from the steely determination of the two very different-looking men who sat opposite her, that they had the facts to refute anything she had to offer. She remained silent, unconsciously biting her lip and staring at the rich dark red of the Turkish carpet.

Peach let this moment of her defeat stretch for long seconds. Then he said quietly, 'Why did you put those hairs beside the passenger seat of the BMW, Jane?'

It was the first time he had used her forename. She wondered if this marked her acceptance of guilt, whether the move to the informal marked some key stage in the arcane rites of police interrogation. She gathered her resources for a last denial. 'I don't know what you're talking about. If Adam had had some floozy in his car, it's nothing to do with me.'

'It was a mistake, Jane. The woman whose head those hairs came from had never been in the BMW. You collected them from another car, with a comb, didn't you?'

She had no energy any longer for denial, only a vague wish for self-justification. At first she spoke slowly, as if she were observing the actions of some other woman. 'They were in the Mercedes. I brushed them up intending to confront Adam with them. But when I heard he was going off for the weekend in the sports car, I thought I'd dump them in there. In case it was some other tart he was bedding!' Only as she spat out the last phrase did she reveal the intensity of her hatred for the man who had been her husband.

'You thought you'd frame someone else for murder.'

A pause. Then in a weary monotone, 'No. I thought he might like to explain away those dark hairs to some blonde he'd picked up for the weekend.'

Peach did not trouble to argue. This might make her an accessory to a carefully planned murder, if it was accepted as an attempt to divert suspicion from Barnes. Or it might be what she said, no more than an attempt to embarrass her husband when a different woman found the clutch of dark hairs in the BMW. Leave that for the competing counsels to argue out months from now in court. It was Northcott, deep-voiced and quietly persuasive, who now said, 'You were at home for the whole of that evening, weren't you, Mrs Cassidy?'

'Jane had nothing to do with this!' Barnes could restrain himself no longer, and the words sprang out harsh and raw in the quiet room.

Jane's hand stole across the sofa and gripped the top of his. When he felt her touch, Barnes uncurled his clenched fist and clasped her fingers in his. Her voice was almost a whisper as she said, 'Leave it, Paul.'

'Jane was trying to save me on Wednesday, by giving me an alibi. But I killed Cassidy, not her. Jane knew nothing about it.'

Peach said calmly, 'In my view, Mrs Cassidy is what our bright lawyers would call an accessory after the fact. But we'll let them argue about that, in due course. You should tell us how you killed him.'

'I didn't plan it, you know. I didn't go up there with the intention of killing Cassidy.'

'If that's a plea for Manslaughter rather than Murder, you should make it at the proper time, with the proper legal support. I'm here to arrest you as the instrument of the law, not its arbiter.'

'I rang Adam on his mobile, on Thursday. Said I needed to speak to him. He asked if it was about Jane and me. That was the first time I knew that he was aware of us and it shook me a bit. But I thought that only made it more urgent for me to see him.'

He stopped. This conversation now seemed to him a long time ago, in a vanished, more innocent world. Clyde Northcott prompted him gently. 'And you arranged to meet him by the A666.'

'Yes. He didn't want to meet me at all, at first. He said he was busy on Friday and was then going to be away for a shooting weekend. I shoot on the moors near here myself, far more regularly than Cassidy ever did, and I sensed immediately that this was a lie. He was off somewhere with a woman for the weekend and I let him know that I'd twigged that. He suggested that lay-by by the A666 himself. I wasn't happy to meet him there, but he said it was that or nothing. I eventually agreed to it, because I was so anxious to have it out with him about Jane and me.'

The lover's need for action, for moving on his suit, whatever the cost. The lover's pressing need to have things decided and his prize securely in his arms. How often did the thrust of passion towards action at any price lead to disaster? They could argue later, when it came to a formal statement, about whether Barnes or Cassidy had determined the place of that lonely assignation; the Crown Prosecution Service would no doubt see it as a key issue in a murder charge. Peach glanced briefly at the distraught woman beside Barnes and then said softly, 'We need your full account of what happened, Paul.'

There was no resistance now. Barnes stared past them, as though seeing the events he was recounting being played out on some invisible screen. 'I'd been there about five minutes when he drove in and parked behind me. It was a freezing night and we were the only two cars there. But he said we should move away a little, so that we could talk without being disturbed. Then he reached into the back of his sports BMW and pulled out his new shotgun.'

'Did that alarm you?'

'It did a little, at first. But it was a Purdey. The finest shotgun you can buy. He seemed genuinely anxious to show off his expensive new toy to me, because he realized that I knew a little about these things and would appreciate it. Perhaps he was trying to convince me that he was really going shooting at the weekend.'

'So you didn't feel threatened?'

Barnes paused for a moment, as if this were important in fixing the reality of his story. 'I don't think I did, really. I was anxious to say what I had to say about Jane, to tell him that we were serious, that she was going to leave him and come to me permanently.'

'Even in that bizarre setting?'

'Even there. The setting didn't seem important. All I could think of was that I'd finally pinned him down and got him to myself, so that I needed to say what I had to say whilst I had the chance. He showed me his magnificent new shotgun in the car park and I expressed the envy he seemed to feel appropriate.'

A smile of contempt flashed briefly across Barnes's fresh-skinned, countryman's face. 'I said I had important things to say to him. That's when he led me away from the car park and through those scrubby bushes. I suppose we'd gone fifty yards or so when I called to him from behind that this was far enough.'

'Were you afraid of what he was going to do?'

'I don't think so. I suppose I was apprehensive about how he'd react to what I had to say about Jane and me, but I just wanted to say it and get it over with, I think.'

'And how did he react to it?'

'He laughed in my face. Told me to get lost. He said I wasn't in his league and that I shouldn't try to compete. I told him he should ask Jane how she felt about it.'

Since he had begun to speak, it was Jane Cassidy who had looked increasingly horrified, whilst confession seemed to be bringing him a kind of release. She slid a little nearer to him on the leather settee, sliding her arm beneath his as she kept their fingers intertwined. 'You shouldn't do this, Paul. You shouldn't make any statements now without a lawyer at your side.'

He glanced at her and looked bemused, as if he had for a moment forgotten her, as he relived so vividly the events of a week earlier. Then he turned back from her and stared straight ahead again, past the detectives who had brought him to this, past the thick stone walls and through the long window to the fields beyond, to the land which he and his family had farmed for two hundred years.

He resumed as if there had been no pause. 'He said I shouldn't confuse an easy shag with a lonely woman with anything more permanent. He said he'd be back to assert his rights and I should piss off out of it, if I knew what was good for me.'

The woman beside him winced a little at the coarseness of these phrases, which he had not recounted to her before, but Barnes now seemed beyond such emotion. 'I think I made a move towards him when he said these things, but I'm not sure of that. I know he raised the shotgun and I think I believed in that moment that he was going to turn it upon me. I grabbed it and the next thing I knew, he was lying at my feet with half his chest shot away.'

There was an involuntary gasp from Jane Cassidy, who had hitherto been shielded from the detail of the death. She stilled a scream in her throat, clasping both hands to her mouth. And this time Paul Barnes did see her and was concerned for her. 'I'm sorry, my darling. That's how it was. I took his phone from his car and left as quickly as I could.'

There was material here for a plea of self-defence, or at least for a nervous, unthinking reaction from a man who had thought he was threatened. But again it would be up to the lawyers to argue this out. Someone else would take these bricks and build them into a wall, whilst the prosecutors would argue how much preplanning was implied by arranging to meet in such a lonely place and how much Jane Cassidy's placing of a clutch of female hairs in the BMW was an attempt to divert suspicion from Barnes.

At a nod from Peach, DS Northcott stepped forward and pronounced the formal words of arrest with his hand on Paul Barnes's unresisting shoulder. It was at this point that Jane Cassidy, her bright blue eyes glittering with horror, said abruptly, 'Can I go to the children? They need me.'

Peach hesitated. 'All right. Don't leave your house without informing us at Brunton CID. There will probably be formal charges for you later and you should take account of that fact and make preparations for it.'

She stood up, then flung her arms suddenly round her lover. It was intense but not prolonged. As she detached herself, she said, 'I'll look after Thomas. He can stay with us as long as you want him to.'

Of all the passions, the one of parting is at once the most intense and the most bitter, thought Peach. Then, as if ashamed of such sentiments, he said gruffly, 'Mr Barnes will travel in the back of the police car which has just arrived. Formal charges will be preferred at the station. If you offer us a guarantee that you will not attempt to escape, I see no need for handcuffs on this occasion.'

Paul Barnes stood and looked at the Christmas wrapping paper strewn on the floor at the other end of the big room, at the half-decorated Christmas tree, at the children's presents, which appeared pathetically naked as they awaited their wrappings. He knew now what he was going to miss, the months and maybe the years of his son's growth which he would never see. He wanted to express the enormity of it all, to assert that one unthinking moment could surely not lead to this tremendous penance. But all he said, evenly and conventionally, was: 'I can't believe this is happening to me.'

Peach and Northcott drove close behind the car in which Barnes sat rigidly upright between two uniformed constables. They passed over the Ribble, running high and dark against its winter banks, and on through a countryside with leafless trees still as sculptures against the low December sun. And then into the town. Brunton was bright with Christmas lights and crowded with Christmas shoppers. Small children, newly released from nursery and infant schools, were crowding into the town-centre stores to meet Father Christmas. As far as the men who had brought him to justice could see, Paul Barnes's head moved neither right nor left throughout his journey.

In that fine new house near the Trough of Bowland, an unnaturally calm Jane Cassidy was talking earnestly to a wide-eyed Ingrid Lundberg. A nanny's duties might need to be redefined and extended, but she would be amply rewarded. If Jane herself was shut away for a time, it was important that Damon and Kate should think the best of their mummy.

Jane gave the startled young woman a strange, abstracted smile. If it was meant to reassure Ingrid, it failed dismally. You couldn't always expect everything to make sense, Jane told her. Sometimes events took you over. Sometimes you became merely players upon life's strange and wonderful stage.